PRAISE FOR THE MARTYR'S BROTHER

"With *The Martyr's Brother*, Rona Simmons has made her mark on the thriller genre, ripping a story from today's headlines and dropping it right down in our own backyards. From the ominous opening to the very end, she dares you to look away or to put the book down. And when you're done, you won't look at the people around you or the places you go quite the same way again."
—**CAROLE TOWNSEND**, author of *Blood in the Soil*

"*The Martyr's Brother* paints people who brush up against terrorism, using great flawed, 3D characters to represent all sides. An intriguing contemporary tale of our times depicting how these factions at war have faces and absolutely none of them is sure of what they are doing."
—**C. HOPE CLARK**, author of *The Edisto Island Mysteries* and *The Carolina Slade Mysteries*

"*The Martyr's Brother* is more than a well-written book; it is a fast and engrossing story that carries us into a world of deception and terrorism that we all fear. Rona Simmons' portrayal of the desperate, the alienated, and the ruthless rings true on every page. Her lean prose and taut pacing draw the reader deeper with every page into a world we know exists but hope never to encounter.
—**DAVID DARRACOTT**, 2015 Georgia Author of the Year for *Wasted*

THE MARTYR'S BROTHER

THE MARTYR'S BROTHER

A NOVEL

RONA SIMMONS

Cyrilla Publishing | Cumming, GA

Published by Cyrilla Publishing in Cumming, GA

Printed in The United States of America

Cover by Cyrilla Graphics

Library of Congress Cataloging-in-Publications data is available upon request.

ISBN 978-1-944193-61-4

First Edition, 2016

10 9 8 7 6 5 4 3 2 1

For Harry

"Very few of us are what we seem."
Agatha Christie in *The Man in the Mist*

JULY, FIVE YEARS AGO

1. SHAFRA

A SHADOW CREPT OVER THE GROUND WHERE SHAFRA SQUATTED. Someone had come behind him without a sound, no crunch of gravel, or rustle of a garment, or audible breath. Shafra lifted his head and squinted at the figure, its face backlit by the sun. "Nadheer, is that you?"

Shafra shifted his feet, but before he could rise, his brother Nadheer touched Shafra on the shoulder and said, "Stay where you are, little brother."

"But— Your hair. You've shaved your head. You—"

Nadheer raised a finger to his lips.

From the house behind them came the sound of a woman wailing. Shafra turned toward the open door of their home and heard another wail, the anguish palpable. Ignoring Nadheer's hand on his shoulder, Shafra jumped up and sped to the door. Before he disappeared inside, he glanced back to where he and Nadheer had spoken a second ago. But Nadheer was not there, he was in the street, standing beside a dust-covered, blue Toyota. The last Shafra saw of Nadheer was his brother's shaven head as he lowered himself into the car's front seat.

In the kitchen, Shafra's mother and father stood in an embrace, his mother's face hidden, his father's blank except for a hint of resignation in his eyes. His mother, who still wailed uncontrollably, slipped through his father's arms and to the floor.

She clenched her fists and pounded them against her chest, her mouth forming and losing words she refused to say.

Shafra's eyes flicked from one of his parents to the other and then to his sister Selam, cowering in the corner, her face in her hands.

"Mama, what's wrong?" Shafra asked. "Where has Nadheer gone?"

"Be quiet," Shafra's father said. The bark in his voice halted Shafra's questions and his mother's wailing. "Do not bring shame into this house," he continued. "Nadheer has brought us a great honor. We should be proud of his achievement."

Nadheer was headed to the checkpoint at the edge of the main square. Nadheer was going to die.

Shafra fled the tiny room and the house. Once outside, he took the path to the center of town, his sandals slapped along the path, his arms pumped at his sides, his nostrils flared. He was quick, the fastest in his school, and he'd beaten Nadheer once last year. He could catch him again now and stop him. He could.

Shafra rounded the corner of the market and entered the square. It was Saturday. Men and women thronged the rows of shops. Here and there, goats and sheep stood tethered to the side of makeshift stalls, waiting with heads bowed, eyes closed. To his left, Shafra spied a neighbor and further away, an uncle. Surely, Nadheer would not harm these people. They were their neighbors, their friends, their relatives.

A line of cars and trucks jammed the road ahead. The line inched forward, squeezing past a truck parked at an odd angle. A horn blared at the driver who had stopped to greet a friend or haggle with a merchant.

Shafra searched the line for a car with a dusty blue roof. At the far end of the procession, he found it and watched as the Toyota turned and pulled away. Shafra raced through the market. He veered to miss an oncoming car, crashed into a merchant's table, and kept going. Behind him, he heard a clatter of objects and a merchant's curses.

When he reached the spot where the Toyota had left the line, the car had traveled ahead another hundred yards up a hill to where the checkpoint stood. A soldier raised his hand, ordering the car to halt. When it slowed, the soldier stepped in front of the car.

The explosion rocketed over Shafra's head and through the market, the force of the blast tossing Shafra to the ground. When he lifted his head a moment later, silence lay thick like a blanket around him. He spat and tasted iron in his mouth. He had a gash across the middle of his cheek.

Shafra stared in disbelief at the surrounding scene. Dust and smoke. Odd pieces of concrete, rubble from a once smooth wall. Mismatched shoes scattered across the ground. A two-wheeled cart on its side, and beside the cart, a goat struggled to stand, its head rising and falling, rising again, not as high the second time, and lower still the next. Then, the animal lay flat on the ground, its glassy eye wide with pain. It opened its mouth and bleated.

The goat's cry pierced the fog in Shafra's head, the sound muffled and distant at first, then sharp and near. A chorus of wailing followed. From all sides, people shouted names. Aamir! Kali! Fahim! But no one answered. Shafra's voice joined them. "Nadheer!" he shouted. "Nadheer!"

AUGUST, PRESENT DAY

2. ALICIA

OVER THIRTY MINUTES AFTER THE BLAST, A COLUMN OF SMOKE twisted above the charred and mangled heap of metal that had been a vehicle. A Humvee, and next to it a crumpled car door. The shell of the car stood nearby, its tires vaporized and its interior blackened. Bodies of the vehicles' former occupants lay in pieces across the debris field, a half halo emanating from the detonation's center.

Half a world away, in Atlanta, Georgia, Alicia Blake sat in her living room staring at the images on her television screen. She watched with one hand to her mouth, the other on the remote. The camera panned across the scene. To one side she noticed a goat or a sheep, she couldn't say which, lying in the dirt. Hooves on its front feet pawed at the ground. Its head rose, fell, and then lay still.

The people in the marketplace who had fled at the sound of the explosion returned. They weaved in and out of the chaos, searching, righting carts, tossing twisted bicycles and broken concrete to the side. They performed their search in a perfunctory manner, the manner of men accustomed to sorting through rubble and stepping over corpses. A handful of women at the periphery knelt in shock and disbelief; others tugged at their children, gathered them close, and disappeared into the shadows.

Alicia watched with the volume off, not wanting to wake her ten-year-old son Kyle who was asleep in his bedroom. Even without the sound, Alicia knew there were sirens, shouting, and cries of anguish. She'd taped the five-year-old news segment years ago and had watched it dozens, if not hundreds, of times. And though Alicia had practically memorized each frame of the scene broadcast into her life and imprinted into her brain, she watched as if it were the first time. She could do nothing to slow her pulse or dull the throbbing in her head, or stop watching. When the scene played out, a reporter stepped into the picture. Alicia pressed the remote's back arrow and watched the action in reverse. The men replaced the pieces of rubble, re-toppled the carts, and walked backward from the scene. Then, Alicia replayed the video from the beginning, this time in slow motion, frame by frame. She focused on the small blurred shapes the network had applied over the body parts. No matter how careful the technicians were, in their haste to release the video, they'd missed an arm, a foot, and a hand torn from a victim's body.

The first time Alicia had watched the clip and witnessed the carnage, she had been alone and she had screamed, not once, but several times. She'd run from the screen and hid her head under a pillow. But, no matter how loudly she had screamed or how tightly she'd clenched the pillow, the Lieutenant's words echoed in her head.

"There are only remains. Pieces. But enough to be certain. Enough to bury," he had said to her when she arrived in Dover to bring her husband's body home.

"What pieces?" she'd asked him.

"I'm sorry, ma'am, I don't know. The paperwork didn't say. Only that they recovered the remains and, after confirming the identity, they airlifted Sergeant Seth Blake's remains from the field of battle to Baghdad. And finally here to Dover Air Force Base."

"What pieces?" Alicia had asked a second time.

"As I said..."

Before they loaded the coffin into the transport, she'd asked about the pieces once more and to view the body.

"I can't refuse, ma'am. But I don't think it's advisable."

Alicia had walked away, stone-faced. She brought her husband home and buried him, or what the Army said was left of him, the pieces, his remains, and tried to remember him as a whole man.

The official war ended. Most of the men Alicia knew through Seth came home, some wounded, some whole. She "moved on with her life" as her sister advised. Moved on for Kyle's sake, as Seth would have wanted.

Unofficially, the war in the Middle East continued. People died there, men, women, and children, many blown to bits, pieces left behind to testify to the carnage. But at home, interest flagged and, with every passing day, the coverage became increasingly spotty. The scenes of carnage like those in the video of the event where Seth had died became less frequent and shorter.

Tonight's news had nothing to show, nothing to keep the memory fresh or reignite the emptiness. Alicia pressed the remote's off button.

She tiptoed to Kyle's room and peered through the half-open door. He was asleep, one leg dangling over the side of the bed and half the covers on the floor. Alicia nudged the window beside his bed higher, hoping for but failing to find a breath of fresh air on the mid-August night. She placed Kyle's leg back under the covers and kissed him twice on the forehead, once for herself and once for Seth. Then, she made her way to her bedroom and lay fully clothed on her bed. She would not sleep tonight.

3. JAVIER

THE COYOTE SMIRKED. "THREE THOUSAND U.S.," HE SAID, DEMAND-
ing twice the going rate.

Javier squared his shoulders to Salvador, the man who was to
take him from Gabriel, Mexico across the border and into the
United States. Salvador was a stocky man, thick and powerful
through the torso, arms, and legs, but lacking Javier's skill and
speed, or so Javier thought.

Behind them, men loitered in clusters the length of the block.
Some of the men squatted on their haunches; some sat cross-
legged in the dirt. Others slumped against the wall of the meat
market below the sign reading "Carniceria" in red script, the *I* and
A mashed together at the end. To Javier's left, a man rested against
the trunk of a tree, its roots trodden smooth by countless young
men who'd passed through Gabriel before him.

Javier, not his real name, needed Salvador more than Salvador
needed Javier. If Javier chose not to pay, another migrant would
gladly take his place. But Javier could not back out and could not
afford for Salvador to know his circumstances.

Salvador explained that fifteen hundred was for Latinos. "De
donde eres?" he asked. Where are you from?

Javier had nothing to gain by confiding in the coyote. "Euro-
pa," he said after a pause.

"Hablas bien." You speak well. "Still, there's something not

9

quite right." Salvador brought his face within a few inches of Javier's and tilted his head back, scenting the air like a cat.

Javier's heart pounded. Rings of sweat grew under his arms and below his collar. He'd studied the language for months, rehearsing until his accent was flawless. And with his hair cut short and a clean-shaven chin, he'd been told he could pass.

"It's the eyes," Salvador continued. "It's definitely the eyes. Too far apart." Salvador spat, the wad of spittle landing a hair's width from Javier's sneaker. "Three thousand."

"You can't do that. Señor Sauza promised me the cost would be fifteen hundred."

"Señor Sauza is in Guadalajara. This is Gabriel. Three thousand." Salvador paused, daring Javier to speak or even blink. When a provincial police motorcycle thundered past, Salvador broke the silence. "You are trouble," he said and turned to go.

"Bueno. Three thousand," Javier said. He had no choice. "Fifteen hundred now. Fifteen hundred later."

"Bueno."

Javier lifted the sweatshirt he'd worn for the last three days and felt for his money belt.

"Not here." Salvador signaled for Javier to follow him into the alley. There, with cupped shoulders, he shielded the transaction from curious onlookers and took the bills from Javier. He counted them twice then stuffed the money in his jeans. "Tomorrow morning. Four o'clock."

"Where?" Javier asked.

"Here. In the alley." Salvador's words trailed behind him and were sucked into the air by the heat.

Javier slid to the ground. Bent kneed, he propped himself against the wall and assumed the air of indifference of a handful of other migrants waiting in the alley. It was a few degrees cooler than the street. Not unlike the alley beside his parent's home, Javier thought, in another desert on the other side of the world.

Across from him, two women sat huddled together. They stared at him with dark eyes. Javier wondered if they'd overheard his conversation or had had a similar one with Salvador. One looked away; the other tossed her hair and lowered her eyes. A moment later, when Javier looked back, the woman eyed him and held his gaze until he turned away.

4. JAVIER

BY SIX O'CLOCK, NINE MIGRANTS, INCLUDING JAVIER AND THE TWO women, had gathered in the alley. Two men stood apart, hands in their pockets, and kicked the dirt with the toes of their shoes. The rest paced back and forth or stamped their feet like restless cattle. Javier sat with his back against the adobe wall, conserving his energy for the day ahead.

Man, woman, boy, girl. They were nearly indistinguishable from one another in their jeans and hooded sweatshirts, backpacks slung over their shoulders, and plastic gallon jugs filled with water. A few days ago, under the watchful eye of an old woman at the back of a stall, Javier had thumbed through stacks of used clothing she offered for sale. He held several sweatshirts to his nose and aloft to check for holes before deciding on the faded blue one, a shirt without insignias or other identifying marks. Like the others, too, Javier carried his possessions in a backpack. His was a hand-me-down as well—but not from a nameless source. His had belonged to his brother, Nadheer.

Of the nine, only one person besides Javier had arrived alone, Ignacio. He was an older man, every bit of fifty. His short hair was thick as bristles and speckled with gray. He had stubble across his chin and skin darkened and coarse from a life in the sun. His sweatshirt bore the words "Just Do It" in bold three-inch high letters stitched across the chest. He made several attempts at conversation with Javier but, rebuffed each time, he soon moved away to a place of his own.

Three brothers, each one as short, powerfully built, and neckless as the other, sat midway along the alley. One of them, perhaps the eldest, kept up a running discourse. He bragged how he and his brothers had made the trip before, worked for a dozen years in America, and then returned home to their wives and children. He boasted too how, within weeks of his arrival home, he'd impregnated his wife only to remember there was no work in the village. With the burden of another mouth to feed, he said he and his brothers were retracing their steps, going back to find work and earn enough money to send home.

Past the brothers were two other men, Manuel and Octavio whose easy banter, though crude, suggested they knew each other. They spent much of their time drinking beer and discussing Manuel's tattoos. A strand of barbed wire in blue-black ink circled Manuel's neck. An intricate scroll of faces, both human and fantastical, ran from each wrist to the shoulder, the left arm a mirror of the right. When he'd drained his last beer, Manuel removed his shirt to reveal another tattoo, bigger and bolder than the others, a number and five letters in gothic script. He rose and paraded back and forth bare-chested, cawing and strutting like a rooster in the presence of hens. The letters made no sense to Javier. The others forced a half smile to their faces or nodded before finding a can or a rock to study.

Bored with the scene, Javier punched his backpack with his fists to plump the middle and tucked it under his head for a pillow. Then, he pulled the hood of his shirt over his head and closed his eyes.

Hours later, a clatter woke Javier.

Three migrants silhouetted against the night stepped past Javier and took a seat. The man nodded at Javier and said his name was Pablo and the two boys were his sons. "It's their first time," he said. The boys nodded but stayed silent and huddled close to their father.

"Vamonos," a man's voice called. All heads turned toward the sound. It was Salvador. He scanned the group, counting, "...Diez, once, doce." Salvador cocked his head toward the far end of the alley and the desert beyond. The twelve charges scrambled to their feet, grabbed their belongings and set off behind their coyote.

5. JAVIER

WHEN SIGNS OF CIVILIZATION HAD ALL BUT DISAPPEARED BEHIND them and the scatter of distant campfires faded, Salvador stopped. He drew a semi-circle in the sand with his foot and motioned for the group to squat facing him. There in the still dark landscape, he gave them a first and, he added, a last briefing.

He said they would walk without stopping until the sun was high in the sky when they would stop for water and a bite of food. He forbade them to take as much as a sip of the water they carried before they stopped. He issued his instructions like commandments: Do not speak. Do not walk ahead. Do not fall behind. Do not do anything unless told to do so. "If you want to make it across alive, you'll do as I say."

To emphasize the gravity of failing to heed his advice, he crossed to a wash ten or fifteen yards to the west. "Come, see for yourself," he said, nodding toward the ditch. The twelve migrants scooped up their packs and scrambled to where Salvador stood.

Flies buzzed unseen in the darkness and a foul scent filled the air. Several of the men covered their mouths and noses with a corner of the bandanas tied around their necks. One woman retched repeatedly until the other pulled her from the edge. What Javier first took to be a small animal's remains was on closer examination a human foot, protruding from a pair of ragged trousers. The five toes were picked nearly clean. But Javier had seen worse, much worse. He stared at the body of the dead migrant, ignoring the flies that pestered his ears and eyes and the stench that filled his nostrils. He stood unmoving until Salvador turned.

The group followed Salvador, their feet scuffling and stumbling, unaccustomed to walking with pieces of carpet tied to the bottoms of their shoes. Salvador had insisted each migrant buy a pair of the crude carpet soles. "To hide footprints from los federales," Salvador had said. Javier suspected Salvador also meant to say from the gangs who hunted migrants, robbing them, raping them, and killing those who resisted. He wondered, as he imagined the rest did, if Salvador were leading them into the path of his own gang waiting ahead. There was no way to know.

For the next hour, the group followed a gravel road, walking single file in one of a pair of ruts until, without warning, Salvador halted and motioned for everyone to stop. He cocked his head to the right and listened without moving or making a sound. "Bajense!" he said. Get Down! Though he whispered his command, the urgency was no less than if he had shouted. He scrambled to one side of the road and tamped his fingers toward the ground. Javier and the others followed, flattening their bodies against the desert floor, ignoring the sharp pebbles biting into their knees and the mesquite and ocotillo thorns gouging their hands and faces.

Everyone settled into their hiding places to wait. Soon, the reason for Salvador's order became clear. A vehicle was heading in their direction, traveling slowly and without headlights. As it neared, bumping across the rutted road, squeaks and rattles echoed across the desert. Twenty yards from where Salvador and his charges lay, the vehicle stopped.

The driver cut the motor and waited. The ticking of the vehicle's engine as it cooled was the only sound for miles. Then, a high-powered light mounted on the vehicle's roof pierced the dark. It swept across the terrain, panning left to right and north toward the border. The beam illuminated a dense stand of mesquite, a tumble of rocks, and a weathered shelter, peering into its dark interior to surprise a lone migrant.

With his heart racing, Javier held his breath. He challenged his body to lie motionless and to ignore the pain where the ground bit into the scar on his cheek. He dared open one eye. Low on the eastern horizon, he found Orion and Taurus, constellations his father had shown him on nights spent in the desert. He wondered whether, in that other desert on this same day, his father had gazed up at the night sky, seen the same familiar patterns, and thought of his son.

Javier slammed his eye shut and chastised himself for losing his concentration. He needed to focus on survival, not tracing patterns in the sky.

After what seemed like an hour, though it had been only minutes, the searchlight switched off and the vehicle left. When the squeaks and rattles faded and the car's taillights glowed dim like fox eyes, Salvador signaled, making the bird sound, *char-char-char*. He had taught the migrants to recognize the sound of the cactus wren's song. It was his signal to gather. It came again, from Javier's left. *Char-char-char*. Wordless, the twelve shuffled to their feet and dusted the grit and sand from their clothes.

Rather than return to the road, Salvador chose a path perpendicular to it, leading deeper into the open desert. The migrants took the same positions they had had earlier, Javier fifth in line, deliberately near the middle, not leading or lagging. They trudged in single file except for the two women who walked abreast at the rear.

6. JAVIER

BY MID-MORNING, BEADS OF SWEAT DOTTED EVERYONE'S FOREHEAD and dampened the bandanas around their necks. Most of the migrants had shed their outer clothing, stuffing sweatshirts and jackets into their backpacks. Once or twice, someone in the line asked Salvador to stop. But the coyote gave no sign of having heard the pleas and walked as he had from the start, at the same pace, in the same direction, without conversation, and without a break for water.

Up and down the line, the sound of labored breathing nearly drowned out the shuffle of feet. But Javier's breathing was unlabored and even. He did not need to rest. His feet were calloused and hardened, his legs strong, with sinewy muscles. As a child, he had walked for miles every day and often run barefoot through his village and into the hills beyond, returning only after the sun had set and his mother's voice echoed up from the valley, calling his name, "Shafra! Shafra!" Javier smiled at the memory of his mother's voice and his given name, one he'd not said aloud for months.

Javier forced the memory from his mind, but another took its place, and then another, his mind a tangle of past and present and future until he remembered his teacher Hussein's counsel. Hussein had cared more for his mind than his body. Hussein had laughed at him. "Shafra," he said, "you must be patient. The body may be strong but the mind must be exercised as well." To prove his point, he challenged Shafra. "Recite al-Fatihah for me."

Shafra knew the verses comprising the first chapter of the Quran. He'd recited them in his daily prayers alone and with his family or the village's imam. He'd practiced them with his brother, reciting them over and over as Nadheer had prepared for his graduation.

Shafra began.

In the name of Allah, the beneficent, the merciful
Praise be to Allah, lord of the worlds,
The beneficent, the merciful
Master of the day of judgment,
Thee alone we do worship. From thee alone we do seek assistance,
Show us the right path, the path of those whom thou hast favored
Not the path of those who earn thine anger nor of those who have
gone astray.

"Good. Now, continue, Shafra. What verse have you selected to complete your prayer?"

Shafra hesitated. Usually, he followed his father's lead in their daily prayers. He had not anticipated Hussein's question and had no answer.

"Perhaps al-Ikhlas?" Hussein said. The Perfection.

With his eyes lowered and hands held open beside his head, Shafra took a deep breath. He knew the passage well, but in that moment he could not remember how al-Ikhlas began.

A fly crawled across Hussein's thobe, the traditional Middle Eastern male's long white shirt. It crept over his right knee, down the valley of cloth between his shins, and then up until it reached Hussein's other knee. Shafra hadn't blinked or looked away even for a second, but when Hussein presented his clenched hand below Shafra's chin and unfolded his fingers, the insect fluttered its wings and took flight.

Hussein laughed. "Come back when your perfection is one hundredth that of this tiny insect," he said. He laughed again and shooed Shafra from his side with a flick of his hand.

Soon afterwards, strangers took over the village and Shafra's education took a turn. A teacher named Mohsan replaced Hussein. And though Shafra continued to practice reciting the Quran, his new teacher never tested his recall. Instead, Mohsan taught Shafra other skills. He taught him how to run and jump and roll, faster, higher, and more deftly. And he taught him the use of knives, machetes, and the AK-47.

Shafra excelled at the new teachings and waited for the day his father would praise him as he had Nadheer. But his father said nothing of his younger son's schooling. And at night, his mother wept.

Javier listened for a moment. He thought he heard weeping, here in the desert. But instead of weeping, there was only someone pleading, "Can we stop for a minute, please?" It was one of the women in the line.

Javier shook his head to clear his mind.

They did not stop. But soon, Manuel and Octavio fell out of line to relieve themselves. When they rejoined the group, they took a place behind the women. As they walked, the men filled the silence with their talking. Every so often, one or the other made a crude comment in a voice loud enough for everyone to hear.

Javier minded his own business. What Manuel and Octavio said or did was not his concern. His concern was surviving the desert.

7. ALICIA

ALICIA GATHERED THE PAPERS STREWN ACROSS HER DESK AND tapped the edges to form a neat stack. "Done," she said. Carlo, Alicia's boss and head of the security team at Riverside Centre, grunted without looking up from his desk. He'd assigned the routine paperwork to Alicia while he spent his days staring at the security cameras or on the phone, his feet propped on a waste can. But he was the boss.

Like most of the other guards, Alicia much preferred being out on the floor, circulating among the public, doing what she was supposed to do, protect the mall property, its tenants, and its customers. But she never wanted to give Carlo the satisfaction of knowing how much she hated the paperwork. So, as she worked she kept a smile on her face and hummed a tune, off key, and loud enough for Carlo to hear. She was quick, and if she tuned out the buzz of computers, phones, and radios, and occasionally Carlo snoring, she could finish the reports and make it back to the mall corridors in no time.

Alicia hit the "print" key and retrieved a copy of the completed report from the printer. The same as last month, just like Carlo wanted, nothing to pique the interest of Ingram Security's headquarters staff. A one sentence summary at the top, the same seventeen words she wrote each month, described the Riverside Centre team's accomplishments. Below that, figures in rows and columns tallied the incidents: thirty cases of shoplifting, twenty-one shoplifters apprehended, three potholes noted, and one abandoned vehicle towed.

Though it hadn't been her first choice, working security at Riverside Centre had its advantages. Surrounded by residential neighborhoods full of tree-lined streets and well-kept lawns, the upscale mall was a safe place to work. It was only minutes from where she lived. And, perhaps best of all, the job offered overtime pay if she worked extra shifts or on holidays, which she often did.

After school, on the days her shift ended early, Kyle took the bus to Riverside and waited for her in the food court. On the days she worked late, Kyle went straight home and stayed with their neighbor Nancy who had a son Kyle's age. When Nancy couldn't oblige, Alicia imposed on her sister-in-law or hired a sitter, her least favorite option.

"I'm going for a stroll," Alicia said.

Carlo gave her a sharp look.

Alicia's primary responsibility was to patrol the mall, "strolling" as she referred to the trip around the complex, a term that rankled Carlo. She waggled her fingers good-naturedly at him. As she exited the office, she set the campaign-style security hat on her head, grimacing. She hated how the hat mashed her auburn hair and left a ring around her head.

It was her last round of the day. Alicia radioed Wade Robida, one of her counterparts out on an inspection tour. They met at Starbucks in the west atrium for coffee. Alicia ordered a special grind and, as she often did, a flavored variety. Today, she asked for a double caramel macchiato with cinnamon and sprinkles. Wade ordered a small cup of regular coffee, black.

"Isn't that close to a zillion calories?" Wade asked.

"You ask the same question every time I order this. I think you really want one."

"Not me. Unlike some people, I've got to watch my waistline," he said, patting his hands against his bulging "spare tire."

Alicia ignored Wade's comment and kept her eyes from his mid-section, not knowing whether he was serious or making a joke at his own expense. But she wondered, as she had the first time they'd met, how he'd passed the Ingram Security physical.

Alicia had the opposite problem, she struggled to keep weight and muscle mass on her thin, five-foot-eight frame. She had a serious work out routine, one she did every night after Kyle had gone to bed. And, for Kyle's sake and hers, she insisted on healthy, well-balanced meals at home. The one exception she allowed herself was a caramel macchiato, or two.

Alicia and Wade scooped their coffees from the counter and carried them along as they made a circuit of the west wing. The two-story mall contained three sections, a west, central, and east wing, with major entrances and exits separating each section. A south facing exit from the food court in the glass-domed atrium sat between the west and central sections. And a north facing exit with a horseshoe-shaped row of restaurants separated the central and east sections. At three thirty in the afternoon, in the middle of the week, with a trickle of shoppers, Alicia and Wade's inspection circuit promised to be uneventful. Starting with the second floor, the two guards walked at a leisurely pace to the end of the west corridor where they turned and started back to the center.

Alicia stepped to the rail of the balcony where she had a view to the shops on the first floor. Wade joined her. The two stood side by side, elbows resting on the rail, adopting an air of indifference for the sake of an occasional passerby. Everything below them seemed normal and unremarkable, but both remained alert. Alicia's eyes flitted from one spot to the next, then fell on an anomaly.

An abandoned bag lay slumped against the side of the Wax on Wicks kiosk. Mall rules were clear and strictly enforced. Vendors were to keep their belongings locked inside their kiosks, not lying around in the open. There were no customers anywhere near the kiosk. No potential owner of the backpack. Gladys, the Wax on Wicks vendor, sat on a stool on the kiosk's far side, arranging merchandise.

"Bingo," Alicia said, "check that out."

"Check what out?" Wade asked.

"That bag, or backpack, or whatever it is. What do you think?"

"I don't know, probably nothing," Wade said.

"Well, I don't like the looks of it."

"All right, let's take a closer look."

The two made their way to the first floor. As they approached the Wax on Wicks kiosk, they split, Wade taking the right side, Alicia the left, both checking the surroundings for something out of the ordinary. They stopped a few feet from the bag.

"We should call this in and clear the area. Quietly," Alicia said.

"I don't know," Wade said. "It's kind of small. And, by the way it's sagging, I'd say it's empty. I don't think it's, well, you know..."

"Yeah. I know. It could be a mistake, or even a prank, but—" Alicia said, breaking off when Gladys looked up from her work. "Hi, Gladys," Alicia said, "do you know whose backpack—"

Gladys jumped from her stool, "Oh my God. I don't know. I didn't see anyone drop it there." She paused. "You don't think it—"

"No, I don't think, but I've got to call this in," Alicia said. "We can't take a chance."

"Alicia, maybe we—" Wade interjected, but Alicia had buzzed

Carlo on her radio. Wade spread his arms wide, halting a handful of approaching shoppers and asking them to keep back. "Sorry, ladies and gentleman, we're closing this section of the mall for a bit."

"What's going on?"

"Closing? What for?"

"Is it a bomb?" a female shopper shrieked, spotting the backpack on the floor.

"Everything's going to be fine," Wade said. "There's nothing to worry about, we just need you to clear the area."

Alicia mirrored Wade, blocking the approach from the opposite side, adding her reassurances. A panic was the last thing they needed.

From a distance, sirens wailed.

In minutes, four Ingram guards joined Alicia and Wade and cordoned off a third of the west wing, evacuating shoppers and staff from the corridor and seven nearby stores. The emergency crew arrived and conducted what was becoming an increasingly common exercise. Two other Atlanta malls had been shut down in the past month for suspicious packages, suffering hours of lost sales, angry customers, and unwanted media coverage.

At the time, Carlo had thanked God it hadn't been Riverside.

It was their turn now, Alicia thought. But Riverside was in luck. Thirty minutes into the incident, as an officer in a heavily padded suit approached the suspicious backpack, Wade's voice came over Alicia's radio. The backpack's owner had come forward.

Wade stepped from the crowd; a teenage girl with earbuds hanging from her ears stood by his side.

Riverside experienced thirty minutes of disruption and was spared a media frenzy. Nonetheless, throughout the incident, Alicia imagined the scene inside the Ingram Security Office: phones buzzing non-stop and Carlo pacing and cursing.

When the last of the emergency vehicles left and a degree of normalcy returned, Alicia sighed audibly.

"It wasn't your fault," Wade said. "We had to call it in."

"Well, if I'd waited another ten or fifteen minutes..." she replied.

"You had no choice."

"I don't know. Maybe. I need to get back and write this up so I can get out of here at a decent hour."

"All right. See you tomorrow," Wade said. "I'm going to make one more loop."

"See you," Alicia said. On her way to the Security Office in the mall's center section, she wondered if Wade would tell Carlo he'd wanted to wait another few minutes before calling in the incident. She hoped not. Like Wade, Carlo already thought Alicia was hyper. Carlo didn't need encouragement from Wade or anyone else.

It really could have been a bomb.

For the last half-hour of her shift, Alicia avoided eye contact with Carlo. She fixed her eyes on the security cameras, searching for shoppers with backpacks. Though she was accustomed to seeing Kyle with his backpack, until today she'd never noticed how many people carried them at the mall. They weren't just school children with books either, but young men, too. Young men carrying what, she wondered.

8. JAVIER

TRUE TO HIS WORD, WITH THE SUN HIGH OVERHEAD, SALVADOR stopped beside an arroyo edged on the near side by half-dead or dormant scrub. When he dropped his pack and drank from his water jug, the rest did the same. "One hour," he said.

Most of the rag-tag bunch plopped to the ground where they stood, too tired to search for shade, too afraid to wander far from Salvador. Javier chose a place within hearing distance beneath a scatter of branches that provided little relief from the sun but screened him from the others. He set his water jug beside him and groped inside his pack for the package of dried beef and bread he'd brought. He laid the food on the ground next to the jug. His throat was parched, but he paused to pray before eating or drinking. In the name of Allah, he said to himself.

A couple of feet away, two packs dropped to the ground. It was the two women. For the first time, Javier noticed they were twins, the same dark eyes, rounded cheeks, and full lips. They were identical except for a birthmark near the hairline on one woman's forehead. The marked woman moistened a cloth and dabbed it across her face. She took several long breaths, her shoulders and back rising and falling. The other smiled at Javier before tilting her head back and taking a long drink from her water jug.

The women chatted between bites of food, their voices low and soft, but Javier kept to himself and his ritual. When he finished his prayer, he wet his lips with a sip of water and tore a corner from the loaf of bread. He ate, concentrating on his body, feeling his heart beat slow and his muscles relax. He had no doubt he could make the rest of the walk, having trained for it and for what lay ahead. But he wondered if the others could make it even as far as the border. Ever since they'd started this morning, the sound of heavy breathing had preceded him along the trail.

He glanced at the two women, astonished they had made it this far. Javier wondered how his sister Selam would have fared under similar circumstances. Selam. He smiled. He hadn't thought of her in days, perhaps weeks. At fourteen, she was half-girl, half-woman. He would not see her again and wondered if she had forgiven him for leaving without a goodbye. His smile faded.

A tap on his arm. Javier's head snapped to the right. The woman who had smiled, the one without the birthmark, stood beside him, a section of orange in her outstretched palm. Javier shook his head, refusing though his throat was dry and swallowing difficult. But the woman insisted, nodding and nudging him again, the section wet and gleaming. He plucked it from her hand and held it on his tongue, savoring the juice.

Her smile broadened. "Me llamo Lupe," she said. My name is Lupe. When Javier did not respond, she repeated the phrase, saying each word more clearly.

"Lupe," Javier repeated.

Lupe smiled her ready smile. "And this is my sister, Ximena." Lupe popped another section of orange into her mouth and rejoined her twin. She placed an arm around her sister who frowned and pulled away. "And you?" Lupe asked.

"Javier," he said, hoping the tone conveyed he was not interested in further conversation. In his village, he did not speak directly with women outside his family. And besides, Mohsan had instructed him to keep his distance from everyone during his journey. Though he refrained from speaking to the women, he could not ignore them; his eyes returned time and again to their bodies. Both had walked with their jackets zipped to their necks and their hoods over their heads. Only the ovals of their faces had been exposed to the rays of sun and the sting of brambles and briars. Now they sat with hoods flopped back and jackets unzipped to catch even a hint of a breeze. A shadow ran between their breasts, mounds of soft flesh visible above the necklines of their tee-shirts. When Ximena, the one with the mark on her forehead, noticed Javier staring, she turned away and zipped her jacket.

Lupe sat as before, not seeming to mind the display of her cleavage. She peeled another slice of orange. The perfume of citrus hovered in the air.

"I'll take one," Octavio said from where he had squatted.

"I didn't offer it to you," Lupe said. She popped the segment into her mouth and wrapped what remained in a plastic bag. She edged closer to her sister.

Rebuffed by Lupe, Octavio stood and grabbed his crotch, then pumped his pelvis. He said a few words Javier did not know or need to know; Octavio's actions said everything. Octavio turned his back to the women, but continued spewing insults and suggestions, a grin on his face. Manuel sniggered from where he sat and added a few remarks.

Salvador, who ate by himself, glimpsed Octavio's antics but finished his lunch without comment. Only when the two miscreants erupted in guffaws and leg slapping did he speak. "Cállense!" he said. Quiet! He crumpled the sack that had held his lunch and flung it over his shoulder.

To Javier's surprise, the men escaped even a mild admonishment and everyone soon forgot the display of obscenity—everyone but Javier. He had come to a strange world with customs he cared nothing for and was thankful he would not have to endure them long.

When Salvador made the *char-char-char* sound, calling the group together, their bodies were barely rested. "Take one more drink. We won't stop again till dark." With a few grunts and groans, they rose, dusted themselves off, and followed Salvador.

* * *

Long after the sun slipped below the horizon, the group reached a ravine. They stood along the rim and looked into the dark abyss, assessing the climb down and the ascent on the far side with weary eyes and aching calves.

"We will rest here and cross over before full light," Salvador said, perhaps understanding the level of the migrants' exhaustion. Everyone breathed a sigh of relief. Most dropped their packs where they stood and collapsed beside them. A couple of men walked away to relieve themselves.

Soon, everyone dispersed beside the ravine, stretched out on the ground, and laid their heads on their packs. Like the others, Javier fell asleep in minutes.

When the snap of a dry twig underfoot woke him, it was dark. Javier had no idea how long he'd been asleep. His body told him minutes, an hour at the most. He waited, his ears tuned to any sound. A second snap sounded, followed by muffled sounds. At first, Javier thought it was Salvador rousing them. But it was too early, the sky studded with stars and holding a slice of the moon.

To his right, something moved. A silhouette against the night sky. It was a woman. She moved away from the others and into the brush, then disappeared. A moment later, he heard a trickling noise and the patter of urine falling to the ground.

Footsteps muffled by carpet soles.

Javier turned over, closed his eyes, and tried to sleep. But moments later, a different sound, words, but not distinguishable. He perched on one elbow and stared into the dark. Whispers, followed by a whimper, and then nothing.

Without making a sound, Javier made his way barefoot through the brush to where he'd heard the sounds, now grunts, animal like, but low.

Octavio sat astride one of the women. He grunted one last time, then set his knife on the ground. As he zipped his pants, he turned and found Javier standing beside him, a knife in Javier's right hand. Octavio flung himself at Javier's feet, tackling him and bringing him down. But Javier proved quicker, if not stronger. He pressed the Latino's face into the sand and drew his knife across Octavio's throat. Octavio gurgled, struggling for a breath, then went limp and still.

The woman had not moved from where she lay on the ground. And though she looked at Javier, she said nothing. Javier rose and shoved Octavio's body to the edge of the ravine where he nudged it once more, sending it into the ravine. The body rolled over and over until it came to a rest with a low thump.

Javier headed back, passing the spot where the woman had been, but she had fled without a sound.

9. JAVIER

SALVADOR CALLED OUT, "LET'S GO." THE GROUP GRABBED THEIR packs and jugs of water and assembled. They took their same places in line as they had the previous day, part instinct, part fear, part superstition, and part trust that what had carried them this far would carry them forward. Eleven migrants stood in the line, groggy and weary but on their feet.

"Octavio," Manuel muttered. There was no answer. Manuel called his friend's name again, louder this time. "Octavio."

"Silence," Salvador said, yanking Manuel's arm. Salvador walked a few paces along the edge of the ravine. He turned, rejoined the group, and made the *char-char-char* sound. Octavio did not emerge.

Salvador shrugged, turned, and started into the desert.

"Hombre, we can't just leave him," Manuel said.

The others moved away, shuffling behind Salvador, some turning their heads, scanning the ground behind them, some focusing on Salvador's feet moving on in the faint light.

"Hombre!"

Salvador continued his steady pace north, ignoring Manuel's pleas. Soon Manuel fell in at the back of the line, behind Javier. Ahead of Javier, Ximena and Lupe walked in silence, one leaning into the arms of the other, one sobbing into her hands.

Later, with the sun up and the temperature rising, several of the migrants groaned and begged Salvador to stop for a few minutes.

"The border's just ahead," Salvador said, without pausing. Twenty minutes later, where the terrain sloped away into a valley, he stopped. At the bottom of the slope, in plain sight, was the fence. Chain-linked and topped with loops of concertina wire, it ran uninterrupted to the horizon in both directions. It was tall, taller than Javier had imagined, and cast a long shadow to the north. An expanse scraped clean of brush and rocks flanked the fence, leaving no place to hide.

"Do we cross now? In daylight?" one of the group asked. It was Ignacio, the older man.

"Yes. There's a trail on the other side of that cut. It's not much further. I'll show you where Ortiz will meet you," Salvador said.

"What? You're not coming with us?" Ignacio asked. The group huddled, eyes flicking from one to the other and to Salvador who fidgeted. He checked his watch.

"I'll take you across," Salvador said.

"Shouldn't we wait till after—" Pablo asked.

"No," Salvador said, cutting Pablo short. "There's no one here. We need to go now."

Each of the migrants took the measure of the fence.

"Are we going to climb over the fence?" Ignacio asked, his forehead furrowed, the folds caked with dust. He had limped, favoring his right leg for the last several miles.

"No. We're going under. I'll show you. Follow me."

Salvador led them into a wash and past several clusters of gray and brown rocks with scars hacked into their sides. The migrants followed, hurrying to keep up with Salvador. Their heads swiveled, checking over their shoulders, back at their feet, up at

33

the sky, and down again. All had ears peeled for the high whine of aerial surveillance or the distinctive *whop-whop* of helicopters, or the rumble of a vehicle.

The wash leveled out. The brush thickened, snagging at their trousers and impeding their progress. Evidence of others having passed this way lay at every step, backpacks with their contents strewn across the ground or caught in the brush, empty water jugs, trash bags, clothes, shoes, hats, scarves, and gloves.

Salvador halted. When the migrants caught up, he tugged at a thicket of dead sticks. A snarl of brush came away in one piece. As he stooped to set it aside, his jacket lifted, revealing the grip of a pistol protruding from Salvador's waistband. Javier had seen it and imagined the rest had as well.

"Through here," Salvador said. He handed one of the brothers a flashlight and motioned him into the tunnel. "Keep going. Be quick."

Javier held back, his eyes on Salvador. When all the other migrants had disappeared inside the tunnel, the coyote picked up the discarded cover and jerked his head at Javier. "Go."

Javier crouched and entered the tunnel. He followed the beam of light splashing the mud walls ahead. The tunnel fell at a steep angle for several yards before it flattened and rose again. In places, it was no more than a few feet tall, forcing the group to crawl on their hands and knees. No one spoke, but panting, groans, and the stumble of feet on rock echoed through the darkness.

Up ahead, one of the brothers shouted, "Gracias a dios, madre mía." Oh, Thank God. There was a rustling sound as he pushed his way through another cover of brush. Light flooded the end of the tunnel.

Javier emerged and took his bearings. The fence lay behind

him now. He was in America. Only one more leg of his journey remained.

Salvador replaced the cover and urged the migrants out of the swale. From there he took them along a narrow path for a mile until they reached another ravine cut through the earth and forming a jagged line pointing north.

"Now what?" Manuel asked.

"Now, you pay me the other half of what you owe me."

"No way, hombre. I'm not paying until I see Ortiz and the van."

"Ortiz will meet you there," Salvador said, pointing to the north and west of where they stood. "See the three peaks on those mountains? You go toward them. You'll come to a river where you can refill your water jugs. Follow the river north until you see a set of power lines. There'll be more water there at a spot marked with blue flags. That's where Ortiz will be. At six."

"Another day of walking?" someone asked.

"I thought you said Ortiz would pick us up once we crossed," Manuel said. He took a few steps forward and stood in Salvador's face.

Salvador stepped back. "Ortiz will be there. It won't take long if you don't waste your time arguing."

"I'll pay you when we reach the blue flags and when we see Ortiz," Manuel said.

"This is as far as I go," Salvador said.

Salvador turned to Pablo and opened his hand. Pablo handed him a roll of bills. Without bothering to count it, Salvador stuffed the money into a pocket on his backpack and moved to the next person in line.

In the distance, over Salvador's shoulder, a plume of brown

dust rose. Javier squinted and made out the form of an approaching vehicle. It was a pickup.

"Is that our van?" Ignacio asked. He had spotted the vehicle as well.

"It's not a van," Javier said.

"Who is it?" Pablo asked.

Questions flew at Salvador, but Javier did not wait to hear the answers. Javier shouted, "Policia," knowing the word would cause everyone to flee at once and in myriad directions, confusing the approaching federales. He shouldered his pack and ran. Behind him, the scuffling of feet as the rest of the group scattered into the scrub.

Javier ran with long, low steps, his shoulders hunched forward. He slipped into a finger of the ravine, skidding just below the ridge and into a cluster of small trees. When the cloud of dust he'd kicked up settled, he raised his head to follow what was happening. To his right, at eye level, a lizard sunned himself on a boulder and studied the unwelcome visitor.

Close by, someone stumbled and fell to the ground. It was Salvador. He buried himself under a shrub. Javier and the coyote kept their heads low and still, only their eyes moved, tracking the approaching vehicle, now clearly a US Border Patrol pickup.

When the vehicle stopped, two men in uniform jumped out. One fired his gun over the heads of Pablo and his sons who had taken off at a run. The trio halted and walked back at gunpoint. The second Border Patrol agent walked up to Ignacio who knelt on the ground not ten feet from where Salvador had stopped earlier. After relieving Ignacio of his backpack, the agent frisked the old man and cuffed him. Pablo and his sons were cuffed as well, then forced to their knees beside Ignacio.

With their captives secure, one agent grabbed a megaphone and called to the migrants hiding in the desert. His words were indecipherable though Javier guessed he asked them to surrender. No one appeared. He called a second and a third time. Still no one showed.

While the first agent waited with the megaphone, the other scanned the terrain with a pair of binoculars. Javier's instinct was to duck. But rather than risk betraying his location with even a small movement, he held his breath, stared straight ahead, and prayed. A long interval of complete silence followed. When the pickup's engine came to life, Javier blinked and exhaled.

The agents loaded the four captured Mexicans into the back-seat of the pickup. The vehicle crawled off to the west. For as long as Javier could see, the agent in the passenger seat glassed the desert. Then, the pickup hurtled off, leaving a trail of dust in the air.

10. JAVIER

SALVADOR MOVED FIRST. "WE'RE SAFE," HE SAID AND STOOD.

"Where's the van?" Javier asked as he rose and swatted the dirt from his pants.

"I told you, it will be under the power lines at six."

"Then I'll pay you at six."

"It'll be there."

"You can try to get what you want from the others, but not from me."

"You owe me. I want it now."

Salvador's hand went behind his back where Javier knew the gun was. But before Salvador could retrieve his pistol, Javier swung his backpack and knocked Salvador to the ground. Then, he slipped his knife from its sheath and thrust the knife into Salvador's stomach. He turned the blade against the man's flesh and pulled upward, using all his strength. A gash opened and Salvador's blood spilled into the sand.

Crouching beside the coyote's body, Javier snatched the pistol from Salvador's pants and stuffed it in the waistband of his own jeans. He patted the sides of Salvador's jacket until he found Pablo's money.

Javier looked at Salvador. He spat in the coyote's face, dirty, twisted, and frozen in a grimace. Before rising, he wiped his knife on Salvador's shirt.

Without leaving his hiding place, Javier scanned the horizon. A couple hundred yards away, Manuel stood facing the remaining migrants. He was gesturing wildly, pointing north and yelling, though Javier could not make out his words. After a few minutes, the group split, Manuel and the other men heading north, perhaps to Tucson seventy miles away, the women to the west and the power lines with the promise of transportation and water.

Javier waited for them to disappear before retrieving his pack from where he had taken shelter. He needed to leave quickly. He guessed another car or van would arrive soon to retrieve Salvador and the money he'd collected from the migrants. Maybe they'd demand more and kill anyone who balked. The others might have come to the same realization.

Javier set out for Tucson, but he'd stay well away from Manuel. He closed his eyes and pictured the map of Arizona in his head. He laughed. Hussein would be proud of his ability to recall the state's main arteries when once the verses of the Quran had escaped him.

He'd have to traverse public and private lands in the open desert until he found the highway. The walk would be grueling and fraught with dangers he could not imagine. Though he doubted anyone would look for the killer of anonymous migrants in the desert, he'd play it safe. He'd walk the distance rather than find a ride at the highway. In Tucson, he'd be just another Latino looking for work or a ride onward. No Anglo would give him a second glance. That was what Mohsan had said. Of course, Mohsan had expected Javier to avoid calling attention to himself—not to leave two dead bodies in his wake. Or to be late. Without a ride to Tucson, he'd be at least three days later than planned.

11. LUPE

HOW THE US BORDER PATROL AGENTS—OR WHOEVER THE UNI-
formed men were—missed apprehending them, Lupe would
never know. When Javier and Salvador scurried into the ravine
and disappeared in the brush, she had grabbed Ximena's arm and
pulled her along, running perpendicular to the fence. The others
ran westward toward a rise in the distance.

"Come, Ximena. Come quickly. This way," she said. Ximena
stumbled behind Lupe, saying nothing.

They ran in a semi-crouch as far as Ximena was able. Lupe
stopped and pulled her sister to the ground beside the trail Salvador called "the freedom trail." Unlike the telltale signs of scattered belongings they'd seen earlier, here mounds of discarded
clothing, plastic bags, sweatshirts, and empty water jugs lay in
deep piles along both sides of the footpath. Lupe pulled a pair of
mud-caked and torn trousers over Ximena's head and propped an
open and empty, sun-baked backpack over her arms. She threw a
jacket across her own legs and crumpled a trash bag around her
head, noting too late the putrid stench of decaying matter. She
had no time to make any better preparation.

"Ximena, keep quiet. Dios mío." My God. "Keep quiet and
don't move," she said. Ximena had not said a word. She'd not
cried or whimpered since the night before when she had crawled
back to their resting spot. Lupe doubted Ximena would say any-

thing now. Nevertheless, Lupe reached inside her pants pocket. She clutched her rosary, closed her eyes, and prayed while her heart thundered in her ears.

The pickup crunched to a stop, and the doors opened with a click. Lupe dared not look up but hoped the agents would pursue the men who'd taken off at a run across the open desert.

"Stop! Halt! Pare!" an agent shouted. One fired a shot. Shoes pounded the ground. Gun belts, ammunition, radios, and other gear clattered then faded as the agents headed away from the women.

Moments later, bits of conversation, half Spanish, half English, drifted toward Lupe. The agents had caught at least one runner. A door slammed, but the vehicle stayed where it was. Voices over a bullhorn called, "Muchachos. Come out. You will not be harmed. You will not survive the desert. Es peligroso." It's dangerous. "Muchachos. Come out. You will not be harmed."

Beneath the trash bag, Lupe crossed herself. She said the rosary for the fifth time and began another Hail Mary for luck.

Hail Mary, full of grace, the Lord is with thee; blessed art thou among women and blessed is the fruit of thy womb, Jesus.
Holy Mary, Mother of God, pray for us sinners...

Footsteps approached, crunching the scrabble underfoot. Lupe held her breath and squeezed her eyes shut. With no time to retrieve her prayer card, she pictured the cherubs and roses surrounding the image of Our Lady of Guadalupe and imagined the feel of the paper between her fingers.

"Goddamn," an agent said. He kicked at something and swore

again. An empty water jug plunked as it tumbled across the field of debris. He fired four shots, one zinging as it passed over Lupe's head. She guessed they were random shots designed to startle a migrant into revealing his hiding place. She and her sister were unfazed. The *pop-pop* was a familiar sound in her village, abandoned brass-studded shells a familiar sight, whether from a drunk exhibiting his bravado after a night of celebration or a drug dealer eliminating a rival. She and Ximena remained as still and lifeless as the debris on the trail.

Doors opened and closed again. The engine fired, idled for a moment, and then grew faint.

Thirty minutes passed before Lupe dared raise her head and open her eyes. She flung aside the garbage bag and filled her lungs with fresh air. Yards away, the three brothers stood with their belongings piled at their feet.

Lupe nudged Ximena. "Come on. Get up," Lupe said.

After pulling Ximena to her feet, Lupe led her sister by the hand out of the piles of detritus to where the brothers huddled. As the women approached, they broke off their conversation and turned their heads.

Luis, the eldest of the three, jutted his chin at Lupe. "You made it."

"Yes. Gracias a Dios. We hid over there," Lupe said, pointing to the field of discarded objects. "Is there anyone else?"

"I don't think so. Looks like it's just us. They took Ignacio and Pablo."

"We heard gunfire," Lupe said.

"Yeah. Just warning shots though. So, what are you and your sister going to do?" Luis asked.

"We'll walk to the power lines, like Salvador said. To the place with the blue flags."

"You're crazy if you do," said a voice behind Lupe.

All heads turned. It was Manuel. As he joined the circle, Lupe put an arm around Ximena and pulled her close.

"What do you mean?" Lupe asked.

"You see Salvador anywhere?" Manuel asked. He smirked. "No. I didn't think so. He's probably halfway back to Mexico City by now. He never intended to take us to Ortiz. I don't trust him for one minute. I'll bet he arranged for someone to ambush us and take what's left of our money. They might be waiting for us now somewhere between here and the blue flags. If there are any blue flags."

"So, what do you suggest?" Luis asked.

"Don't look at me, hombre. I'm no coyote. I don't know about these things, but I'm going north until I find a highway where I can hitch a ride into Tucson," Manuel said, giving Lupe and Xi mena a long look before leaving. He walked a few paces, paused, and called back, "Good luck, my friends. Adios."

"I think we'll go with him," Luis said, looking to his brothers for a sign that they agreed. They nodded. Luis turned to the women. "What about you two?"

"Us?" Lupe asked. "Ximena, what do you want to do?" Ximena looked at the peaks in the distance though Lupe didn't know if she were answering Lupe's question or merely avoiding looking at Manuel. "We'll walk to the power lines. It can't be too far," Lupe said.

"Don't drink all your water," Luis reminded them. "And don't get lost."

Lupe's shoulders slumped. "We'll take our chances. We'll go

quickly. And, besides, I don't want to go with that one," Lupe said, pointing her chin at Manuel in the distance.

"Suit yourself, I'm following Manuel," Luis said. The brothers shouldered their packs.

"Did anyone see which direction Javier went?" Lupe asked.

"No. He disappeared like a rat down a sewer," Luis said. "Besides, I don't think he's anyone you want to follow."

"Why not?"

"He's trouble."

"What do you mean?"

"Nothing. Just what I see. You coming with us or not?"

"No," Lupe said. "We'll go on our own."

"Well, good luck to you," Luis said. "But don't hang around here. Who knows who will show up next?"

The three walked away, leaving Lupe and Ximena alone for the first time in days. When they were out of sight, Lupe took a sip of water from her jug and passed it to Ximena. "Go ahead, take a sip now. We won't take another until we reach the river."

12. LUPE

SHE DIDN'T HAVE A WATCH, BUT FROM WHERE THE SUN SAT LOW ON the horizon, Lupe guessed it was well past six and that Ortiz would have come and gone. She'd not kept up Salvador's pace and instead walked at Ximena's, losing precious time. Worse, she'd taken several breaks for water, despite having vowed to wait until they reached the river and the power lines.

A dull thud caused Lupe to glance back over her shoulder. Ximena had dropped her backpack and collapsed to the ground. "No more," she said.

At least she had spoken, Lupe thought. Kneeling beside Ximena, Lupe cupped her sister's chin and said, "Mena, look at me."

Ximena raised her eyes.

"We have to keep going. We have no choice." Lupe shook Mena gently. "Do you understand me?"

"Someone will come."

"No one is coming. If we stay here, we will die. It's only a little further." Lupe tugged at her sister's arm and pulled her up. "Put your arm around me. You can rest a little that way. But we must keep going."

An hour later, Lupe heard what sounded like water flowing. She quickened her step and crested a small ridge. "Mena, look. Look. It's the river. We made it." Lupe clapped her hands and hugged her sister.

Lupe had pictured a torrent of water rushing through a canyon. The river running below them was little more than a steady trickle, brown with silt as it meandered through the rock-strewn landscape. But it was a river, and the mesquite trees along its banks would give them shade for the rest of the afternoon and shelter for the night. Lupe held her water jug aloft. Little more than an inch of clear liquid sloshed at the bottom. She and Mena drank until they had drained the jug. They'd fill both of their jugs in the morning before setting out to the north. Salvador had said the power lines and flags lay to the north, but not how far away or how long it might take to reach them.

She prayed Ortiz would come back. Prayer was all she had left.

At the sound of men's voices, Lupe bolted upright, one hand grabbing for the water jug, the other for her sister. To her left, a group of eight or ten Latinos emerged from the brush and rushed to the river, one calling to the next, "Water. Water. It's here!"

By Lupe's reckoning, they were heading north, perhaps to the same spot with blue flags. She waved her hand above her head to signal them. "Hola! Hola!" she said, scrambling to her feet.

A round-chested, dark-skinned man in jeans cut away at the knees turned his head at the sound of Lupe's voice. He approached, eyeing the sisters. "Are you alone?"

A lump formed in Lupe's throat. She wondered whether she had made a mistake in hailing him. While he waited for Lupe's answer, the group of seven men edged closer, surrounding Lupe and her sister.

"We...we are. But Ortiz is coming for us. At the blue flags. He is bringing a van for us," Lupe said with as much confidence as she could muster.

"Yes, there's a truck coming for us, too."

"If we miss Ortiz, can we go with you?" Lupe asked, her hopes rising.

"Our truck is full," the dark-skinned man said.

"Oh. Do you think there'll be another?"

"Quien sabe?" he said. Who knows? "It depends."

"Depends on what?"

The man raised a hand in front of her and rubbed his thumb against his fingers.

"We can pay," Lupe said, assuming the man was the coyote. She hoped he'd be satisfied with money and nothing more.

"Then we will make room," he said.

13. CYRIL

GREG STOOD UP ABRUPTLY, KNOCKING HIS CHAIR AGAINST THE wall. "It's him," he said. "It's him."

"No shit! Are you sure?" Cy asked, scooting his chair closer to Greg's desk. Greg Nothwang and Cyril Westfall, or Cy as he preferred to be called, were working late. The two freshly minted Federal Bureau of Investigation agents were on loan to Peter Olson, a Supervisory Special Agent in Cyber Intelligence. They were the last two on the fourth floor of the FBI's Atlanta Field Office. The only lights on the floor were the ceiling lights above their shared cubicle and the blue glow of their computer screens.

Peter, the agent running the sting hadn't heard from Rasil Khan, a suspected terrorist, for two weeks, and feared Khan had grown suspicious and fled underground. Cy and Greg were to monitor the FBI's Twitter account for messages from Khan and a handful of other suspects. But Khan was the prize. Peter Olson believed he would lead them to one of the FBI's most wanted and well hidden terrorists, a man named Qasim Bousaid.

The message on Greg's screen read: "Can you get me money for the ticket?"

"What do we do now?" Cy asked. "Should we let him wait till tomorrow when Olson is here?"

"Wait? You mean we should ask permission?" Greg asked.

"Yeah," Cy said, "as in make sure we don't blow this thing."

"Okay. You call Olson." Greg tapped the face of his watch. "Two in the morning. He'll be glad to hear from you. You want him to think we can't manage for six hours without his help?"

"Maybe. What's your plan?"

The two stared at the computer screen, a cursor flashing in the empty reply box.

A new message appeared on the screen: "You there?" Khan again.

"We can't wait," Greg said. "Khan hasn't shown his head for weeks."

"Yes we can. You haven't responded to his first message. He doesn't even know we're here. We can wait."

Greg keyed a message using Olson's undercover name, Omar.

OMAR: Yes.

"Shit," Cy said as Greg hit the enter key, sending the message to Khan.

KHAN: First, I need proof.

OMAR: What proof?

KHAN: Proof you are who you say you are.

OMAR: You met Mohammed. You know him. He can be trusted.

Cy held his head in his hands, reading the messages between his open fingers. Greg was bringing up Mohammed, the FBI's informant and middleman to reassure Khan. Mohammed was the face Khan knew.

KHAN: I don't know. I only know him through Facebook. And through you.

OMAR: How do I know you are who you say you are? Maybe you are FBI?

"Christ!" Cy said.

KHAN: I don't know.

OMAR: What do you mean?

No response. Cy and Greg stared in silence at the screen.

KHAN: I don't think I can go through with this.

"He's blown. You've got it right there," Cy said. Both agents were aware they could not encourage a target who expressed doubt to go forward with their plan, in Khan's case to travel to Syria to join the Islamic fighters. Encouraging Khan now could bring a charge of entrapment.

OMAR: Don't worry. Mohammed will bring you the money.

OMAR: Tomorrow.

"Greg, you have to stop. You can't deliver on this, anyway. And he's blown."

"Maybe, maybe not. Olson wouldn't just walk away. He'd want us to save this."

Us? Cy's stomach tightened. It was true. Olson had enlisted them to work the sting as a team under his supervision. A first "field" assignment for the two and a welcome change from the paperwork assignments he'd had since joining the Bureau's Atlanta Field Office. Greg was more hyped than Cy, which might explain his eagerness and his casual stretching of Olson's leash.

But Cy was in this with Greg. Four years of case studies at Cornell had drilled the idea of teamwork into him. Graduate school and training at the FBI's Academy reinforced the concept. Nevertheless, teamwork went against Cy's nature and, he thought, that of Jerald Westfall, his father.

The senior Westfall had spent his entire career at the FBI, excelling at every post. Last year, he'd been promoted to Associate Executive Assistant Director, or AEAD, of the Criminal Investigation Division, a high ranking position a couple of rungs below the Director himself.

Jerald Westfall never let Cy consider anything other than joining the FBI when he finished school. Still, Cy thought he might make a job at the FBI work out. He broached the subject of working in intelligence analysis in the National Security Branch, reminding his father of the critical thinking and analytical skills honed over his exorbitantly expensive, seven-year education. They'd gone to his father's study to talk, or in Cy's case to listen and to shift endlessly from side to side in one of the mahogany-colored leather chairs.

Jerald acknowledged his son's abilities, tipping his glass of amber-colored whiskey to Cy. But Jerald said he wanted Cy to "get his feet wet" first. AEAD Westfall was old style FBI. In Cy's head, a grainy black and white film played, men running, jumping, climbing ropes, firing handguns, and wrestling fellow recruits to the ground.

Cy had been miserable throughout the twenty weeks of training and had barely passed. All his genes had come from his mother, a frail woman even in her earliest family photos. One shot he favored was of his mother standing behind him and helping him blow out the candles on his fifth birthday. He liked the photo, because that's where the memories of her as a healthy, vibrant woman started and stopped. To this day, he remembered tears had welled in his eyes when he'd missed one candle then evaporated when a warm sweet-scented breath behind finished the job. The memory was suspect, though, aided as it was by the photo.

On graduating, Cy started in the Atlanta Field Office's Criminal Investigation Division, a division in his father's chain of command. If his plan to work in intelligence analysis was to succeed, Cy needed to complete his first few assignments with high marks. After that, he could apply for a transfer with or without his father's approval.

OMAR: Wednesday. At the cafe.

There was no reply.

Greg waited five minutes before repeating the message. He waited through another five minutes of silence, then he typed a new message.

OMAR: You there? Silence.

* * *

By six the next morning, Greg and Cy were back in front of their PCs. They'd gone home only long enough to shower and change clothes. Olson was due any minute.

"What do you mean, gone?" Peter Olson asked when Greg and Cy completed briefing him on the overnight activities.

"That was the last message we received," Greg said. "He signed off, or at least he didn't answer again."

Cy left the talking to Greg and kept his own eyes on the transcript of the social media conversation. The last thing he wanted to see was the look on Peter's face.

"Am I mistaken or did I not specifically ask you to let me know when we heard from him?" Peter asked.

"You did, sir," Greg said.

"And despite my instructions, you decided to handle the contact yourself?"

"It was a mistake, but he was blown, anyway."

"Is that your experienced assessment?" Peter asked.

"It was a mistake," Greg repeated.

"And you, Westfall?"

"It was a mistake," Cy said, repeating Greg's answer.

"I don't need to tell either of you it's taken three months work, day in and day out, to get to this point. To identify this guy, determine he had intent, and gain his confidence."

"No sir," Greg said.

"I don't need to remind you, do I, that Khan was our link to Bousaid? Or that Bousaid managed to come here, become a citizen, God only knows how, and fund every goddamn plot we've uncovered? And now, in one night, it's all lost," Peter said.

"No, sir. I mean yes, sir. It seems that way," Greg said.

Cy stared at the table and did not answer.

14. JAVIER

AT DUSK, JAVIER ENCOUNTERED THE FIRST SIGN OF HUMAN HABITA-
tion, a barbed wire fence, three rows of wire strung pole to pole
as far as he could see. In places, the wire had worked its way loose
from the pole and sagged to the ground.

Javier chose one of the low spots to cross. Before he'd gone
more than a hundred yards, two riders on horseback came into
view. They were traveling toward him, the horses in a walk. Javier cast a glance back over his shoulder to the point where he'd
crossed. Even at top speed, he'd not be able to outrun the riders if
they came after him. He squared his shoulders to the riders and
planted his feet.

The horsemen were not two men. They were an older couple,
in their sixties, Javier guessed, not an expert in guessing ages of
white Americans.

The man spoke first. "You lost?" he asked. "Perdido?"

Javier had to choose between responding in English or Spanish. "No. Voy a Tucson," he said, staying in role.

The man on horseback accepted Javier's answer whether or
not he believed him.

"Are you hungry?" the woman asked.

"Or thirsty," the man said, noticing the near empty plastic jug
tied to Javier's backpack. "Thirsty?" he repeated and raised his
hand to his lips to mimic drinking from a cup.

Javier answered in English, saying he was thirsty, not hungry.

"Where are the others?" the man asked. "Los otros?"

"No others," Javier said in English, at which the man eyed the woman on horseback.

"You didn't save any for this part of the trip," the man said. "Well, it's even more difficult and dangerous up ahead than what you have been through. You can fill up at our well, but then I want you off my property. No armas? No drogas?" he asked.

Javier shook his head.

"Come on up," the man said. "You can ride with me to the well. I'll give you a lift." He offered his gloved hand, implying Javier was to ride with him. To his female companion he said, "Why don't you head on back, Honey? I'll be along, there's just one more stretch of wire I want to fix on the way."

The woman nodded and rode off, her horse kicking up dust as she galloped north to whatever lay beyond the crest of a small hill.

Javier took hold of the man's gloved hand and hoisted himself behind the rider. They veered toward the fence and the spot where Javier had crossed over the loose wire.

There, the man dismounted.

"My name's Chester," the man said. When Javier said nothing, he repeated his name, "Ches-ter," emphasizing the syllables.

"Ches-ter," Javier repeated.

"That's it."

He didn't ask Javier's name and Javier didn't volunteer.

"You can give me a hand here, if you don't mind," Chester said.

After mending the broken section, they mounted the horse again and poked along, checking the fence line as they went. They rode in silence, Javier tracking their route in his head and keeping sight of the crest of the hill over which the woman had gone. He wondered if the slow and deliberate pace Chester took was to give "Honey" time to reach their home and call the police.

With a free hand, Javier felt behind him and found both the knife and the pistol.

Chester shifted in the saddle. "We're almost there," he said. "Diez minutos mas. Bueno?" Ten more minutes. Okay?

"Bueno," Javier answered.

At a corner in the fence, they came on a small hutch. It was nothing more than a crate with a tin roof tacked to it, the crate mounted on the corner fence post.

"Agua," Chester said.

They dismounted and Chester opened the crate for Javier. But as Javier wrestled to free his empty water jug from where he'd tied it to his back, the gun slipped from his pants to the ground. Chester spied the gun at once. His jaw dropped. "Goddamn it," Chester said. "You said no guns." Chester reached for the pistol, but Javier beat him to it and grabbed the gun.

Javier pointed the barrel at Chester.

"Get off my land," Chester said. He kept his eye on the young man as he mounted the horse.

It took two shots, the first hit Chester in the arm, the second, square in his back. He fell from the horse and collapsed in a heap to the ground, his hat tumbling away into the brush. Startled, the horse ran a short distance away before stopping.

Javier walked a few steps toward the horse. He'd never ridden a horse and was unsure whether he wanted to try or just tie the animal to the fence. But when Javier came within a few feet, the horse ran, leaving Javier no choice but to continue on foot.

He would have to kill the woman. If she hadn't called the police before now, she would when Chester failed to return.

As he crested the hill, Javier spied the woman's light bay horse tethered to the rail of an adobe-walled house. Javier eyed the surroundings and the horizon. There were no signs of the authorities, no farm hands, no dogs. No sign of anyone.

When he was a few yards shy of the front porch, the door opened. Honey emerged, drying her hands with a dish towel, a quizzical expression on her face.

"Where's Chester?" she asked.

"Calle 86?" Javier asked.

"That way," Honey said, pointing to her left. "Where's Chester?" she asked again, her voice an octave higher this time. "What have you done to him?" The muscles in her face tightened, her eyebrows knit together. Honey dropped the towel and ran inside the house.

Javier found her in the kitchen, her hands fumbling with the phone. In a single motion, with one hand he grabbed the knife from its sheath and with the other Honey's hair, arching her head back and slitting her throat. He let her fall to the floor, then wiped his knife clean. He rinsed his face and refilled his water bottle at the kitchen sink. As he stepped over Honey's body, he noticed a table set for three with sandwiches and fruit. Javier placed the sandwiches in a sack, picked up an apple and took a bite, then walked out the door and into the desert toward Calle 86.

15. LUPE

AT MIDNIGHT, THE BUS PULLED AWAY FROM THE GREYHOUND BUS Station in Tucson and wound its way through the city and to the highway headed east. Tucked into the window seat with her head braced against the window, Ximena fell asleep, allowing Lupe to relax. They'd made it to America. They'd survived the walk, near capture, exhaustion, and a cramped ride to Tucson with another group of migrants. True, Ximena had suffered something more and would not speak to Lupe or anyone else. But she, too, had survived.

Lupe fingered the beads of her rosary. She closed her eyes and gave thanks.

Some hours later, Lupe woke and gazed out the window at the dark landscape. For a while, Lupe worried they had not really escaped. The terrain had changed little, still as flat, arid, and devoid of life as the desert had been. Even the cities through which they passed had familiar names, Las Cruces, El Paso, and San Antonio. But at midday on the second day, they veered north, and the countryside changed. Meal stops were in places where Latinos were in the minority, where people stared.

In Montgomery, still hours from their destination, Lupe and Ximena remained on board during the stop. "We'll wait till we get to Atlanta," Lupe told Ximena. "It's not far now." The truth was she wanted to save the rest of their money. She feared arriving in Atlanta without enough left to find their father.

* * *

Then, forty hours after they had departed Tucson, the bus pulled into the Atlanta Greyhound Station. Lupe barely understood the driver's announcement; instead, she relied on the word "Atlanta" in foot-high letters above the entrance to confirm they had arrived.

Everyone disembarked, though for some passengers this stop was not the end of their trip but a chance to visit the restroom and purchase food for the next leg.

Lupe swallowed her hunger, opting for a long drink from a water fountain inside the station. With their belongings strapped to their backs, the sisters watched the crowd disperse. Some greeted waiting families with hugs, others simply shuffled away. Summoning her courage, Lupe tapped the arm of the only female nearby, an Anglo, but an older woman with a child. "Perdon," she said. "Address."

The woman started at Lupe's touch. Without so much as a glance at the wrinkled slip of paper Lupe offered, she said, "Taxis are out there." The woman pointed toward the exit.

"Gracias," Lupe said. Then, mindful of the woman's use of English, she followed with, "Thank you."

The woman nodded and urged her child forward.

Lupe had much to learn.

* * *

Forty-nine Willow Road. The taxi driver, a dark-skinned man, glanced at the words on the page Lupe held out for him. "You have thirty-five dollars?" he asked in words strung together, rising and falling like a melody.

"Thirty-five?" Lupe repeated to make certain she'd understood.

"Yes, thirty-five dollars." He held up three fingers on one hand and five on the other.

"Yes," Lupe said. She reached into the pocket of her backpack, removed two twenty dollar bills, and offered them to the driver.

He shook his head. "When we get there," he said, again song-like. He swiveled in his seat, gave her a second glance in the rear-view mirror, and edged the cab away from the curb.

A half hour later, the driver turned onto a narrow street. He drove slowly, scanning the houses as he went, his head shifting left and right to spot the number, while at the same time to avoid the deep potholes in the road. Lupe spotted the number above the door of a ramshackle house, twice the size of her home in Saltillo but in a greater state of disrepair. "Cuarenta y nueve," she said, tapping her fingernail against the window to alert the driver.

* * *

The women stood side by side, staring at the front of the house.

"Is this where Papa lives?" Ximena asked. One of the few questions she'd asked since they'd left Tucson.

"Yes, I think so," Lupe said. "I don't know if he's home or not, but we can't stand here forever."

Lupe grabbed her backpack and followed the foot worn path through the yard to the front door. Raucous music and a jumble of voices yelling over each other came from inside the house. Lupe tapped on the front door, but no one answered. She made a fist and knocked harder, several times. The music stopped. Seconds later, the door opened to reveal a young Hispanic male dressed in nothing more than a tee-shirt and shorts. He ran his fingers through his matted hair though the stiff strands settled as disheveled as they had been when he'd answered the door.

"Bueno," he said.

"Soy Lupe. Mi padre se llama Alfonso." I'm Lupe. My father is Alfonso.

"Alfonso. Ah. Sí." The man stepped aside, making way for Lupe and Ximena. Inside, two men sat on the floor beside a mattress on which another man sprawled. They eyed Lupe and Ximena. One smirked and bobbled his eyebrows at the other.

"Disculpe," Lupe said. Excuse me. "Donde esta, mi papa? Alfonso." Where's my father?

A door in the hallway opened, and a man stepped into view. Ximena pushed past Lupe and ran to him, crying, "Papa, Papa," ignoring the stares of the men in the front room. When she reached her father, Ximena flung her arms around him. Lupe did the same, causing Alfonso to stumble backward into the room he'd exited a moment ago.

"Quien es?" Who's there? It was a woman's voice.

Both women wheeled to their right, to another mattress on the floor. A wedge of light streaming through a drawn curtain too short for the window illuminated a half-naked woman. She propped herself on one elbow but made no attempt to pull the sheet over her breasts.

Alfonso scratched himself then ran his hands over his face. "Come with me," he said, walking his daughters back into the hallway and toward the front of the house.

"Don't go, Alfonso, don't go," the woman pleaded. But Alfonso pulled the door closed behind him.

"So, you made it," he said, stating the obvious. "It's good to see you. I...I didn't know how soon you'd get here. Your, ah, your mother told me you were on your way."

Lupe stole a glance at Ximena, wondering what thoughts were going through her sister's head. As twins, they often found they shared the same thoughts. With a half-open jaw, Ximena was surveying her father. Her eyes moved from head to toe and back again. Clearly, they were thinking the same thing.

Lupe remembered her father as a proud man, clean-shaven and meticulous in his appearance. Even on the days he'd come home from work in the fields, he rushed to bathe before sitting down to dinner. The man facing her now was unkempt and had grown a paunch. The bloated stomach pressed against a discolored undershirt that had seen better days. A several-day growth of stubble lined his jaw.

"Lupe," Ximena said, "let's go."

"Go? Go where?"

"I don't care," Ximena answered. "We can find a place."

"I'm sorry, girls. I can make space here for you until tomorrow. But then—"

"I'm not staying here," Ximena said.

"I'm not going to argue with you. As you can see—"

"Alfonso, venga!" Come here. It was the woman's voice coming from the hallway, pleading for him to return.

A man in the front room laughed.

Alfonso opened his mouth to say something but changed his mind. "Un momento," he yelled down the hall. "Let me show you how to get to the church. They'll help. They help everyone when they first arrive."

16. LUPE

XIMENA WAS OUT THE DOOR AND HALFWAY ACROSS THE STREET BE-
fore Lupe stepped from her father's house. "Wait for me, Ximena,
wait," she called. "You don't even know where you're going."

"No I don't. But I know I'm not spending one more minute in
that house with that woman."

"Don't think about it right now. Here. Let's look at the map
father drew. We go two blocks on Willow, then we make a right
at the next corner, and then a left. He said we could spot the
church from there. It will be okay. You'll see."

The Iglesia Santa Maria, nothing more than a storefront,
stood at the end of a row of buildings. A middle-aged woman
answered the door. Latina. Relieved, Lupe took a deep breath
and explained their circumstances, making their long story as
short as she could.

"Come in. Please, come in," the woman said. She led the sisters to a room at the back of the building. "My name's Isabel.
You must be exhausted. You can stay here for the night. But first,
you should eat something. In the morning we can talk about
next steps."

Isabel's words were like a balm to Lupe who was weary of
being Ximena's sister, mother, and caretaker. She surrendered
herself to the kindly woman.

After a spare meal of bread and soup, Isabel showed the two

sisters their room. It was the first bed the sisters had seen in weeks and both fell asleep at once.

The next morning, over a cup of strong, dark coffee, Isabel said she knew a young woman who needed a roommate. "Her name is Mercedes Guzman. She comes from Saltillo, too. Do you know her?"

Ximena shook her head.

"It's a big city. Not like here, of course," Lupe said, "but, no, I don't think so." Saltillo. Almost family, Lupe thought. If it didn't turn out as they expected, they could search for another place to stay. But for now, the apartment was a roof over their heads and a place to sleep.

"She'll be here this morning for services. I can introduce you. You can decide then."

Isabel dropped a few tortillas into a paper bag. "For later," she said.

* * *

"My roommates left a few days ago," Mercedes said. "They moved in with their boyfriends. I figured they would leave sooner or later, but they said nothing to me until the day they left. There's plenty of room if you want to stay with me. Just as long as you tell me ahead of time if you decide to change your mind."

"Of course," Lupe said. "We have nowhere else to go, anyway."

"Well then, come on up and take a look."

Ximena and Lupe climbed the stairs behind Mercedes, Lupe gripping the handrail and testing the vibrating metal staircase for soundness with each step. Settling in took five minutes. Lupe and Ximena had nothing to do but unpack their backpacks and stack their clothes beside one of the two cots in the front room of the apartment.

When Mercedes offered to fix them dinner, the women protested. "Here, Isabel gave us these," Ximena said, holding one of the paper bags aloft. Neither had eaten the tortillas. They'd saved them, not knowing when they would have their next meal.

Mercedes pulled open the bag and laughed. "Isabel is a sweet lady, but you can't exist on one tortilla. You can pay me back when you have a job. I understand. Remember, I came here with nothing a few years ago. I understand."

Later, after Mercedes had gone to her bedroom, the twins climbed into their cots. Lupe whispered, "Did you hear her say we might find work at the place where she works?"

"She said 'might' find work. And she works in a greenhouse," Ximena whispered to Lupe. "What do we know about working in a greenhouse?"

"I told Mercedes how we planted vegetables at home, and watered them, and removed weeds, and harvested—"

"You don't know anything about flowers—"

"I know we need a job and a place to live. You saw for yourself how Papa lives. How—"

"Don't ever mention him again. I don't want to hear his name. I don't want to see him. He lied. He lied to mother. He lied to us."

"I know, but—"

"Don't make excuses for him. He told mother he had a place for us. He told us how we could come here and get jobs and how we'd be able to send money home. So, what happened to those promises? What has he spent his money on over the last year when he said he didn't have enough to send home? Huh? What do you think?"

Ximena turned away, the thin cot bouncing as she shifted position.

Lupe had to admit to herself if not to Ximena things weren't quite what she expected. Still, they were in America. They had survived, found a place to stay, and a chance of work.

17. ALICIA

CARLO LOOKED UP FROM HIS DESK. HE MADE A SHOW OF CHECKING his watch: pulling back his sleeve, grabbing his left wrist, and cocking the dial to keep the glare from the overhead lights off the watch face. He squinted, pursed his lips, and nodded.

Alicia ignored Carlo, as usual. He was well aware she left the Security Office every afternoon between two and two-thirty to make her last inspection tour of the day. He knew, too, on this tour Alicia checked that Kyle had made it safely to the food court.

"Why don't you give that kid a key?" Carlo asked. It was a question he'd asked on more than one occasion.

"He's not old enough to be home alone," she answered.

"No? But he's old enough to walk a block, cross the parking lot, and find his way into the mall alone?"

"Yes, in daylight. And when I'm waiting for him."

"Right."

From the start, Alicia had assured Carlo that having Kyle meet her at the mall would not interfere with her work. Quite the contrary, she had said, she'd have less to worry about and be better able to concentrate on her work.

Alicia picked up her radio and fastened it to her belt. "I don't know how you can stare at that thing without a break," she said to Carlo as she made her way to the door. "It makes my eyes hurt."

"Walking on concrete makes my feet hurt," he said, sitting with his feet propped on the edge of the trashcan next to his desk.

Though it crossed her mind that a walk might do him good, Alicia resisted the temptation to say so and instead smiled and said, "I guess that makes us a perfect pair."

"Well, don't forget your new fandangled contraption."

Alicia patted her pocket. "Got it," she said with a smile. "R2D2 on duty."

Carlo grunted at her use of the nickname he'd given her after Ingram Security installed the new system. He'd complained every day since, taking particular pleasure in pointing out how many times the system crashed. "Never happened with the old one," he said, banging a fist against the computer tower.

"Well, you have to admit the cameras are a lot better than the old ones. But remember, you can track me on the digital layout. I'm the blue dot. Number three."

"I'll admit, they do show more detail. I'll find you on the cameras if I need you," he said. "And on the radio."

"Suit yourself, but you have only thirty more days before the old system is history."

Alicia pressed the power switch on her new Personal Digital Assistant and on the backup system, the old-style, two-way radio. She tapped the microphone and listened for the feedback from the central console, confirming her signal.

Satisfied, she exited the office and, out of habit, tugged the door handle to make sure the latch caught. She had thirty minutes to patrol the west wing and reach the food court in the atrium before Kyle arrived. More than enough time to complete a check of the west wing emergency exits and delivery hallways. Riverside had six of them, long, bare linoleum corridors, their walls striped with black marks where loading carts had caromed off the walls. Store clerks often came and went through them to avoid the crowded corridors. Though it was against the rules, a few clerks used them for smoke breaks and occasionally forgot to lock the doors on their return.

Alicia checked the hallways and access doors one by one, finding none unlocked. She continued patrolling the west corridor, stopping only when a patron approached her to ask directions. The questions were always the same and frequently asked by shoppers who stood just feet from one of the directories displaying the mall's floor plan. Still, Alicia smiled and answered each question politely.

She recalled a lecture from Ingram's recruiter, cautioning against being lured into complacency by the monotony of the job, though he might have used the words "routine nature." Either way, he was referring to the endless inspection tours. "You will be playing a vital role in ensuring the public's safety and could be called upon to respond to almost any situation at a moment's notice. Possibly..." and here she remembered he had paused for effect, "at great personal risk."

So far, the only personal risk Alicia had placed herself in was dodging an umbrella-wielding shopper. It had happened on Black Friday last year when she escorted a woman from the mall for attacking another shopper. Alicia even had a tiny scar on her elbow as a reminder.

She couldn't take unnecessary risks now, not with Kyle having already lost one parent. Once, Alicia had wanted to follow in her father's footsteps and join the local police force. She'd even run the idea past Seth before he left on deployment abroad. Seth knew her father had served for thirty years with the Atlanta Police Department and that he'd given his life for the job, killed in the line of duty. The latter was a fact Seth chose not to mention at the time. Seth hadn't said "yes," but he hadn't said "no" either, at least not so far as Alicia remembered. He'd asked her to wait until he returned from his tour of duty. And, in a perverted way, she had. But with Seth gone and facing the task of raising a son alone, Alicia needed a less demanding occupation. And, if she were being honest, a job that paid right away and allowed her to work overtime when necessary.

* * *

Alicia scanned the food court. Kyle's instructions were to wait in a booth, one well away from the din from the food vendors and the jingle of the carousel. She had a clear line of sight to his normal booth. It was empty. Her heart skipped a beat.

It was four o'clock by her watch and the same on the British-style, street clock in the atrium. Kyle should have been there. Alicia checked the lines in front of the fast food vendors, starting with Lone Star, Kyle's favorite. There was no sign of him there or at the burger stand, his second choice.

Alicia passed through the food court, forcing herself to take deliberate, measured steps toward the exit and to keep a smile on her face. By the time she pushed through the double doors, her heart was hammering. She craned her neck to see across the sea of car trunks and hoods in the Blue lot.

A half dozen rows of cars away, the distinctive peak of an Ingram Security guard's hat caught Alicia's eye. It had to be one of the guards on an exterior inspection.

The guard stepped into the open. It was Wade and, she sighed, Kyle was beside him.

"Hey, Wade, what's going on?" she asked, speaking slowly and calmly to disguise her concern. Alicia reached her arm out and pulled Kyle to her side.

"Not to worry," Wade said. "I got a call to checkout an incident in the Blue lot. Got there in time to see a couple of guys up to no good and your young man here." Wade nodded at Kyle.

Alicia raised an eyebrow at Kyle.

Before she had time to say a word, he said, "I wasn't doing anything. I was walking along and then these guys were there."

"Did they say anything or do anything to you?" Alicia asked Kyle.

"I think they were trying to shake him down," Wade said.

"I didn't say anything to them. And I tried to walk away, but they kept following me."

"Okay. It's all right, Kyle." Turning to Wade, Alicia said, "Thanks."

"We're good. I took their names, checked their licenses. They were older guys. Twenties. Didn't look like they were here to shop."

"Coming in?" Alicia asked. "I'll get Kyle situated and meet you for a coffee. My treat."

"That's okay."

"No, I insist," she said.

"Well, if you insist, sure."

Alicia hovered beside the table as Kyle settled into his regular booth.

"You stay right here and don't move an inch. Not until I get back."

"Yes, ma'am."

"And don't be talking to anyone."

Wade waited a few feet away, glancing toward Alicia every few seconds.

"Go on, Mom. I'm fine."

"Not an inch."

Kyle pulled a notebook and pen from his backpack. He spread the notebook on the table.

"And remem—"

"Yeah, I know. No games until my homework is done." Kyle bent over his book, adjusted his glasses, and dismissed his mother.

Once they were out of Kyle's sight, Alicia picked up the thread of conversation with Wade. "What do you think they were up to?"

"No good, I'm sure. You never used to see that around here. Now I see it every day. Kids roaming around with nothing to do but make trouble. I'll write it up when I get back to the office."

"The usual," Alicia said, smiling at Amy, one of the Starbucks baristas.

Alicia grabbed her double caramel macchiato and handed Wade a plain black coffee.

"I thought we'd escaped the toughs and the crime when we moved out of the old neighborhood. But I guess not."

18. CYRIL

"COULD YOU STOP WITH THE LEG THING, ALREADY?" STEPHEN BART-
lett asked.

"Sorry," Cy answered. His foot was propped on the ledge underneath his desk, and he'd been jiggling it up and down so hard
it had shaken the panel separating their cubicles. It was a nervous
tic. A tic he'd not been aware he had until the first day on his new
assignment with Stephen.

Cy had reason to be anxious. He was facing a meeting with
Ivan Druitt, Assistant Special Agent in Charge of the Atlanta
Field Office and liaison with the FBI's Intelligence Division in
Washington. The meeting was the first with Druitt since his and
Greg's reassignment.

Cy hadn't been this nervous since his senior year when he
told his father he would not be graduating with the rest of his
class. There'd been a mix up of sorts. Cy's advisor had deemed
one statistics course he piled into his self-designed curriculum to
be "substantially similar" to another, depriving him of the credits
needed for graduation.

Cy had the opportunity to appeal the decision but elected
to finish over a ninth semester. His father had not been pleased,
to put it mildly. Nor was he any happier when, at the end of the
summer, Cy announced he'd enrolled in a graduate program. But
then Cy hadn't pleased his father in some time.

The FBI work reassignment, like the stain on his degree, would not sit well with the old man. Besides reflecting poorly on his father, the way Jerald would see it, Cy would also be out of his father's direct chain of command. At least, Cy didn't have to look his father in the eye. Two years ago, a month after Cy's mother's funeral, the elder Westfall had sold the family home in Atlanta and relocated to the District of Columbia. Cy had never thought of Washington as home and preferred the familiar, more humane pace of life in Atlanta. He liked having the distance between him and his father, too. That didn't hurt.

"Come on in, Cyril," Mr. Druitt said, motioning Cy to a chair. "Shut the door, if you will."

Between them was a standard issue executive desk, one approved for the level of Assistant Special Agent-in-Charge. A single item sat in the middle of the desk: Cy's performance review in an open manila folder. Even the phone, pens, tablet, and photos of Mr. Druitt's wife and children were relegated to the credenza behind him. Cy speculated the arrangement allowed Druitt to get right to the topic and avoid distractions that might extend the meeting beyond the ten minutes he had scheduled.

Mr. Druitt checked the time on his watch then flipped through the pages of the review. Cy had trouble reading the words from where he sat, but the boxes with check marks were obvious. On the last page, a "3" had been typed in the box for overall rating. Cy shifted in his chair and placed a hand on his left knee to quell its twitching. A "1" was the highest level of performance, "Exceeding Expectations" in Human Resource parlance. A "2" was "Meets Expectations," a "3" was death. Officially, it signified "Needs Improvement." Unofficially, it meant the recruit had ninety days to rectify their performance and unending reports of bullshit to file over a ninety-day probationary period. In Cy's case, as son of an AEAD level executive, Mr. Druitt would tread lightly, but still Cy would have to abide by the rules.

Cy didn't expect anything different. The problem was he should never have received the low performance rating, not if Greg Nothwang hadn't stepped out of line. Greg had blown the sting. They should have called Peter Olson like Cy had suggested before responding to Khan's message. Maybe Olson should never have given them access to his files. And whose idea was it to assign two fresh recruits to the sting, anyway? But Cy was not about to point fingers, a high-risk tactic. He toed the line and cast his fate with Greg.

Their timing could not have been worse. The incident occurred the week before their performance reviews. Peter Olson had given them a "3" rating and recommended reassignment to projects with close supervision and restricted decision making. On the bright side, as far as Cy was concerned, the reassignment put him in the intelligence division, even if for the mind-numbing task of audio surveillance.

"I confess, Cyril, it really distresses me to see you have a '3' for your first performance review. I know you have greater potential than what this suggests. You do understand the seriousness of this?"

"Yes, sir. I do." Cy thought what really distressed Mr. Druitt was knowing AEAD Westfall would call within minutes of the performance rating being entered in the system. But, as Cy knew, not before the senior Westfall called Cy.

"And you're willing to do whatever it takes to address the deficiencies noted in your performance report?"

"Yes, sir."

"First, we'll ratchet your responsibilities back a tad. Let you have a chance to show what you can do in Intelligence. Then, we'll do another assessment at the end of October. If all goes well, I'll do what I can to get you back into your cohort before the end of the probation period. How does that sound?"

"Much appreciated, sir."

Cy signed the form beside Mr. Druitt's signature, took his copy and exited. On his way to the elevators and his windowless cubicle on the fourth floor, Cy passed the supply room where he slid the performance review into a shredder. The sooner he completed his share of today's work requests, the sooner he could access the FBI's mainframe computer for his own special project.

SEPTEMBER

19. LUPE

MONDAY WAS NO DIFFERENT FROM TUESDAY, OR WEDNESDAY, OR any other day of the week. One day bled into the other, the routine the same. Each workday, Lupe and Ximena rose well before dawn, showered, ate a breakfast of tortillas and beans, then walked with Mercedes to work. Sometimes they took the most direct route past the corner where the Latino men loitered, waiting for work as day laborers. Though shorter, the route had its disadvantages. As they passed, the men erupted with catcalls and taunts, complaining the women were taking their jobs or suggesting the women were better suited to other pastimes.

Lupe hated running the gauntlet and imagined Ximena felt even worse. Both preferred the longer route, across an open field behind their apartment complex, through an alley, and along the back of a shopping center. Few people frequented the half-shuttered place. Three stores remained, a self-service laundry, a check cashing and money transfer store, and a former fast-food restaurant converted to a shop selling tortas, thick-breaded sandwiches filled with chopped or ground meat, cheese, and other toppings.

The longer route was safer, too, as Lupe and Ximena had learned their first week in town. As they had approached the corner, a black car slowed and pulled to the side of the street. On the hood and forward doors of the car the letters P-O-L-I-C-E. The vehicle halted beside the group of Latinos. Lupe's heart stopped beating for an instant.

"Get back," Mercedes said. Though she did not run, she hurried back to their apartment. Lupe and Ximena followed, matching her pace. They kept silent and their eyes forward.

Once safely inside, Mercedes poked two fingers through the slats in the window blinds and peeked at the activity in the street.

"What's going on?" Ximena asked.

"It happens now and then," Mercedes said. "They stop especially when there's a big crowd hanging around."

"Will they come in here?" Lupe asked scanning the small room, preparing to evacuate if Mercedes gave the word. Against the far wall, Ximena stood beside their clothes with a backpack in one hand as if she were ready to shove everything inside and run. Lupe crossed the room and took one of Ximena's hands in hers, anchoring her, steadying her sister and her own nerves at the same time. Then, Lupe drew Ximena to the window and the two peered outside over Mercedes's shoulder.

On the corner, two uniformed men spoke to three or four of the laborers. The rest, those who the police had not addressed directly, wandered away one by one, slowly and purposefully. Cars and vans of potential landscape crew and construction bosses approached the corner to hire an illegal for the day. They slowed, but sped away as soon as they spotted the police.

"Will the police arrest them?" Lupe asked.

"No. They'll question them. Ask them what they're doing and tell them they can't hang around on the corner. Basically, harass them. They don't do anything. They just cause trouble. They'll make the men late for work or keep them from finding work altogether today."

"Will they ask to see their papers?"

"Ha!" Mercedes laughed. "The police know the men don't have papers, but they can't ask to see them. As long as they break up and disappear for a while, the police won't do anything. Wait ten minutes. You'll see. They'll be back. Let's go. We'll take the long way around. But we need to hurry."

* * *

A few minutes after the top of the hour, the women slid into their stations. Ricardo, the foreman, followed them with his hooded eyes. We're ten minutes late, Lupe thought. Only ten minutes. She scooped a handful of black earth from the mound in the center of the table and stuffed it into a black plastic pot. She scrambled, working double time to show Ricardo she could make up for being late.

Ricardo had a green card, so Mercedes had told them. "Usually, he hires only Latinos with work permits, but sometimes, for some women, particularly attractive women, like you two, he makes an exception. Just watch out that he doesn't try to take advantage of you."

Convinced Ricardo was staring at her, Lupe avoided looking up from her work, avoided doing anything more than fill the eighteen plastic pots in her tray. Working frantically, she was the first of the half dozen women to finish. Lupe caught her sister's attention and signaled her to speed up, but Ximena ignored Lupe. She held a plastic pot in one hand and a clump of dirt in the other. She filled the pot with precise, efficient motions, at her usual pace and not a hair faster.

To break the routine they'd settled into, Mercedes suggested they go to the mall on Friday.

"For what?" Ximena asked.

Mercedes hadn't stopped describing the place and singing its praises since they arrived, but the twins were wary.

"We can't go shopping," Lupe said. "We don't have any money." Between what they received for their first weeks of work and what they spent on food and contributed to the rent, they had a handful of dollars left. Not enough to justify sending home to their mother. Lupe refused to admit, let alone say anything to Ximena, but she had an inkling of how difficult it had been for her father to send money home. At least what he had at first.

"We don't have to shop. We can just go and walk around. What do you say?" Mercedes asked.

Lupe looked at Ximena.

"It'll be fun. You'll see," Mercedes said.

"Not me," Ximena said. "I'm tired. I'm going to stay here and take a bath. But you go ahead, Lupe, if you want."

20. LUPE

FOR CLOSE TO AN HOUR BEFORE THEY LEFT FOR THE MALL, MER-
cedes walked in and out of her room, modeling a different outfit
for Lupe and Ximena. "How does this one look?"

"You look fine in any one of them, Mercedes," Lupe said. In
truth, they all looked the same. Mercedes carried a few extra
pounds, most of which had settled around her waist. Nothing,
and especially not her penchant for wearing bright colors and
horizontal stripes, disguised her flaws.

Ximena stayed out of the conversation and left the two to
their wardrobe discussion while she went to bathe.

"All right, then. This is it," Mercedes said.

"Okay, let's go," Lupe said as she rose from her cot.

Mercedes took one glance at Lupe in her jeans and tee-shirt
then shook her head. The once white shirt bore streaks of brown
from where Lupe leaned against the potting and plugging tables
at work. "Just a second," Mercedes said as she disappeared. In a
minute, she returned with a pink jacket over her arm. "Here," she
said, "try this on. I can't wear it anymore, anyway. I think it will
fit you."

Lupe donned the jacket and zipped it over her tee-shirt until
only the neckline showed. "How does this look?" she asked.

"Wait." Mercedes unzipped the jacket half way. Then, smiling,
she tugged at the shirt's neckline to expose Lupe's cleavage. From

her pocket, Mercedes pulled a pink ribbon the same shade as the jacket and tied it around Lupe's ponytail. "That's better," Mercedes said, standing back to admire her handiwork.

Lupe checked her reflection in the hallway mirror and blushed. She smiled.

* * *

A mile from their apartment, Riverside Centre was everything and more than Mercedes had said it would be. There were gleaming white marble floors that ran forever, bright lights, music wafting overhead, and no end to the aromas spilling from the open entryways. Mercedes and Lupe walked up one corridor and down another in what to Lupe was an endless expanse of wealth. It was the America she had pictured in her head ever since she'd left Saltillo.

"Ximena will never believe me when I tell her about this place," Lupe said. Her eyes flitted back and forth from one strange and wonderful sight to the next. She couldn't wait until she had the courage to navigate this America as easily as Mercedes.

Soon, reeling from the experience and near exhaustion, Lupe asked if there were a place to sit. "Of course," Mercedes said, "there's a food court up ahead."

"Food court?"

Mercedes laughed. "Just wait, you'll see."

Until Mercedes mentioned food, Lupe had not realized how hungry she was. Now, surrounded by stores offering every imaginable choice of food, Lupe stood transfixed. Hundreds of shoppers talked at once. Food vendors called out over the sizzle of meat on their griddles and handed out samples. Chairs scraped against the floor as people came and went. Conversation was difficult. "Ximena will never believe this," Lupe said, raising her voice over the din.

"What would you like to eat?" Mercedes asked.

Lupe surveyed the array of choices. With its Hispanic name, La Parrilla stood out to Lupe. She started toward the store promising familiar fare and then stopped. "I'll just have a Coca Cola."

"Not me, I'm starving," Mercedes said.

"Un dollar y cinquenta," the young Latino cashier said. A dollar fifty. Lupe groped in her jeans for the two dollars she had brought with her, two of the five she'd saved this week. Two Lupe did not tell Ximena she'd removed from the small stash in a box under her bed. As she waited for her drink, Lupe unfolded the bills and put them on the counter, running her fingers over them to smooth the creases.

Mercedes ordered four tacos and a drink. When her order came, the two headed for a table near the center of the atrium.

"Here," Mercedes said. She pushed two of the tacos across the table.

"Oh. No, I—"

"Yes, you can. You can pay me back later."

* * *

From over Lupe's shoulder came a cry, "Chica!"

Mercedes looked up and smiled.

Lupe turned to see four young Latinos about her age.

86

"Diego, que tal?" What's up? Mercedes greeted the young man and motioned for him to sit.

The four grabbed empty chairs from the nearby tables and arranged them around the two women. Mercedes made introductions and let Lupe know the group lived together in a house a mile or two from their apartment.

One of the men, Margarito, had a muscular chest, well out of proportion to his short legs, making him appear top-heavy. He said little but ogled Lupe, his eyes dropping to her breasts and the cleavage on display through her open jacket. Lupe blushed. She might have to omit that detail when she recounted the events of the evening to Ximena later.

Just as Margarito leaned across the table to say something, a few bars of music pulsed through the food court, startling Lupe. She jumped and turned to the source. At the far side of the atrium, a carousel had come to life, hundreds of lights twinkling from its canopy and children squealing as the amusement lurched forward and gained speed.

Everyone laughed, including Lupe. This is the America I imagined, she thought.

21. LUPE

AFTER DINNER AND WITH THE MALL CLOSING IN TEN MINUTES, THE men had suggested they move their impromptu party to their car parked outside Macy's.

"You have a car?" Lupe asked, her eyebrows arching high on her forehead. Here was yet another discovery to add to the many she'd catalogued tonight.

"It's my uncle's," Margarito said. "He let me borrow it tonight."

"But, I didn't know you could get a license here, that is…" Lupe wanted to say "as an illegal immigrant," but she hesitated.

"Well, I don't have one," Margarito said, eyeing the nearby tables for an eavesdropper. "But, I'm careful."

"You'd better be," Mercedes said. "If you get stopped—"

"I won't get stopped," he said with a hint of confidence in his voice.

* * *

Later, as the women climbed the stairs to their apartment, Mercedes laughed, remembering Margarito's bravado. "He's crazy! 'Won't get caught,' he says. Maybe not, but if he does, he'll be heading home, or worse."

"What could be worse?" Lupe asked. *Hic.*

"Jail. Especially if he has an accident. This guy I know. He was drunk—drunker than those guys were tonight—and he ran into another car. He hurt a gringo. Hurt him pretty bad. He's still in a jail somewhere. Or at least I think he is."

Hic. Hic. Lupe's hand went to her mouth to stifle her hiccups. The two exploded in laughter as they entered the darkened front room.

"I think you're drunk!" Mercedes said. "It's a good thing you're not driving."

Hic. "You're right. But we're safe. I don't know how to drive."

"What's that?" Ximena woke and propped herself up on her elbows. "Who's drunk?"

"Your sister is," Mercedes said. "One beer and bam!"

"Where have you been?" Ximena asked.

"Oh, you won't believe where we've been and what we've been up to," Lupe said. "I can't wait to tell you everything." She sat on her bed and kicked off her shoes, letting them tumble to a rest between the two beds.

"You don't need me for this," Mercedes said. She yawned. "I'm going to bed."

"Okay. Good night, Mercedes," Lupe said.

"Is she right? Are you drunk?" Ximena asked, reaching across the floor to switch on a lamp.

Lupe crossed to Ximena's cot and collapsed against her sister's shoulder. "Not drunk. I just had—" *Hic.* "One beer. But let me tell you. You have to go with us next time."

"For what? Do they give away beer there?"

"No, no. That was later. With these guys from Honduras." Lupe kept Ximena up for another half hour regaling her with tales of her evening out with Mercedes and the wonders of the mall. A dimple above Ximena's right eyebrow signaled skepticism. Ximena's face was a mirror of her own. One Lupe could read so well. Beneath the skepticism, she read disdain, and beneath that Ximena's new found fear of men.

"It's okay," Lupe said, "it was harmless. And we didn't get in the car with them. We just talked in the parking lot."

"Just talked," Ximena said, parroting her sister.

"Yes. Just talked. But forget them. They're not the point." Lupe reached across Ximena for the light switch.

22. JAVIER

WHEN HE TRANSFERRED BUSES IN HOUSTON ON THE LAST LEG OF HIS
Greyhound bus trip, a young man took a seat beside Javier. He was
friendly and said his name was Honorio. Javier humored the man.
Traveling with him made Javier appear less like a loner, less suspicious, less likely to draw unwanted attention. The trade off being
Javier had to be polite and talk to Honorio for the rest of the day.
Even so, it required little more of Javier than to nod now and then,
grunt occasionally, and once tell Honorio he had a sister. "Selma,"
he said when prodded, his answer a fabrication but as close to the
truth as possible.

Honorio, more boy than man, like most of their fellow trav-
elers, was making his third trip through the United States. The
first time, after an uneventful six months, Honorio had run into
trouble and fled back across the border. At home, he found a job
as a taxi driver. Each week he set aside part of his meager wages
until he saved enough to pay a coyote a second time. That stay
ended a year and a half later.

"Cinco de Mayo," he'd said. "Big mistake. We were drunk.
Very drunk. And the cops were ready. They were waiting for us to
leave and get in our cars. Wham! We hadn't gone a block when
they pulled us to the side."

Javier shook his head as if he understood and sympathized
with Honorio's predicament.

"You want my advice? This is your first trip, right?" Honorio asked.

Javier shrugged. Let him believe what he wants.

"Right. Well, don't go to bars. Not when you have to drive. Comprende?" You understand?

Javier nodded.

"Yeah. I'll play it safe this time. Well, for as long as I can, anyway."

Honorio's advice on how to avoid deportation continued for the better part of the day. But Javier's thoughts drifted, returning only when Honorio paused. He'd nod or shrug and Honorio would pick up and go on for another several minutes. Eventually the patter faded into the hum of the tires on the road and the drone of the engine. Javier dozed.

At one in the morning, the driver shifted gears and slowed the bus to a halt at a traffic signal. Javier woke and pressed his face against the glass. Stores lined the still dark streets. Above him, buildings reached to heights he'd never imagined possible. Towers of cement and glass, studded with lights glowing in the windows. They'd arrived.

"Hombre," Honorio said, as if he'd never slept or missed a part of his monologue, "you have a place to stay?"

Javier had his instructions to make contact on arrival. But at this hour of the morning in a strange town, he was unsure where to go. Atlanta, from what he'd seen over the last few miles, was as intimidating if not as crowded and congested as Dubai and Mexico City through which he'd passed.

"I thought so," Honorio continued. "You can stay with me. My brother has a house with plenty of room. He has five or six friends staying with him now so I don't think anyone will mind or even notice one more." Honorio laughed, "Not for a day or two, anyway."

* * *

Javier lay on the carpet in the front room of Honorio's brother's house. His hooded sweatshirt was rolled beneath his head for a pillow, his backpack tucked between his knees and the wall, and beside his pack his sneakers with soles worn thin.

It was Sunday. Honorio, his brother, and the other five Mexican laborers were staying home. Probably a good thing, Javier thought. Their party had been going strong when Honorio and he arrived. Javier had begged off, pleading exhaustion. Now a steady rhythm of snores surrounded him, some from the room where Honorio slept with his brothers, others to Javier's left through an alcove. They'd assigned Javier the front room with a couch and two wooden chairs but no mattress. Javier had started out on the small, stiff couch. At some point, he'd rolled off the couch and crawled next to the wall where he slept.

Javier had no sense of the time, but the sun bathed the front room in light. He pulled on his sneakers and sweatshirt and rubbed his fingers across his head. Without a sound, Javier picked his backpack off the floor and exited.

A few blocks from the house, Javier spotted a gas station, S-H-E-L-L in large red letters on a lighted sign above the station. The place Honorio said he could find work and purchase a cell phone. He wasn't seeking work, but he needed a phone. He also needed to dispose of Salvador's gun. He'd been fortunate not to be caught with the pistol when he boarded the bus in Tucson and again in Houston when he changed buses. He didn't want to press his luck now that he'd arrived at his destination.

Javier watched people come and go, fill their cars with gas, enter the store and return a few minutes later with newspapers or packages, and jump back in their cars. An attendant exited the side of the store and dumped a plastic bag into a metal trash bin, then went back inside the store. Javier crossed the street, reached his hand deep inside his backpack, withdrew the pistol from the bottom, and tossed it into the bin.

Inside the store, dozens of cell phones were arranged in a glass case next to the cash register. Javier pointed to one. Without a word or a glance at Javier's face, the black man behind the counter accepted Javier's money and slid a plastic wrapped phone across the counter.

* * *

At the other end of the line, a man answered, saying one word, "Yes."

"It's me, Javier," Javier said.

There was silence and then static and a fumbling noise. Someone cleared his throat.

"Yes," another voice said.

"It's me, Javier," he said again and followed with the phrase Mohsan had him memorize, "I'm looking for work." He spoke the words in English and he did not use the man's name. Mohsan had warned Javier not to use Arabic on the phone. He'd said

94

conversations in their native language could be detected from among the millions flowing over the wires. How that was possible, Mohsan did not say. He had also said never to use Qasim Bousaid's name. Never.

"One one zero five Grant Street. Grant," the man said. He spelled the word, "G-R-A-N-T" and coughed.

"Okay, 1105 Grant Street. Can you—" Javier wanted to ask for more information, but a tone sounded from the earpiece. The man with the rasp had disconnected the call.

23. JAVIER

A MAN WITH THICK GLASSES AND SEVERAL-DAY-OLD STUBBLE across his jaw answered the door at 1105 Grant, a gray clapboard house. He made eye contact once and then shuffled back inside the house, leaving the door half open. He withdrew a key from a cabinet, returned to the front door, and handed the key to Javier. The key had a tag with the numbers 9-0-5. The man pointed to his right where three nearly identical clapboard houses sat, each the same shade of years-old gray paint. When Javier turned back, the door was closed. The transaction was done. He'd not given his name or his signature. He'd not presented or been asked for identification or money. The transaction was done.

The house next door had the numbers 1005 over the door and the one next to it 905.

Javier turned the key in the lock, noticing as he did a discolored indentation on the doorframe. The mark was the size of a man's heel, or the end of a club, or another blunt instrument. Carpeting, if the threadbare sculpted fabric on the floor could be called carpeting, ran from wall to wall. Javier speculated as to the origin of the splotches on the carpet—some no doubt were food and drink but others could have been blood. He dropped his pack inside the door and stared at the empty room.

Honorio's apartment was palatial and well appointed compared with Javier's new home. To his right, down a short hall, were a bedroom and a bathroom no bigger than a closet. Off the front room was a small kitchen with a window overlooking the backyard, its patch of thin grass sloping toward a fence and a set of railroad tracks. Javier ignored the view and instead craned his neck to check the angle of the sun and his bearings.

He pulled a cylinder of fabric from his backpack and spread it on the carpet in the front room. Again, he checked the orientation through the window and returned, adjusting the head of the cloth to the Kaaba in Mecca. He removed his shoes, set them against the wall, and stepped onto the rectangle of fabric. For the first time in weeks, Javier felt safe from prying eyes and free to put aside foreign words and customs. He opened his eyes, placed his hands palms up near his head, and recited his prayers.

* * *

For over a week, Javier stayed inside his house, venturing outside once to purchase food and the most basic of supplies. By day, he sat on the floor in the front room, praying at the specified times. When not praying, he studied the pattern of stains on the floor, imagining the hilltops of his village, the muzzle of a horse, and the shape of a hand. The rest of the time, he stared at his watch and prayed for his phone to ring.

He set the cell phone on the linoleum counter in the kitchen. Better there, he thought, than inside his pack where the sound might be muffled.

Mohsan had not said how long Javier might have to wait. His one instruction was to make contact on arrival, find the address given to him, and wait for a call. Every morning when he woke, he checked the phone, convinced either the battery had depleted or he'd missed the call. When the battery dropped ten percent, he recharged the phone. He left nothing to chance.

At the end of the third week, Javier checked the phone. It had a full charge. On the display were two words, Name and Date. For the first time, he realized though he'd activated the phone he'd not set it up according to the directions in the package. Out of boredom, he flipped through the menu and set the date and time. He entered and erased a variety of names in the settings until the phone beeped a warning. Worried his tinkering might have caused the phone to malfunction or a call to go to voice mail, he checked for a dial tone. Satisfied the phone was working, he shut it off and returned it to the kitchen counter.

Javier squatted beside his backpack and the stack of his clothes. He unfolded the shirts and his spare pair of jeans, ran his hand over each to smooth the fabric, aligned the hems, and refolded everything. He set the stack against the wall.

The activity had consumed ten minutes. Boredom returned with a vengeance. Javier paced back and forth across the front room like a caged animal, except he had no one or nothing outside his cage to watch. He changed his route and circled the room, and then after one or two laps, he added the hallway and unused bedroom.

At least he had the Maghrib prayer to look forward to after sunset. Javier prepared by clearing his throat. He prayed aloud, delighting in the sound of his own voice. With one exception, his was the only voice he'd heard in weeks. Last night, after dark he'd walked Grant Street from end to end, keeping to the far side away from the other houses. At 1005, the door was open and a couple of empty beer bottles sat on the front steps. It was as if someone had enjoyed a drink then gone inside for more, except the two empties had been in the same place for the last week. The voices of two women quarreling spilled from the open door. They talked over each other, the volume and pitch rising as the argument continued. Javier listened as he passed and then doubled back, caring nothing for what the women said but appreciating the sound of their voices.

Later, when he finished the Maghrib prayer, he put away his prayer rug. It was time for his exercises. He did them every day, twice a day immediately after his morning and evening prayers as if they were another pillar of Islam, another requirement. The routine covered each muscle group, from squats, to sit-ups, to push-ups, using his body as a weight. At the end of his thirty-minute routine, he collapsed on his back, his arms and legs throbbing. He wondered if he was growing soft or lacking motivation. With Mohsan's threat-laced encouragement, he'd once done twice the number of repetitions as he had tonight, all without raising his heartbeat.

Javier rolled over and did another round of push-ups, counting to fifty before he let himself rest. He sat back on his haunches and leapt from the floor to his feet in one motion. I am ready, he said aloud. I am ready.

Javier grabbed the phone from the kitchen counter and dialed the one number he'd memorized. Two rings. A man cleared his throat. "Yes," he said, as if speaking a single word required an extraordinary effort.

"It's me. Javier. I need to speak to someone."

"You must wait."

"But, I have been waiting, I—"

"Do not call here again."

The phone went dead.

Javier stuffed the phone in his jacket and left his apartment. He walked to the end of Grant and continued to the streets beyond. He passed a storefront from which the odor of corn and warm cumin with a bite of hot pepper emanated. A group of young laborers exited, walking in front of him carrying the pungent scent with them for another block. They turned, going deeper into the Latino community, but Javier continued down the street. He passed the grocery store where he had shopped. From there, he entered unfamiliar territory. He walked without regard to direction, or distance, and found himself at a busy intersection. Ahead, bright lights studded a soccer-field sized parking lot. Welcome to Riverside Centre, the sign above him read, a series of decorative swirls and dots ran below the words.

24. LUPE

LUPE HAD NOT STOPPED TALKING ABOUT RIVERSIDE SINCE HER VIS-
it with Mercedes. Still, her descriptions had not drawn even half
an arched eyebrow from her sister. She'd have to take Ximena
there to see the mall for herself. First, though, she had to pay back
Mercedes and replace the money she'd taken from her savings.

The next week, on Friday, after Ricardo handed out the week's
wages, Lupe announced she was taking Ximena to the mall. Once
again, Lupe borrowed the pink jacket from Mercedes and though
their roommate offered Ximena another, she declined. Instead,
Ximena donned the olive sweater she'd bought from a local thrift
store. The weather had turned cool, surprising the sisters who
were unprepared for the coming winter. They had each purchased
a sweater for four dollars at the store, Ximena the olive one and
Lupe a dark blue. But Lupe preferred the pink jacket with its
zippered front.

As Lupe had on her first visit, Ximena stared at the array of
stores and merchandise, her jaw as slack as Lupe's had been. Lupe
chuckled. She had worried all day the tableau might not be as wonderful as she remembered. But it was, and though she tried to pretend a certain familiarity, she too gawked at the riches on display.

This time, Mercedes sauntered into the women's department at
Nordstrom, the twins following a few steps behind, looking right
and left as they went. They stopped in the shoe department with

row upon row of every imaginable style of shoe. There, Mercedes astonished Lupe by picking up a high-heeled, leopard-print shoe. She dropped it to the floor and slipped her foot inside the shoe.

"What do you think?" Mercedes asked, lifting the leg of her jeans and twisting her ankle one way and then another.

"I think you had better put it back before someone comes," Ximena said.

"Nonsense," Mercedes said. After returning the shoe to the stand, she led the way deeper into the store, past piles of sweaters and racks of blouses, slacks, and skirts. She stopped abruptly as they passed a row of gleaming cases on top of which sat an array of boxes in pastel shades of pink and blue, topped by glass bottles of amber liquid.

"Try this," Mercedes said. "Here, give me your wrist." When Ximena hesitated, Mercedes grabbed Ximena's forearm, pushed back her sleeve, and sprayed a fine mist on her wrist. Ximena's jaw dropped. "Don't worry," Mercedes said. "It's free. It's a sample. Here." She turned the bottle toward Lupe and spritzed the fragrance near the twin's ear lobe and then on her own neck.

"Where are we going now?" Lupe asked, halfway up the elevator, a cloud of Estee Lauder floating behind her.

"You'll see, it's right over there."

At the entrance to the evening-wear department, a floor-to-ceiling glass case held a mannequin in an evening gown embroidered with sequins. The dress shimmered under a spotlight in the case's ceiling. And behind the display, a rack of more gowns in billows of chiffon, taffeta, and silk.

"Aren't these the most beautiful things you've ever seen?" Lupe said, stroking the lace sleeve of a dress on the rack.

"Is there something I can help you with?" It was a woman's voice, low and lacking inflection.

The three women turned in unison. A tall, painfully thin woman glared at them and at Lupe's hand on the sleeve. Lupe dropped her hand and cringed.

"No, no señora," Mercedes said. "Thank you, we were just looking."

The woman stepped between the three friends and the display case.

"Vamonos," Ximena whispered. She pulled Lupe away from the gowns.

Lupe risked a glance back over her shoulder. The woman was a few steps behind, following them across the store, turning back only when the three boarded the escalator to the ground floor.

"We shouldn't have gone in there," Ximena said as she took a seat in the food court.

"Why not?" Mercedes asked. "We weren't doing anything wrong. Just looking. We can look, can't we? There's no law against that, is there?"

"I don't know, but we don't need to go looking for trouble," Ximena said. "It's dangerous."

"Forget it," Lupe said. "It was worth it. Those gowns were so beautiful. I want to have one with lace sleeves just like the one we saw."

Ximena grabbed Lupe's hand and held it in front of Lupe's face. "Take a look at this, Lupe? Do you see this? Do you see your hand with its dirty fingernails? You pot plants." She dropped Lupe's hand. "You need to understand where you are and what you have. Which is nothing. And you're not going to have anything either. How many years do you imagine it would take you to save to buy something like that? Huh? And, oh yes, in case you forgot, we have to send something to mother this week." She repeated, "In case you forgot."

Lupe put her hands in her lap, folding her nails into her palms. Ximena was right as always. "I haven't forgotten. But I can dream, can't I?"

"Girls, it's none of my business, but you can argue all you want tomorrow," Mercedes said. "Right now, we should be enjoying ourselves. Right?"

"Right," Lupe said. "Look, Ximena, it's the carousel. Remember I told you about it?"

"It's starting up again," Mercedes said. "We can ride for a quarter."

"Really?" Lupe said. "Okay, let me buy a ticket for each of us. Come on Ximena."

Lupe was glad they did. Once on the platform with the lively music playing and the lights glowing, the mood became festive again. A Hispanic woman boarded beside them and lifted first one and then the other of her children onto the horses. When the carousel lurched forward, one child wobbled in her seat. Ximena instinctively reached out a hand and steadied the young girl. The woman smiled at Ximena. "Gracias," she said.

By the third revolution, Lupe had forgotten the fright in the evening wear department and the argument with Ximena. She relaxed and closed her eyes, swaying to the melody piping from the center of the carousel. When she reopened her eyes, she spotted a young man standing against the wall near the exit. Her eyes lingered on his face. There was something familiar about him. She craned her neck as the carousel continued around but lost him behind a pillar. She came around again. And again, she stared at the man. Javier. The name came to her at last. It was Javier from the desert.

The pillar intervened once more.

"Ximena, look over there." Lupe pointed at a spot now behind her. "Wait. Wait till we come around," she said with her head swiveling over her shoulder.

As the carousel came around, Lupe pointed. "There," she said, "right there. See?"

"See what?" Ximena asked.

"He was there," Lupe said. "Right there, by the door."

"Who?"

"Javier," Lupe said. But he had vanished. Nothing was there but a blank wall and a glass door.

25. JAVIER

FOR OVER A WEEK AFTER HE'D STOPPED BY RIVERSIDE CENTRE, JAVI-
er had trouble sleeping. The sights and sounds and smells stayed
with him, haunting his thoughts and invading his dreams. He
remembered a couple who passed by him, the man clutching the
woman to him, his hand finding and fondling her backside, her
hand tucked into the back pocket of his jeans, and her arms bared
for everyone to see. And later, a group of young people, no more
than teens, arms and legs entwined, clothing clinging to their
bodies and accentuating their curves.

He prayed harder and more often, but still he slept fitfully.
He dreamed of being at the market at home with its familiar
scents of livestock, warm wool under a hot sun, and fresh-baked
bread. It was a prosperous time. He'd gone with his father to
sell the family's excess harvest of onions. Javier filled an old
woman's sack with onions. But the onions became gold and
silver bangles, shoes and belts of fine leather, yards of silk, and
bottles of perfume, the old woman a temptress who ogled Javier
and his father. Javier screamed and ran from the market as fast
as he could.

Javier woke, out of breath and panting.

Mohsan had been proven right again. He had lectured Javier
on the ways of the west. He had said, "The temptations will be
great. You must be vigilant at all times." And the temptations

had been especially great at Riverside. Javier had felt unclean and walked for miles after dark to erase the thoughts.

Nothing worked. The dreams returned each night. He needed to go to a mosque where he could pray with others and speak to an imam and be cleansed.

* * *

Javier made discreet inquiries, asking no more than one or two questions of the same person and never within earshot of another. Mostly he asked women he encountered in the self-service laundry. Women who had explained how to operate the machines, choose the proper soap, and set the timer. Women who looked to be his mother's age.

He asked one woman where he could find a place to eat. While their clothes tumbled in adjacent dryers, she took him by the wrist, ignoring his instinctive recoil, and escorted him to the end of the block. She pointed across the road to a row of buildings, a money transfer shop at one end and Iglesia Santa Maria a storefront church at the other, and a taqueria in the middle of the row.

Javier asked another woman how to find a watch repairman. The woman had shrugged, saying she didn't know but told him to check the circulars, a few of which lay strewn across the folding tables. Another said to ask the manager when he returned. A third introduced him to what she called the "yellow pages," a book filled with names and addresses of places on pages colored, as she said, yellow. She turned the pages until she found the word "Watches" at the top and a list of repair shops with phone numbers and addresses.

Javier waited until the woman folded her laundry and left. When his clothes were done, he passed the table and scooped the book into his bundle of folded clothes. In the privacy of his apartment, he searched the book for the words Islam and mosque and found a half dozen entries.

When Javier asked for directions to Copeland Street, the name he copied from the yellow pages, he omitted any mention of the Islamic Center, and asked only for the address on Copeland. It proved to be easy to find. The words "Islamic Center" were carved into a concrete footer running the length of the building and the structure itself occupied an entire city block. Javier read the name over and over with delight. He was tempted to cross the street and go inside the Center to pray openly with his brothers, but Mohsan's repeated warnings to avoid revealing himself rang in his head. For now, he took comfort in knowing a community of faithful Muslims was near.

That night, he dreamed not of home or Riverside Centre, but of praying in the middle of a long row of brothers, one of many rows of many faithful in a cavernous structure. He fell deep asleep, waking as the light rose in his windows. Javier washed his face and hands and began his day, reciting the dua:

All praise is to Allah who gave us life after having taken it from us and unto Him is the resurrection.

He added a prayer, asking Allah to give him the courage to enter the Center and for forgiveness if he asked for Qasim Bousaid, a man whose name he'd never spoken aloud. Javier vowed to pray twice as often as he already did if Allah would grant his wish. It would not be a violation after all, he thought, he would be among his brothers.

The next morning, after dressing in a fresh set of clothes, Javier set out.

He returned to Copeland Street and waited on the corner, a newspaper folded in his hands, his head angled over the words, but his eyes on the door across the street. A man approached, knocked, and was ushered inside the Center. In a few minutes, five more arrived and entered. Javier tossed his newspaper into a trash receptacle and skipped across the street.

An elderly man in traditional robe and skullcap answered the door. Javier's heart leaped and though he tried to maintain his composure, joy shone on his face. The man examined him from head to foot without saying a word.

After a quick glance around and seeing no threat, Javier said, "Assalamu alaikum," his voice a whisper. Peace be upon you.

"Wa 'Alaykum Asalaam." The man spoke the traditional response then swung the door wide.

"Qasim?" Javier said.

"Qasim?" the elderly man repeated, leaning closer as if to be sure he had heard Javier correctly.

"Yes. I am looking for Qasim Bousaid. Have I come to the right place?"

"Wait there," the man said pointing to a bench. As Javier took a seat, the man disappeared.

While he waited, Javier listened for any talk of the stranger at the door, but the only voice he heard was a child's reciting a verse from the Quran. After a moment, the child paused and began again, this time joined by other young voices. Javier held his hands chest high, palms skyward. He recited the verses silently along with those he imagined were being tutored in the Quran. Whether he'd come to the right place, whether he'd find Qasim, and whether Qasim would be angry with him for violating his orders, Javier did not know. But he felt a calm he'd not enjoyed since leaving his village in what now seemed a lifetime ago.

When the lessons ended, three young boys emerged, slipped their feet into the shoes they'd left beside the door, and darted through the entrance. Not one noticed Javier, or if they did, they found nothing remarkable about him. Javier relaxed. He was among his kind.

After the boys had gone, the Center fell quiet. Moments later, a conversation began in Arabic, the words unintelligible from where Javier sat. A patter of feet on the floor followed, people moving from one room to another, a door opening and closing, and then silence again. Javier remained in the quiet alcove for over an hour before he heard another sound.

"Assalamu alaikum," a man Javier had not seen before said. Like the elderly man who had spoken to Javier earlier, this man wore a thobe so clean and pure to Javier's eye it sparkled. On his head, a kufi. On his face, brows drawn together with two deep furrows between them.

Javier rose from his seat and returned the greeting. The man said nothing more as if he were waiting for Javier to speak first. "Qasim Bousaid?" Javier asked.

"No, there is no Qasim here. I am Imam Ata Nahidian."

"Imam, I have come to..." Javier started to mention praying at the Center, but the imam held up a hand. "You have disobeyed your orders," he said.

The words struck like knives thrust into Javier's chest. He trembled, the sense of calm and excitement of a moment ago replaced with shame and fear, but not regret. Having had the chance to be near his brothers was worth the risk, even if a room away and for such a brief period.

Javier found his voice. "Imam, forgive me. I thought I had been forgotten. I feared I would not be called to my duty."

"Have patience. Was patience not one of the reasons you were chosen? Do you not remember?"

"Yes, Imam."

"You must have patience and courage and faith."

"Yes, Imam."

"It will not be much longer, God willing. Now, go. And remember your instructions. Do not come back here again."

Javier headed back to his house on Grant Street. For the first few blocks he kept his eyes lowered, avoiding eye contact with passersby, fearing they could tell he was a Muslim and he'd visited the Center. At one corner, he waited for the crossing signal and risked a glance at the woman standing beside him. She ignored him and when the light turned crossed beside him. With a lighter heart, he continued but followed a route different from the one he'd taken earlier. This path took him to parts of the city he'd never visited. He crossed railroad tracks buried in asphalt, wide boulevards with fast moving traffic, and nearly empty streets of neighborhoods of small, doll-like homes. He ambled, not caring where he went or how indirect a route he took.

When he passed a placard advertising hamburgers and hot dogs outside a fast food restaurant, Javier remembered he hadn't eaten since breakfast. He quickened his pace.

Near home, the sound of meat sizzling on a hot griddle and the aroma of corn and warm tortillas welcomed him. People at the familiar taqueria did not ask questions and did not judge.

Javier ordered and stepped aside, joining the line of customers slouched against the wall as they waited for the cashier to call their number.

"Veinte y un. Torta de carne asada." Twenty-one. Grilled beef sandwich. Javier checked the number on his receipt before picking up his sack of food. Every chair inside was occupied or pulled close to one of the red-topped tables set helter-skelter around the room. As he turned to go outside, he caught sight of a woman with a birthmark on her forehead. Their eyes met. She reached across the table and tapped her twin on the arm.

Surprise and delight lit Lupe's face. "Javier!" she said, blurting out his name and causing everyone to look her way and then toward Javier at the door.

26. CYRIL

CY SLID INTO HIS CHAIR AND PICKED UP HIS HEADSET.

"How'd it go?" Stephen asked. He fingered the rim of his left ear, pink from where the headset rubbed.

"Fine." Cy had no interest in discussing his performance review with anyone. For all Stephen Bartlett knew, Druitt had welcomed Cy to his new assignment, a gesture reserved for new agents with fathers in high-level positions. Cy chose not to disabuse Stephen of the notion. He adjusted his own headset and returned to his tapes, avoiding further discussion. Out of the corner of his eye, Stephen swiveled back to his computer and donned his own headset.

Cy didn't look up again until Stephen tapped his shoulder. "Hey man, I've had enough hours in the dungeon for one day. I'm out of here. Want to grab a beer?" Stephen's monitor was dark, his workstation swept clean.

"No, thanks. I still have a good bit more to do."

"Suit yourself," Stephen said, giving Cy a mock salute as he left.

Stephen was fast, which went a long way with some of the higher ups. Probably a lot of "someones," Cy mused, the people more interested in complete and prompt reports than in what they could glean from the information in them.

Cy wondered if Mr. Druitt had intentionally paired him with Stephen so Cy would have a role model on his new team. The team idea had proven disastrous in the incident with Greg. Cy, a loner by nature, would not make the same mistake twice. And though, like his old man, he preferred to take his time, he would have to push himself to make good before the end of his probation period.

With Stephen gone, Cy paused the tape he'd been monitoring and pulled up a program from his personal file space, a program he'd been tinkering with from his first months at the Bureau. Now with the circumstances as they were, he was ready to do more than tinker. He was ready to bet his career on the program—one that played to his strengths in analytics.

He had a few ideas on identifying the bad guys, terrorists, "evil doers," and the lot, a few theories rolling around in his head, and a basic framework in code. The upside of the new desk assignment was he might have a chance to build out the program and test his theories with live data.

Cy had made sure he had permission from Druitt for access to the databases he needed. "I'd be doing it in my spare time," he'd said to Druitt. He'd worked it into an innocuous question on protocols near the end of his interview.

As Cy suspected, Druitt was eager to move on to his next appointment. He granted Cy his request with one last admonishment. "If I sense it's impacting your work, I'll put a stop to it."

"Understood," Cy said.

Working on his own and after hours, he'd be the first one to call it quits if he found he was chasing data down a rat hole.

For the rest of the evening, Cy pored over files on the FBI's server, their own data and data the National Security Administration had shared. He started with the basics, the file structures and content formats. By nine, when he pushed back from his desk, he had added several blocks of code to his framework and filled a legal pad with notes. He skimmed over the pages again, priming his brain to work through the jumble later.

On the first page, he'd captured financial data sources including banks, finance companies, money transfer agencies, and their Islamic equivalent, the hawalas. On another, data on communications from telephone intercepts, traditional sources listing originating and receiving numbers, call locations, and call length. He'd devoted several pages to nontraditional social media information, including the obvious Facebook and Twitter sites with data on everything from the number and duration of visits to comments and replies. At the bottom of one page, Cy had circled new sources to check. They included online gaming sites with data on the flow of dialogue between players, much like the flow of phone calls, but with their own unique patterns.

Cy had once shared his ideas with his father, a mistake he realized as soon as he'd opened his mouth. Cy knew from what he'd read of the Bureau's analysis of 9/11 that blame had been levied against each of the agencies with a hand in defense or domestic or foreign intelligence. Each had known something about the terrorist plots, but not one had put the picture together. Jerald defended the Bureau, saying it was easy to spot the terrorists afterwards when all the data pointed to them, but ahead of the event it was nearly impossible. And that was before they became awash in data. "You're looking for the proverbial needle in the haystack," Jerald said.

"Actually," Cy said, "a needle in ten thousand hay stacks."

"My point exactly, son. Data works, after the fact," he said. "We'd have been better off with a little more old fashioned intelligence gathering. The kind you get by being out there among them. By engaging on a human level, gaining the confidence of the right people, and keeping our eyes and ears open to what's happening. You young folk always think there's an easy way. Well let me tell you..." Cy had maintained eye contact but tuned out otherwise. He'd heard the lecture before, several times.

Cy wasn't sure his father gave enough credit to how much the internet had done for surveillance. Jerald was more concerned for the new constraints imposed on the Bureau after the 2013 exposé of government spying activities. It made Cy's task harder, not impossible, just harder. A challenge he readily accepted.

Cy closed his eyes and pinched the bridge of his nose to clear his head. The amount of data was overwhelming and growing so fast he thought the Bureau would soon drown in data. As it was, he and the other agents were treading in water up to their necks.

He needed a break, time to consider his next steps—to find a better way to sift through the information and to learn from the changing patterns of data, as nimbly as the country's adversaries did. That was where he'd apply his theories on recognizing patterns in what seemed to be random pieces of information.

* * *

Cy's cell phone swam across the nightstand, the vibration at the maximum setting. He blinked awake and grabbed the phone. The time 12:09:01 was visible on the bright display.

"Well, Cy," his father said after Cy punched "accept." Dressed only in his briefs, Cy rolled out of bed and moved to the hall. He preferred to stand when he spoke to his father. "I didn't wake you, did I?" his father asked.

Cy didn't answer. Neither "Yes" or "No" was an appropriate response.

"I couldn't call earlier or I would have."

Cy waited again.

"Were you going to tell me yourself or leave it to your boss, what's his...oh yes, Druitt?"

"I was sure the news had reached you."

"Well, yes it did, finally. It was something of a surprise, I'd say."

"Sorry about that," Cy said.

"I suppose you are. And I suppose you have a plan to make sure your performance improves. I can't say how disappointed I am."

"I do. Mr. Druitt said if I prove myself in the first thirty days, he'll try to push the schedule for me. Get me back in place."

"Well, Mr. Druitt can't do it alone."

"No, sir."

"And so?"

"And so, I'm doing what I need to do. That and more. A special assignment Mr. Druitt and I have worked out." Cy's heart had not skipped a beat, his tongue had not tied. He'd woven in the fabrication of Mr. Druitt's approval of his extracurricular assignment without hesitation.

"Okay. Keep me posted."

The words "call ended" flashed before Cy could say goodbye. As usual.

Cy made his way back to bed. He placed the phone face down on the carpet to muffle the sound and light when the phone woke and buzzed with the next message. The FBI never slept.

He slipped beneath the covers and pulled himself close to Yasmeen and the warmth on her side of the bed.

27. JAVIER

THOUGH JAVIER HAD TRIED TO ESCAPE WITH A NOD BEFORE EXIT-
ing, Lupe had jumped from her table at Tacos El Mirasol and
blocked his way.

"You weren't even going to say hello?" Lupe asked. The tips of
her fingers rested on his forearm.

"Hello," Javier said. He scanned the room. Most of the pa-
trons had returned to their conversations and meals. Those whose
eyes lingered in his direction strayed no further than Lupe. She'd
changed, Javier thought. She wore a tee-shirt he couldn't imagine
would fit Selam. The pink fabric stretched across Lupe's breasts
and was cut low enough to show a tanned neckline and cleavage.
After one glance, Javier kept his eyes averted, looking to the right,
to the left, above Lupe's head, toward the window, and back to
the right again. With no place else to look, he fixed his eyes on
the gold earring threaded through her left ear lobe.

"Come. Bring your lunch over here. You remember Ximena,
right? We have an extra chair. Eat with us. Please."

Lupe must have sensed Javier was on the verge of making
an excuse because she took his arm and coaxed him through the
maze of tables and chairs.

"Mena, see who I found," Lupe said.

"I see."

Ximena offered nothing more and returned to her meal, leaving Javier with the feeling she would rather not have run into Javier or anyone who shared their history in the desert. Lupe ignored Ximena's sullenness and began a litany of questions about how Javier had traveled to Atlanta, where he'd found work, how he liked where he was, and on and on to other topics.

Javier offered brief answers, words he'd rehearsed for such an occasion. And when he failed to ask the same questions of them, Lupe supplied their side of the story.

After their meal, Lupe followed Javier out the door, leaving Ximena behind alone. Lupe kept pace with Javier and launched into another stream of questions, where he lived, where he was headed, and when she would see him again.

Javier did his best to avoid answering, but Lupe would not surrender.

"Okay. I'll see you tomorrow." The sooner this is over the better, he thought.

"Perfect. I'll meet you here. We can go to Riverside. I know you've been there. Mena and I saw you there a week ago, but by the time I caught up to where I'd seen you, you had gone. Anyway, I'll show you around. Seven o'clock?"

"Seven o'clock."

"Promise?"

"Promise."

* * *

At six o'clock on Sunday, Javier was on the verge of ignoring the appointment. Lupe didn't know where he lived, not exactly, as he'd only given her a general sense of the area. Nor did she know where he worked, which was nowhere. However, as Ximena said, it was a small world, and they were very likely to meet again. If they did, he could claim he'd forgotten, but he had promised; he'd given his word.

When Javier arrived at the rendezvous point, he was surprised to find not only Lupe, but also Ximena and a third woman, their roommate Mercedes. Javier had never been on his own in the company of three young women his age. Where he came from, it would not have been tolerated. If they'd been discovered, their families would have forbidden their daughters to go out again without the company of a brother or uncle.

Although he'd become accustomed to seeing young women and men together and unsupervised, Javier could not rid himself of the sense of being unclean. He cringed at the touching and hugging everywhere he looked, stranger touching stranger, girl touching boy. He vowed to cleanse himself when he returned home and to spend the night praying.

Shortly after they arrived at the mall, Mercedes said she wanted to get a coffee and then sit and watch the shoppers. When she invited the others to go with her, only Ximena agreed.

"Not now," Lupe said, "I want to show Javier something. We'll be back in a few minutes. Go ahead, get your coffees. We'll join you later."

Lupe threaded her arm through Javier's. He wanted to pull away, but each time he moved his arm, she tightened her grip. As they walked, Javier recited verses from the Quran to himself, nodding whenever Lupe took a breath.

Lupe led Javier deep inside one store. They walked along wide corridors and rode escalators, moving stairs he remembered seeing in the airports he'd passed through on his journey west. She walked confidently, head up, ponytail and pink bow bobbing at the back of her head as if she'd been there a thousand times, as if she'd never been anywhere else.

She stopped short of one department and pointed. "They're in there, but you can see them from here if you stand on your tip toes. See?" Lupe pointed toward a rack of long garments. They were unlike any garments he'd seen before, with threads of silver and gold and colors from red to orange to blue. They shimmered and sparkled like jewels.

"And look how the men dress. Very handsome, no?"

In a glass case on their right, a male figure in a tuxedo stood frozen in place next to a female figure wearing one of the department's gowns. Their plastic faces were set with permanent smiles.

"That's how I want to dress when I'm an American," Lupe said.

"When you're an American?"

"Yes. I'm going to stay here and become an American. I'm never going back to Mexico."

"What if they find you and deport you?"

"It doesn't matter; I'll just come back again. What about you? Will you go back home?"

"I'm never going back," Javier said.

"So there. We think alike."

Javier shrugged.

"All right, I can tell you're not impressed. Still, you would look very handsome, I mean, more handsome in an outfit like that."

They retraced their steps across the white marble floors and through the cascade of scented candles, perfume, and leather. Back at the atrium, while Lupe scanned the heads in the food court, looking for her sister and friend, Javier tried to recall the scents of home.

"I don't see them anywhere," Lupe said.

Just then, over the din of shoppers and the carousel's melody, a woman screamed. Heads turned toward the mall's atrium entrance where two women stumbled into the corridor.

"What? Dios mío!" Oh my God. "Mena! Mena!" Lupe ran toward her sister who stood bent over a gray-haired woman kneeling on the floor. The woman had one hand to her head, the other holding her torn blouse together at the neck.

Gasps erupted across the crowd. Someone cried for help. Someone screamed. Someone yelled for Security. A family of four rose from their table and fled, the parents pushing the young ones ahead of them. A couple looked up from their meal, rose from their seats to see what had transpired, then returned to their conversation.

Javier turned on his heels. He headed back into the maze of shops, matching his pace to the ambling shoppers, keeping to the center of the crowd until he found another exit.

28. ALICIA

WHEN THEY PASSED THE COFFEE STAND A SECOND TIME, ALICIA turned to Wade. "One for the road?" she asked.

"Not for me. I don't know how you do it," he said.

"Do what?"

"Swallow a gallon of caffeine and then go home and sleep."

"I don't know. It just doesn't bother me," Alicia said.

"Double caramel macchiato," the barista called from the end of the counter. As Alicia reached for the cup, a scream echoed through the atrium. Wade looked up and toward the screaming.

"Darn it," Alicia said, "hold on to that."

Alicia left her coffee on the counter and ran to the far side of the atrium; Wade waddled behind her as fast as he could go.

"Over here," a man yelled on spotting the Ingram Security hats over the heads of the other shoppers.

Alicia pushed through the onlookers standing around two women, an older woman on her hands and knees, sobbing hysterically, the other crouched beside her. Wade spread his arms and shooed people back, then he pressed the switch on his handheld radio, ignoring the new PDA mounted on his shoulder. "Unit Two to Central. We have a disturbance at the food court, south entrance." As he waited for acknowledgement, Alicia knelt beside the woman in distress.

"Central to Unit Two." It was Carlo.

Between heavy breaths, Wade responded on his radio. "Unit Two. We're here."

"What's the nature of the incident?"

"We've got a woman on the ground. Might have fallen and cut her head. Hold on a minute."

"Ma'am," Alicia said, using her most reassuring tone and patting the woman's forearm. "It's okay. Everything's going to be all right." The audible sobbing subsided, but the woman's shoulders rose and fell and her hands trembled. Alicia noted the woman's disheveled gray hair, a tear in her blouse, a wet stain on her back and the seat and leg of her pants, as if she'd been lying in water. "Where are you hurt?" she asked.

The woman reached a hand to her head and pushed her hair back to reveal an abrasion across the side of her face. Alicia peered at the wound and satisfied herself it was superficial. "It's not serious, just a scrape, but we'll get you some medical attention. What's your name?"

"Pol...Polly," the answer came.

"Are you hurt, too?" Alicia asked the woman crouched next to Polly.

The woman shook her head, her ponytail of thick black hair, sweeping from side to side, a birthmark on her forehead.

"And your name?"

"Ah." It was Polly, her hand to her neck and a smear of blood on her fingertips.

Alicia pushed Polly's hand aside and noticed a small cut on her neck. "It's nothing, Polly, just a small cut. It'll be fine," Alicia said, then turned back to where the second woman had been. But the woman had disappeared, slipping away through the crowd.

Polly raised her head and took in the surroundings. Uniformed personnel, badges, shoulder radios, and utility belts of flashlights and notepads. She stopped crying.

"That's better, Polly," Alicia said, now cupping the woman's elbow in her hand, and remembering to use her name to establish a connection. "Do you think you can get up and sit over there?" Alicia pointed to a nearby bench.

Polly nodded.

"Ladies and gentlemen," Wade said, "please, give us some room. Unless any of you are witnesses to what just happened to this lady, please go on about your business. We have this under control." He shooed the onlookers away and then radioed Carlo in the Security Office to request medical attention.

Alicia took a seat next to Polly on the bench and asked her what had happened.

"A man. Outside. He...he attacked me. I was going to my car. He was waiting there and he had a...a knife."

"Did he cut you?" Alicia asked as she pulled the woman's hair back from her forehead. The skin was broken and flecks of debris pocked the wound, but the bleeding there and on the spot on her neck had stopped.

"No, but, he said he would if I screamed." Polly reached her hand to her neck.

"He threw me to the ground and pushed my face against the pavement. But...a woman came by. He looked up and ran. She helped me up and helped me back here."

"Polly, do you see the woman who helped you?" Alicia surveyed the few bystanders who had ignored Wade and continued to stare at the injured woman. Polly followed Alicia's gaze.

"No."

"Do you know her name?"

Polly shook her head and fumbled with the tear in her blouse.

"Do you remember what she looked like?" Alicia asked.

"Not really. It was dark. She had some kind of scar on her forehead. But I didn't really get a good look. She had a ponytail, I think. I don't know. I don't really remember."

"That's okay, Polly. You're doing good. What about the man who attacked you? Do you remember what he looked like?"

Polly looked away.

As Alicia thought, it was too early after the event. Polly had not recovered from the trauma. Alicia would have to leave it to the cops who had arrived and parked near the exit, their blue lights flashing.

To Polly, Alicia said, "It's all right, Polly. We'll get you taken care of first. Maybe later you can look at some pictures. Okay?"

* * *

Enough vehicles and emergency responders arrived to quell a minor riot. The ambulance, fire department, and police crews cordoned off the area, keeping the onlookers at a respectful distance. Oh, God. Carlo will be beside himself, Alicia thought as she stood up, yielding the scene to the medics and summarizing what she had gathered for the cops. When the ambulance driver said they were ready to go, Alicia and Wade checked on Polly. She lay inside resting on a gurney, a blood pressure tourniquet on her arm, a temporary bandage across her forehead.

Wade asked Polly for her car keys and if she remembered where she had parked her car.

"We'll take care of it for you until you can come back. I'll put one of my cards in your purse," Alicia said, flashing her card above Polly's head. She tucked it into a pocket on the side of Polly's purse. "Please call me when you're ready and we'll meet you." Alicia wanted to be there when Polly returned. She hoped after a good night's sleep, Polly would have a clearer head and be able to recall other details of the attack.

Alicia and Wade followed the police to the spot where Polly had parked and waited as the cops made a quick inspection. When they left, the guards headed back to the Security Office.

"Did we miss inviting anyone to the party?" Wade asked as he held the door for Alicia.

"Better safe than sorry," Alicia said. "I'm sure Carlo doesn't want to give her a reason to say she received anything but the best treatment."

Outside the Security Office, Wade took a deep breath before opening the door. "Time to face the music."

29. ALICIA

CARLO WAS ON HIS FEET, HIS GOUT MOMENTARILY PUSHED ASIDE. "Goddamn it." He banged a fist against the wall. Minor incidents made it into the daily security reports and were accumulated for statistical purposes, but they never prompted calls from management. Even parking lot fender-benders, pick-pocketing, and the occasional car break-in were chalked up as part of the business of running security at a mall. However, an assault on a woman resulting in an injury, one described as an attempted rape, was another story.

Carlo would have to meet with the police and pass on any information he could gather. And before he closed up for the night, he'd have to report the incident to Ingram Security headquarters.

"Kia Soul. Green lot. Section C. Row Three," Wade said, consulting his notepad. "She said she got here at five or five-thirty."

Carlo had made a first cursory review of the footage from cameras inside the mall as he waited for Wade and Alicia to return to the Office. He switched his monitor to the parking lot cameras and rewound the tapes, hitting pause when they reached five o'clock. There, he started the camera forward in slow motion.

At five fifteen, Polly's car, a dark Kia Soul, entered and parked between a Buick and a Ford 150. It was the only open spot for several rows. She exited and walked to the mall entrance. The cameras captured no one in close proximity. Carlo punched fast-forward on his console. Cars came and went. At eight, a figure in dark clothing came into view. He placed himself between the Kia and the Buick and stooped as if he were tying a shoe or picking something off the ground. He wore a hoodie and kept his head bowed.

At eight-ten, the camera picked up Polly returning to her car. She headed straight to the driver's side without breaking her stride.

"She doesn't see him," Wade said.

"You're right. Look, he's moved in front of the Buick," Alicia said, pointing at the screen. In her head, she screamed, Stop! Turn around. Run!

As Polly fumbled with her keys, the figure emerged from his hiding place. He grabbed her from behind and tried to pin her arms to her body. Polly struggled and dropped her purse. With her free arm, she flailed in the air. Then she froze. In the next few frames the figure, only slightly taller but much heavier than Polly, slammed her to the ground. And, in the next, he had knelt or squatted over her.

The cameras and lights were mounted on a pole twenty-five feet above the pavement and two rows away. The assault took place in near darkness. Carlo tried to zoom in for a closer look. The camera captured a few pixels of gray and white in the attacker's hand.

"Not going to get much on him," Carlo said. "He knew what he was doing. Kept his face hidden, his head covered, and may have worn gloves. Probably not his first attempt."

"Wait," Alicia said. "On his right arm. Look. It's not much, but it looks like a stripe around the sleeve of whatever he's wearing."

Carlo backed the tape up, started and stopped it again, and zoomed in as close as he could to the attacker's sleeve. "Could be a stripe or two," he said, "but it's hard to tell." He rolled the tape forward. Two figures approached. First, their shadows came into view, long faint shadows cast by the same distant lights. One of them, a woman judging by her shape and stature, stopped and pointed toward the Kia. The other put their hands to their head. The figure in the hoodie scuttled between the cars and headed away toward Chattahoochee River Avenue. The rest of the footage showed a woman with a ponytail putting her arm around Polly and helping her toward the mall. The second woman passed outside the camera's view.

"Okay, that's it," Carlo said. "I'll go back over this. Alicia, you want to take the interior and see what more you can get, if anything, once they're inside the mall? Wade, you take the rest of the exterior cameras and see if our guy shows up again as he's making his escape. See if we can tell if he gets away on foot. Whatever. Eight ten was it? Let's do what we can to wrap this up now. I don't want to take shit from the cops and have to listen to what they say a true professional security team could do," Carlo said.

It wasn't the first time Alicia or Wade had heard Carlo worry aloud about the cops. He'd retired from the force years ago, but several of the officers remembered him. If they had a reason to stop by the office, they never passed up an opportunity to rib him for taking a "cushy," second-rate job.

Alicia logged on to her computer and scanned the videos for the south exit. Eight-ten. As the mall closed at nine o'clock, the traffic flow was decidedly one way. Eight-twenty. The right most of the double doors opened. Two people stepped aside to allow someone to enter. It was Polly in her white blouse and dark slacks. She was leaning on the arm of a woman with long dark hair tied behind her head. The woman in a long sleeve sweater or jacket led Polly to a bench, but Polly crumbled to the floor in the middle of the corridor. A crowd gathered and then thinned, most passed as far from the two women as possible, hugging the wall and only turning their heads to look back when they reached the door. Some came closer, circling the women. The long-haired one looked up at them, reaching her hands out, looking as if she were asking for help. The woman's face came into view, the birthmark evident.

"Bingo," Alicia said. She tagged the frame, made note of the time stamp and frame number, and sent the frame to the printer. She switched back to a view of the food court and searched for better photos of the mystery woman and Polly, hoping to find a clear one of a stalker. Even so, Alicia suspected the perpetrator had never entered the mall and had been waiting the whole time in the parking lot. Wade would find out from his sweep of the exterior.

Frames buzzed across Alicia's screen. Her eyes were having a hard time focusing, but she was not ready to quit. Not yet. Any minute the police would show up to see what they had. Alicia rose and poured herself a cup of coffee from the office's communal pot. She grimaced at the taste of the stale and bitter liquid. It would have to do.

Revived by the infusion of caffeine, Alicia went back to work. Through one of the other cameras, she spotted Polly exiting a store earlier in the evening. She made a note of the camera and time stamp and studied the image for any clues it might yield. Behind Polly was a woman with long dark hair in a ponytail. She was walking arm and arm with a guy in a dark-colored sweatshirt. A hoodie. He looked up straight into the camera. There was some kind of mark on his face near the mouth. The woman looked at him and followed his gaze, the camera catching her full in the face.

"What?" Alicia said aloud. She rewound the footage and sent both frames to the printer. Alicia grabbed the woman's photo and held it up beside the earlier one she'd printed. They were identical, except for the birthmark. "Wade. Carlo. You have to see this."

30. LUPE

"THERE YOU ARE. WHERE DID YOU GIRLS GO?" LUPE ASKED XIMENA who was lying in bed when Lupe returned home. "I looked all over the mall for you."

"We left after having coffee," Ximena said. "Two coffees, as a matter of fact. We gave up waiting for you."

"And?" Lupe asked.

"And nothing."

"What do you mean, 'and nothing?' I saw you with that old lady at the exit. What happened?"

"I don't want to talk about it."

"Mena, it's me, Lupe. What's wrong? Who was she?"

"I don't know who she was. Mercedes and I were leaving. We were crossing the parking lot when we saw this man..." Ximena paused and took a deep breath.

"Go on."

"This man was attacking a woman. He was...on top of her. I just stood there watching. I couldn't move. I couldn't breathe. Mercedes yelled and, gracias a Dios, the man ran." Ximena crossed herself before continuing. "Mercedes didn't want to get involved, but I couldn't just leave the woman there on the ground. So I walked her back into the mall where I thought she could get help. She was hysterical. Everyone was looking at us."

"That's just when Javier and I returned," Lupe said. "I saw you."

"The police came. I couldn't hang around any longer. I left before they could start asking questions. I left and came back here."

"By the time I made my way through the crowd," Lupe said, "you were gone. And then I lost Javier, too. There were so many people trying to see what was going on. I looked everywhere, but I couldn't find him or you, so I gave up and came home."

"We can't afford to get involved," Ximena said. "Not with the police. They ask too many questions."

"I suppose Javier thought the same thing. But it was weird. He was gone, just like that," Lupe said, snapping her fingers for effect.

"You need to stay away from him, Lupe. He's not one of us."

"What do you mean? He's nice."

"He's different. Find someone else. Please."

"I don't want to find someone else. I like him. And you're wrong. He's just like us, away from home and in a strange place. He was afraid to get involved, too. Afraid of getting in trouble and getting deported."

"He's not afraid of anything. He couldn't be and do what he did. Or have you forgotten?"

"I haven't forgotten. But he was setting things right back then. Octavio was a pig. He deserved to die after...after what he did to you."

"I don't want to talk about it, Lupe. Go to sleep. And stay away from Javier."

"But—"

"Go to sleep," Ximena said. She rolled over to face the wall.

31. JAVIER

TO AVOID RAISING MORE SUSPICION BY RETURNING TO PRAY AT THE
Islamic Center, Javier visited a second mosque. He found it the
same way he had located the Islamic Center, asking directions
to the street name but never for directions to the actual mosque.
He took the same precautions, too, first observing the mosque
from a distance. This mosque sat at the end of a row of shops,
most abandoned and shuttered. In fresh paint above the door,
the words Masjid Al-Rahman proclaimed the mosque's presence.
Behind the paint, a shadow of the words Wash & Dry 25¢ was
etched into the siding by the sun.

Javier stood on the corner and observed people coming and
going at prayer time. A hand on his shoulder startled him. "Assalamu alaikum," the man said. Peace be upon you. "Are you here
to pray with us?"

Javier answered in Arabic, "Wa 'Alaykum Asalaam." And on
you as well. "Yes, I would like to pray with you."

"Why don't you come inside, then?" the man said. "Come with
me. My name is Ali."

"Are you the imam here?" Javier asked.

"Me? No," Ali laughed softly. "You have already met our imam,
Ata Nahidian."

Javier's heart fell to the floor. He had difficulty putting one
foot in front of the other. Ali must have known who Javier was

when he approached him on the street. And he knew Javier had met Ata Nahidian at the Islamic Center. If so, he knew too that Ata Nahidian had warned Javier against returning to the Center. Now, Ali had something more to tell Ata Nahidian, that Javier had violated Ata's instructions and come to Masjid Al-Rahman. But Ali stood expressionless as he waited for Javier to remove his shoes.

Javier took a long, deep breath to calm his nerves, then followed Ali inside the mosque. It was not what he expected. The prayer room was a large bare rectangle. A line on the linoleum floor marked where washers and dryers had once sat, collecting lint and dirt and leaving small circular impressions where the appliance feet had stood. And despite the fragrant smoke from incense burning on the far side of the room, a distinct aroma of soap and bleach and electrical heat permeated the place.

Ali smiled and spoke as if he had read Javier's mind. "A mosque in a laundry. Would our families believe it if you told them?"

Javier shook his head.

"Let us pray with the others," Ali said as he gestured to two rows of men kneeling on prayer rugs.

At the front of the room, to Javier's further surprise and dread, Ata Nahidian knelt with his eyes closed, his back to the worshipers, the men to one side of a plywood panel running half the length of the room, the women on the other.

Javier, reeling with questions that flooded his head, took a place at the end of the back row. He couldn't concentrate and resorted to mimicking the actions of the faithful beside and in front of him. He bowed when they bowed, kneeled when they kneeled, and touched his head to the floor when they touched their heads to the floor.

As soon as the prayers ended, the room emptied except for Javier and for Ali who knelt behind him on the floor. With his disobedience known, Javier had little to risk. He took a deep breath and asked, "Does Qasim Bousaid come here to worship, too?"

Ali did not raise his head and only spoke after a long and obvious pause. "I do not know anyone named Qasim Bousaid. Perhaps at another mosque." Ali smiled and rose. He shook Javier's hand and then retreated to the back of the mosque and through a door, closing it behind him.

As Javier slipped on his shoes, two women talked on the other side of the panel. To Javier's astonishment, they spoke to each other in Spanish.

* * *

A few blocks away, while he waited for a green light, Javier tilted his head back, letting the sun warm his face and settle his nerves. He was still reeling from the day's events. He missed the crossing signal and waited through another red light while making plans to return to Masjid Al-Rahman. Ata Nahidian had said not to come back to the Islamic Center, but he had not forbidden Javier to go to any other mosque, not in so many words. And the imam had been at the mosque today and had the opportunity to tell Javier not to return. It was an opportunity the imam had not taken.

When he'd gone another block, Javier had a sense of being followed. He slowed his pace and halted at the next storefront, one with a plate-glass window. On display inside were party dresses for young girls, one prominently displayed made of gaudy violet and pink netting over a sateen-like fabric. His father would have slain Selam himself if she had so much as looked at the dress. But, Javier reminded himself, he was not here to look at dresses. Also visible in the window, through its reflection, was a figure behind him and across the street. It was a woman. Javier continued to the end of the block, rounded the corner, and waited. The soft patter of rubber soles on the pavement, were faint but approaching. When the woman turned, Javier stepped into her path.

The birthmark.

"Ximena, what—"

"No, you tell me. What were you doing in there? Who are you?" she asked.

"What do you mean? Why are you following me?"

"I want you to stay away from Lupe."

"You'd best ask Lupe to stay away from me, if that's what you want. I've not made any attempt to contact her."

"Who are you?" she repeated.

"What do you mean, 'Who am I'?"

"I mean. You're not Latino. You can pretend to be, but you aren't. What were you doing in the mosque?"

Javier sidestepped Ximena's question. "What do you know about mosques?"

"Nothing. Just that Latinos don't go there."

"You think? Well, you're wrong. In fact, come with me." Javier started back toward the Masjid Al-Rahman but turned when Ximena made no move to follow. "Well?"

"Well what?" she asked.

"Let me introduce you to someone. Just for a minute. Come with me."

"I can't go in there. It's dangerous," Ximena said.

"That proves you know nothing. Come."

* * *

"Did you forget something, Brother?" Ali asked. Then, spying Ximena behind Javier in the doorway, he added, "Ah! And who is this?"

"This is...a friend. I want to introduce her to one of the sisters," Javier said, repeating the request in Spanish so Ximena would understand.

"A Latina. I see. One minute," Ali said.

He craned his neck around the plywood room divider. "Sister Yasmeen," he called.

A woman's hand grabbed the edge of the plywood panel and pushed it outward. Beneath a black abaya, was a face, olive skinned and free of adornment. "Brother Ali," she said.

"Our guest has brought you someone," Ali said.

In Spanish, Javier introduced Ximena to the woman Ali had called Yasmeen. Yasmeen responded in fluent Spanish. Ximena's jaw dropped. Javier blinked but otherwise held back his surprise.

Ximena stared at Yasmeen, at Javier, and then again at Yasmeen.

"Ven, por favor," Yasmeen said. Come here, please. She stepped aside and invited Ximena behind the panel.

32. JAVIER

A HALF-MILE FROM MASJID AL-RAHMAN, JAVIER'S CELL PHONE VI-
brated inside the pocket of his jacket. To his knowledge, only
one person had the number. Qasim Bousaid. Although, he knew
little about cell phone technology, having never owned one before coming to the west, he had heard the phones could be used
to locate people. He sprinted ahead, putting as much distance
between himself and the mosque as he could.

On the fourth buzz, he answered. "Yes."

There was a cough and the sound of a man clearing his throat.
"Come back," the voice with the familiar rasp said in English.

"Back?" Javier asked. Did he mean to Masjid Al-Rahman?

"Come back," the voice said.

Qasim hung up before Javier could say more or hang up himself. Javier had no time to ask how Qasim had known he'd just
come from Masjid Al-Rahman. Ali or Ata must have sent word
to Qasim. Still, he had no way of knowing if Qasim would welcome him or chastise him for coming to the mosque, for bringing Ximena, an infidel, inside, for speaking Qasim's name and
for asking to see Qasim Bousaid. Javier retraced his steps, going
as fast as he could without sprinting or running and call attention to himself. When he reached the mosque's door, perspira-
tion ran from his temples to his jaw. Beneath his jacket, his shirt

was soaked below the armpits. Javier wiped his forehead with his sleeve and entered.

For the second time today, Javier removed his shoes and placed them beside the door. He glanced to the right of the crude partition where he'd seen Ximena disappear with the woman Yasmeen. Neither was there now.

The sound of socked feet padding on a bare floor drove all thoughts but those of Qasim from his mind. But the man who appeared was not Qasim. It was the imam, Ata Nahidian.

"Brother Shafra, you came so quickly," the imam said.

"I was expecting Qasim Bousaid," Javier said. "He called." From his pocket, Javier retrieved his cell phone. He stared at the dial, wondering whether he should call Qasim.

With his hand, Ata covered the face of Javier's phone.

"He has sent me in his place."

On the one hand, Javier was relieved that Ata admitted to Qasim's existence. On the other, he feared what Ata Nahidian would say about Javier's disregard for Ata's instructions. Javier said, "Imam, I am your servant, ready to do as you bid. God willing."

The imam led Javier through the empty prayer room where he had knelt earlier and through the door where he had seen Ali disappear. Ata Nahidian pointed to a seat cushion next to a low square table. Javier took a seat, arranging his legs cross-legged. The cushion was warm as if someone had recently vacated the spot. The imam padded to the other side of the table.

Between them lay two cylinders of rolled papers. Ata Nahidian spread one across the table and weighed down the edges with stones.

"This is a map of your neighborhood. You live here," he said, pointing to the intersection of Grant and Beechwood. Javier nodded. The imam slid his extended forefinger across the page to an oblong shape bounded by two main thoroughfares, Chattahoochee River Avenue along the south and Etowah River Drive on the north. A series of connected boxes snaked across the heart of the oblong, the words "Riverside Centre" along the spine.

"And here, a shopping mall. You must become familiar with the area, the streets from your home to Riverside Centre." Ata jabbed his forefinger on the word Riverside. He allowed Javier to study the map for a moment. "You know how to find this place?"

Javier nodded. "Yes, Imam."

"This exact place?"

Another nod. "Yes, Imam."

Ata removed a weight, allowing the flattened page to roll into a cylinder again. He picked up the second cylinder and unrolled the paper on the table, shifting the stones to the new diagram. This one was a scale drawing of Riverside Centre with labels for the major stores, Macy's, Von Maur, Nordstrom, and Bloomingdale's. The imam swiveled the diagram on the table so the south side faced Javier, the familiar Chattahoochee River Avenue side.

"Here. This is Riverside. I showed you this place a moment ago. You see this symbol on the diagram?" The imam pointed at a spot on the outline of the mall. The spot was marked with a double line and a tiny gray arrow, its tip pointing to the double line. "This is an entrance." Ata tapped his finger just inside the double lines. There, opposite the arrow, was a triangle hand-drawn in red ink. "The food court is just inside these doors. A carousel off to the right, here. And on the left several stores. These are of no importance." Ata paused a second time to give Javier a chance to get his bearings. Then he continued, "Beginning tomorrow, you should visit this place. Go to the food court. Eat your lunch there. Learn every detail you can. Learn how long it takes you to go from your house to Riverside and how long it takes you to walk from the bus stop on Chattahoochee to the south entrance of the mall and to this spot." Ata's finger touched the red triangle. "Exactly how long. How many minutes and seconds. This is your assignment."

The imam's face was a blank.

"That's all?" Javier asked.

"That is all."

"But, what—" Javier stopped in mid-sentence. The imam had allowed the page to roll back into a cylinder, but not before Javier noticed a second triangle at another set of double lines with a gray arrow, another exit. This triangle was inked in green. There might have been more, but the other double lines and gray arrows, and triangles if there were any, had disappeared inside the roll of paper.

The imam was halfway to the door. Javier scrambled to his feet and followed. At the door, Javier bade the imam goodbye saying, "Assalamu alaikum," and shaking Ata's hand.

Javier retrieved his shoes and hurried across the street before he dared look back. At the corner, he stopped and pulled his cell phone from his jacket. Someone had warmed the cushion opposite Ata before Javier. He wondered if a third person would arrive to sit on the cushion he had just warmed.

Javier held his cell phone to his ear, nodding if a passerby gave him more than a quick glance. All the while, Javier watched the side door of the mosque. He was tiring, his stance and continued nodding growing suspect. Then, a young man in traditional dress arrived, knocked at the side door, and was whisked inside.

The green triangle? Javier wondered.

33. CYRIL

CY UNPLUGGED HIS EARPHONES AND LEANED BACK IN HIS CHAIR, the headset still resting on his head. He pinched the bridge of his nose between his fingers. He needed caffeine.

He scooted his chair back and headed for the coffee machine in the small lunchroom on the second floor. A sign on the machine said, "Out of Order." Cy cursed and dug for change in his pocket, opting for a caffeine laden soda from the vending machines. He glanced at his watch and banged a fist against the machine as the can dropped. He'd sworn he'd be out of the office by nine, but one string of recordings, one he'd first listened to a little after seven had piqued his interest. That one led him to another and then another and now it was ten o'clock.

When he returned to his desk, he set an alarm for midnight. He'd give himself two hours, tops, to complete his write ups and send them to the Supervisory Agent-in-Charge, and then spend what was left on his "after-hours" project.

The whole transcript review process rankled Cy. It was inefficient at best, he thought, with no feedback from higher up and no sharing of information between the agents who listened in Hindi, Chinese, or Arabic or any of the other languages the FBI found necessary. But Cy knew little of the FBI's inner workings, surprising for someone who'd grown up so close to the Bureau. His father had been appropriately tight lipped about his work, rebuffing questions from his young son so often Cy had stopped asking.

After joining the FBI himself, Cy hadn't gone to his father for information. He hadn't bothered with the new agent networking events, either. All they did was rehash lore of past Bureau failures and successes and stories from "unnamed sources," following everything with the popular but tired refrain, "I'd have to shoot you if I told you."

No one with any real insight talked about what they did or did not know. And no one Cy knew had answers to his questions, those that dealt with the Bureau's lack of understanding of the contents of what they had gathered, parsed, and stored in the FBI's massive databases. Further, the rapid buildup of the amounts and types of data being gathered was exacerbating the problem.

Cy had pulled together his thoughts on how to improve the process. In true FBI-style, he'd given his idea the code name Cycle. He liked the sound of it, though he'd only ever spoken the name aloud to himself, his team of one. He couldn't share it with anyone until he had fine tuned his hypothesis and then tested and retested and proven his theory. Many more late nights and early mornings lay ahead.

Cy pinched his nose again. He saved the surveillance files he'd completed, crafted a cover letter summarizing his findings, attached the files to the letter, and hit the send button on his keyboard. He had one hour left to work on Cycle.

* * *

"Goodness gracious, Cy. What time is it?" Yasmeen asked, her voice throaty. She'd been sound asleep.

"One o'clock," Cy said as he slid into bed. "And before you say anything..."

"I'm not saying anything."

Cy kissed her on the lips and pulled her to him. He was drained from the long hours and high stress level and too tired to make love, but he knew Yasmeen understood. Yasmeen Fakhoury worked for the FBI, too, though her home office was in Washington where they'd met during training at the Academy. He hadn't approached her during those weeks, though he'd been captivated by her exotic look, dark eyes, dark hair, olive skin, and her easy smile.

At the end of their training, Cy had returned to Atlanta. He'd lost track of Yasmeen until earlier this year when she called him from the Atlanta airport. She said she was in town for an assignment and asked him to join her for dinner. Dinner followed dinner until they became inseparable whenever she was in town. Then, when the FBI extended her assignment for another ninety days, Cy made room for her in his closet and his life. She traveled every other week, Washington mostly, but other places too, places she chose not to name. For now, it made for a compatible relationship.

Cy put his head on his pillow and was out before Yasmeen.

* * *

"So, where are you off to?" Cy asked the next morning.

"Can't tell you. You don't have clearance," Yasmeen said.

"Right."

"Dallas," she said with a chuckle. "But just for a few days. I'll be back on Friday night."

"Good, maybe I can get caught up by the time you get back."

"You'll never get caught up, Cy. You know that."

"I will. I have to complete this before the end of the month. There's no way I want to go into the year-end review cycle without the record being fixed."

"Something else will just take its place."

Cy studied Yasmeen's face.

"Cy, I understand. It's okay. If I expected anything else, I'd be spending my days in Washington instead of here in Atlanta. Besides, I feel better about my being away so much. You have your tapes and your codes to keep you warm at night." Yasmeen laughed, kissed him full on the mouth and grabbed her briefcase from the kitchen counter. "See you Friday."

"How late?" Cy asked.

"Late enough, but I'll probably still beat you home. Try to have the weekend free."

Cy let the jab roll away and bit off a corner of toast. He waved. Yasmeen blew a kiss and exited, sculpted calves and leopard skin spike heels, slipping through the doorway.

Outside, the sun peeked over the roof of the building across the street. Cy wondered if he had an all-nighter left in him. He hadn't pulled one since graduate school. Tuesday, Wednesday, Thursday, Cy counted the days on his fingers. Yasmeen would be back on Friday. He smiled. He had all the time in the world.

34. ALICIA

ALICIA STOOD IN THE DOORWAY TO HER SON'S BEDROOM. KYLE SAT with his bony shoulders hunched over his PC's keyboard, unchanged since the last time Alicia checked on him. "It's time, Kyle."

"Just one more minute," Kyle said, his fingers pecking frantically over the keyboard.

"One minute in your lingo could mean five or ten."

"Just one more."

"Okay, sixty seconds. And I'm counting." Alicia marked the exact time on her watch, the sweep second hand at ten past the hour.

She left Kyle to his video game, one she recognized and had vetted before allowing Kyle to play. From his chest of drawers, she pulled out his favorite pajamas, the red and black ones splashed with Spider-Man action figures. With the pajamas draped over her arm, she watched the sweep hand on her watch round the top of the dial and return to the ten mark.

"Ding. Ding. Sixty seconds. One minute. Exactly."

Kyle exhaled, long and loud. A sigh meant for Alicia's benefit, but he lowered the lid of his computer. "Okay," he said, reluctance evident in his voice.

"Here, take your PJs and go brush your teeth."

A moment later, he returned and climbed in bed. "Okay, Spidey," she said as she plumped his pillow, "Sleep well."

"Don't call me Spidey."

"Oh, well, excuse me. I didn't realize Spidey was no longer your bedtime name."

"Spidey's for kids."

"I see."

Alicia tucked the sheets around his neck. She held back a smile as Kyle slipped one web-covered arm out and crooked it under his head.

"So, if you're not going to be Spiderman for Halloween, who are you going to be?"

"Fifty Cent."

"Fifty Cents? What kind of character is Fifty Cents?"

"Not Fifty Cents, Fifty Cent. He's a gangsta."

"Gangsta? What's a gangsta?" Alicia said, pretending to be unfamiliar with the term. She'd seen more than she wanted to see of "gangsta-wanna-bes" in their old neighborhood where juveniles roamed unsupervised when they should have been in school. They'd parade with their hats sideways, backwards, or down over their faces, their hands clutching the waistband of dropped-crotch pants that impeded their walk or defined it like a trademark.

"They're these cool guys," Kyle said.

"Cool, huh?" Alicia twisted one side of her mouth and arched her eyebrows. She would not discuss the merits of "gangstas" with Kyle at this hour. He'd never go to sleep. "We'll see."

"No, not we'll see. I know what 'we'll see' means. Whenever you say 'we'll see' you mean no."

"Good night, Kyle," she said, avoiding calling him Spidey. Alicia leaned forward and kissed her son on the forehead, twice, though his eyes were already closed. As she left the room, she gathered his computer and power cord in one hand and pulled the door close behind her with the other, but was careful to leave a crack. Kyle still wanted a sliver of light visible from the hallway if he woke in the night.

Alicia poured the last of the coffee into a mug, inhaling the soothing aroma of the Sumatra-grown Arabica. She drank it black at home, no cream, no sprinkles. Slouched on the sofa with the coffee by her side, she woke Kyle's computer from its sleep state. The computer had parental controls installed, but she wondered how long it would be before he learned how to subvert her monitoring.

Everything appeared routine, his game sessions, a chat session with "Chatter6", whom Alicia knew to be Philip, one of Kyle's friends, and Kyle using the pseudonym "SpiMan." She shivered, there it was, the word "gangsta." Alicia slowed to read line by line, but found nothing other than back and forth on plans for Halloween and the boys' costumes.

Still, the recent encounter with the thugs might have left more of an imprint on Kyle than Alicia realized. She'd nip Kyle's budding fascination at breakfast. Alicia closed the lid and set Kyle's computer aside. She had her own screen to stare at for the next couple of hours.

News of a terrorist incident in Europe had filled the airwaves all day, but Alicia had not had a chance to catch the details until now. She flipped up the lid to her computer and logged on to the newswires. Television was all chatter and entertainment and talking heads. Alicia typed a few keywords into the browser's search bar: news, bombing, Europe. A page of results filled the screen.

Alicia clicked on one of her preferred sources, one with the headline, "Bomb May Have Been Carried in a Backpack." Below the headline were a half-dozen grainy photos and a video. She played the video without sound. Ambulances and police vehicles sped to or from the scene, blue and red lights flashing. Newscasters held mikes to their chins and pointed an arm to an area roped off with tape and an impromptu barricade of fluorescent cones. White tarps covered the bodies in the street; others were pixelated out of recognition.

For more information, Alicia returned to her bookmarks. This time, she clicked through sites reporting from eastern Europe and the Middle East. These sites contained less sanitized information. They were sites ranting against everything western and explaining how to make a bomb or sever a human head. She'd forced herself to visit the sites to educate herself. Pretending they didn't exist or that the events were not happening on her doorstep was to ignore the truth.

Once Alicia had tried to show Carlo what she'd found. She'd logged on to one of the graphic sites from her office computer. Carlo had eyed the screen for less than a second before he looked squarely at Alicia.

"What the hell are you messing with stuff like this for?" he'd asked.

"Because it's happening. It's happening right under our noses."

"It's happening in Syria and Iraq and Afghanistan and other godforsaken places."

"Yeah, and in Germany, and Italy—"

"And it's being carried out by a bunch of crazies. Lunatics. Lone wolves."

"You think it can't happen here?"

"I didn't say that. But it's all hype. We plaster their faces over the TV which is just what they want."

Alicia closed out the site. Ingram Security's logo, the gold badge with a blue lightning bolt across its center, floated across the screen like an untethered child's balloon.

"You need to stop looking at that stuff. No wonder your imagination is running in high gear. Don't you have something better to worry about?"

The security radio on Carlo's desk had squawked, ending their conversation. "Unit Three to Central. Child trapped in elevator. East Corridor."

Maybe Carlo was right. Maybe she was inventing worries. Still, the unfinished war in the Middle East was not far from her thoughts, nor was the evidence pointing to its spread further and further from the epicenter. The incidents in the United States were, so far, nothing more than pinpricks. But people had forgotten there was a day in the not too distant past when they'd not seen or heard of bombings, and suicide vests, and snipers. Alicia, though, had not forgotten.

She and Seth had talked at length about the events spiraling out of control. Seth was convinced the terrorists had to be contained inside their borders and not allowed to spread their violence to other countries. He'd been even more adamant than Alicia had. She was the one who had used the word contained. Seth had said eradicated.

Alicia woke several times during the night with the images of the events in Europe playing at the back of her head. Relax, she told herself. Leave it to the professionals. With Seth gone, all she could do to keep people safe, Kyle in particular, was to do her small and insignificant job. Tomorrow would be another day like yesterday, she sighed. She'd make her rounds, check doors and locks, offer directions, walk a shopper to their car, and watch for shoplifters and other troublemakers. That was it, for now.

OCTOBER

35. ALICIA

ALICIA HAD BREAKFAST WITH KYLE BEFORE DRIVING HIM TO HER SIS-
ter-in-law's house for an overnight stay, one she arranged every
month or so. It was a chance for Kyle to experience what family
life was like, a family with both a mother and a father and two
boys, not one. Even better, the two boys, Vince and Max, were
close to Kyle's age.

Alicia knew Kyle enjoyed being in a busy, noisy house-
hold, despite his reticence to discuss the time away from home.
Last month, he'd given a tepid response to her asking how the
time went.

"It was okay. We played one of Vince's new video games and
helped Uncle Scott in his workshop," he'd said.

"And?"

Kyle pushed his food around on his lunch plate and took his
time answering.

"That's all?"

"Mom, okay already. It was fun. But I also like being at home
with you."

Alicia pinched Kyle's cheek. She smiled. "I like being at home
with you, too, but it's okay to have fun with your friends." In a few
years, he'd be gone from home more and more often, whether she
wanted him to or not. And Alicia wanted to assure him it was
normal and something they could discuss.

"See you tomorrow!" she called as he ran to the Blake's front door. She watched until June Blake answered, ushered him in, waved hello from the doorway, and closed the door behind Kyle. He'd be safe until Sunday. She could worry about him again then.

Saturday passed without incident, and Carlo left at three, leaving Alicia with the other guards on the night shift, including Wade. When Wade rose to go on patrol, Alicia begged off with a wave of her hand. "You go ahead. If you don't mind, I'll catch up on a few things here. Take David with you." David was one of the newer guards and just discovering how boring desk work could be. He jumped at the chance to do a stroll.

"No problem," Wade said. "Want me to bring you a coffee back?"

"Huh?" Alicia said, already lost in thought as she fumbled with the cameras. "Oh, sorry, no thanks. Not now."

Wade's eyebrows bobbled over his eyes. Alicia ignored him and scooted closer to her screen, squinting at the black and white images. She'd relaxed for one whole week, or if not a week, at least one whole day. On Tuesday, Carlo had even complimented her on how calm she'd seemed of late. Wade had overheard the conversation though he hadn't contributed. And by the way he looked at her later, he hadn't been fooled. Each day since, her thoughts returned to the incident more and more often, until she was back to her old ways, glued to the cameras or frequenting the atrium at Riverside.

Tonight, though, the cameras offered little to catch Alicia's eye. No backpacks, no one skulking in the corners or loitering near the rest rooms or exits, no one following a shopper too closely. Alicia had read an article on a new technology designed to identify potential pickpockets with a direct feed from security cameras. A computer program analyzed pedestrian walking patterns, honing in on the proximity of one person to another, angle and speed of closure of approach, and a few other traffic patterns. Nice, but it was not a feature of the technology system rolling out at Riverside. For now, all Alicia could do was practice, testing the concepts in her head as she monitored the cameras. She ignored the individuals passing through the camera's line of sight and instead took in the whole crowd at once, tuning her eyes to pick up anomalies of motion. She might never catch the professionals, but the amateur pickpockets and other troublemakers stood out.

Alicia switched cameras to view the feed from the food court. She set two images in her mind, a hoodie with stripes on its sleeves and two young women with long dark ponytails. Having grown up on Agatha Christie novels, Alicia was in the camp that believed sooner or later perpetrators returned to the scene of their crime. She bet the man who attacked Polly would show up at Riverside again, in the parking lot or near the south entrance. And she wanted desperately to be the one to find him.

From her desk drawer, Alicia retrieved a manila folder and glanced at a photo inside, an image from the night Polly had been accosted. She fixed the grainy image of the man with the mark on his cheek into her head and stared at her monitor, looking for a match. At eight o'clock, she found what she was looking for. She punched the print button, tapped her foot and cursed under her breath while the printer warmed up and loaded a sheet of paper.

Alicia tore from the security room. In her hand, she clutched a printout of a man with close cropped dark hair, a mark across his cheek, and three stripes on the sleeve of his hooded sweatshirt. The other guards swiveled in their chairs at the click of the office door opening, but Alicia was in too big a hurry to explain. She kept up the full sprint until she rounded the end of the service hallway and entered the public area. There, she changed to a brisk walk, never looking left or right, determined to catch up to the man with three stripes on his sleeve.

By the time she reached the food court, he had vanished. Alicia checked outside the atrium exit. Nothing. Back inside, she filtered through the faces in the crowd, finding no one who matched the photo on her printout. But she saw something she hadn't seen on the camera.

In the food court, three women were eating dinner. The two facing her were Latino. Sleek, deep brown hair pulled back behind their heads, broad smiles, and perfect teeth. It was the twins, identical as far as she could tell, except for the birthmark on the woman to the right.

36. ALICIA

ALICIA REMOVED HER HAT AND TUCKED IT UNDER HER ARM. SHE walked toward the three women but avoided making even a passing glance at them until she stood next to their table. With a broad smile on her face, she leaned forward and placed a hand on the back of an empty chair, sending what she hoped was a nonthreatening signal.

"Hello ladies," she said, keeping the smile going. "Excuse me, but may I ask you a question?" Alicia paused to see if the women understood English.

The twins eyed each other but said nothing. Their lone companion returned Alicia's glance. "Sure," she said.

"I was wondering if any of you know or might have seen this person." Alicia placed the photo of the young man on the table and oriented the page to the twins' advantage. The twins looked at the photo, at each other, and then at their companion. "Go ahead, take another look," Alicia said. "He's not in any trouble. I just want to talk to him."

"No. We don't know him," the single woman said.

"No. No. We don't know him," the twin without the birthmark said, echoing the woman's statement. To emphasize her point, as if she was not sure of her words, she shook her head from side to side. An exaggerated shake. Alicia would not get anywhere with them, but judging by their reaction, she was convinced they recognized the man in the photo. Still, if they did and if they knew he was connected with Polly's attack, Alicia wondered why they were hesitant to say anything.

Alicia tried a different tactic. "I recognize you," she said to the birth-marked twin. Alicia recognized both, the one with the birthmark who had helped Polly and her twin, but the one with the birthmark looked more vulnerable. "You were here a couple of weeks ago when you helped the woman in the parking lot."

"No. We don't know him," she said.

"Yes, I understand that," Alicia said, nodding her head as if she needed validation the woman understood. "But, you were here that night. Correct?"

"No. No correct." More shaking of the woman's head, her ponytail flailing at her shoulders.

Alicia was ready to admit defeat until she turned and saw the young man in the photo exiting from the men's restroom. He was wearing a hoodie with three stripes on the sleeves, and he was heading toward her. Alicia slid the photo from the table, folded it in half, and stuffed it in her pocket.

The young man stopped in the aisle a few feet away as if to show he was just passing by and not about to take a seat. He was close enough for Alicia to see the mark on his face. It was a scar running from the corner of his mouth halfway across his right cheek.

"This is him, no? The man in the picture?" Alicia asked.

"No," the lone woman answered.

The twins kept their silence.

The young man fidgeted and looked as if he wanted to leave. Perhaps, since Alicia had removed her hat, he'd not noticed until now she was a guard. He reached inside his jacket then stuffed both hands in his pants pockets, fumbling with something metallic, coins or a set of keys.

As she waited, hoping one of the women would add a comment, Alicia glanced to the table and noticed a fourth cup of soda, half finished, on the table in front of the empty chair. On the one hand, everything made sense. On the other, nothing did. Alicia was as confused as she had been earlier. Though Javier was the man she had caught on camera with the twin exiting the store behind Polly, and though he had a hoodie identical to the one Polly's attacker had worn, and though everyone was reticent to say much about him, he was not Polly's attacker. Polly had been adamant her attacker was light skinned and had sandy hair. This young man had an olive complexion, perhaps even a shade darker than olive, and close-cropped black hair.

The one remaining thread connected with the attack was the sweatshirt.

"Javier...," the unmarked twin said. She paused after uttering the one word, realizing she'd said the young man's name. She dropped her head and stared at her hands in her lap.

Alicia spoke in her place. "Javier, is it? I was just asking these young ladies about someone. Someone with a sweatshirt just like yours." Javier said nothing. "Your shirt. Can you tell me where you bought it? Someone I'm looking for was wearing that same shirt."

"I found it," he said.

Alicia noticed his cheek twitched and his brows flicked, giving his face an odd expression, a mix of shame and fear. She wondered if he were ashamed to be wearing a shirt he had found and afraid of being arrested for taking someone's property.

"Someone left it in the parking lot," Javier said.

"Did you see the man who left it? Would you recognize him?"

"No, I didn't see anyone."

"Could you show me the spot where you found the jacket?"

"No. It was on the ground. Somewhere out there," he said, waving a hand toward the exit.

"Okay. Never mind, my mistake." She smiled at the three. "Enjoy your evening," she added.

Before she took a seat at her desk, Alicia pulled the photo of Javier from her pocket, wadded it into a ball, and threw it into the waste can. She rocked back and forth in her chair for several minutes, fuming.

She was missing something.

As she waited for her computer to boot, she banged the side of the tower in frustration, as she'd seen Carlo do. She cringed, thinking his habits were wearing off on her

Alicia brought up the video from the night of Polly's attack and each Saturday since, scanning for a man in a hoodie. In no time, she found him. Alone, near the atrium exit each time. She checked an odd day or two during the week and found him again, twice. In three of the frames, the man with the scar on his face carried a backpack. A large backpack.

Alicia leaned over, retrieved the photo from the waste can, and flattened it on her desk.

* * *

The following Saturday, Alicia found one of the twins sitting alone in the food court, a single soda on the table in front of her. Alicia approached, carrying a black Arabica coffee in her hand. "Hello, there. Remember me?" she asked.

The woman looked up, her eyes widened, but she smiled.

Surprised, Alicia thought, but not afraid.

"Yes," she said.

"Mind if I join you?" Alicia put her coffee on the table and scooted back a chair but she waited for the young woman's assent.

"Please. It's okay."

"I'm sorry, I don't even know your name," Alicia said, as she took a seat.

"Lupe," she said.

"Lupe," Alicia repeated.

"It's really Guadalupe, but everyone calls me Lupe."

"Guadalupe. I like that."

Lupe smiled, teeth showing this time.

"Are you alone? No friends today?"

"Just me. But I'm waiting for a friend."

"The young man? Javier?" Alicia asked.

"Yes. I hope he comes soon."

"He seems like a nice young man. Where are you and your sister...ah, what's your sister's name?"

"Mena, for Ximena."

"Lupe and Mena. That's nice." Come on, Alicia said to herself, don't overdo it now. "Where are you from?"

"We..." Lupe hesitated. Alicia looked away and sipped her coffee, as if to convey the woman's answer was inconsequential, asked more from politeness than genuine interest. "We're from Saltillo."

"Saltillo, it's a city in the north, no?" Alicia had no idea where Saltillo was, but by saying "north," she sounded like she knew more than she did, plus she had a fifty percent chance of being right.

"Yes, not too far from Monterrey. Do you know Saltillo?" A broader smile now and eyes that matched.

"No. I've never been to Mexico. But I'd like to go some day."

"You'd like Saltillo, except that it is very dry there," Lupe said.

"Well, it has rained a lot here, lately, but we have dry spells, too."

Lupe nodded and sipped her soda through the straw, dipping her head to the cup rather than lifting the cup off the table.

Alicia continued, "And your boyfriend, Javier, is he from Saltillo?"

"Oh, he's not my boyfriend. Just a friend," Lupe said, lowering her head.

"Sounds as if you'd like him to be your boyfriend."

"Maybe. But my sister Mena doesn't like him."

"I see. But you knew him from Saltillo, so it's good you found a familiar face here."

"No, we met a few weeks ago. He's not from Mexico."

"No?"

"No." Lupe smiled broadly this time. "You have to speak Spanish very well to know."

"Where is he from?"

Lupe opened her mouth to speak then paused. Her brows knit together. "I don't know," she said.

Alicia didn't press Lupe further. She checked her watch for the time and said she had to go back to work.

As soon as she reached her station in the Security Office, she tapped in the code for the food court camera. The young woman she now knew as Lupe was in the same place Alicia had left her, nursing her soda. Alicia panned the atrium and spotted Javier leaning against the far side of a column near the exit. His backpack lay at his feet. He remained in the same place in the same position for an hour before he left without ever approaching Lupe. As far as Alicia could tell, Lupe never saw him.

37. LUPE

SQUEALS OF DELIGHT AND CANNED LAUGHTER BOOMED FROM THE tiny television. Lupe ducked her head inside Mercedes' room. Mercedes lay sprawled on her bed, her head propped on her hands, eyes glued to the set. Ximena sat on the floor beside the bed, working a needle and thread through a shirt sleeve.

"I'm going to bed," Lupe announced. Just as she had the week before, Lupe had gone to Riverside and stayed long after Mercedes lost interest and went home. She'd waited in her usual place at the food court until just before nine, but Javier had not shown. When an announcement came over the loud speakers saying the mall would close in ten minutes, Lupe kept her seat. She waited until the security guards began a sweep of the atrium, but he did not show.

"Hush," Mercedes said, waving a hand in the air. "We have to see who wins."

More shrieks. Mercedes this time. Ximena flicked her eyes to the screen then returned to her mending.

"Don't you want to watch?" Mercedes asked.

Lupe rolled her eyes. She'd have joined them for a telenovela, a Spanish-language soap opera, but not for one of the mindless game shows to which Mercedes was addicted.

* * *

On Sunday morning, Lupe woke to a sunlit room. She yawned and stretched, but did not get up, relishing the luxury of not having to go to work. Mena lay with her back to Lupe.

"Girls, you're going to be late." It was Mercedes.

Lupe lifted her head. "What time is it?"

"Almost ten," Mercedes said.

"Oh, Dios mío," Lupe said. Oh my God. She threw back the bedcovers. "I'll hurry. Wait for me," she said as she ran to the bathroom.

When she returned moments later, Mena still had not moved. "Aren't you coming with us Mena?"

"No. Go ahead."

Mercedes and Lupe didn't argue with Mena. It was pointless. For the last several weeks, Mena had refused to go to church with them.

"She's just going through a low spot," Mercedes said as she and Lupe walked the few blocks to Iglesia Santa Maria.

"I don't know. She's been acting oddly. I've never seen her like this."

"Maybe she misses home."

"I'm sure she does, but it's more than that," Lupe said.

"If you mean what happened in the desert, I know. She told me."

Lupe halted. She put her hand on Mercedes' arm and turned to face her. "She told you?"

"Yes."

"I can't believe she told you. I never thought she'd mention it to anyone else, except maybe to God. She used to pray to God, asking him to turn back the clock. She stopped asking a while ago. And now she won't even go to church."

"Maybe she needs to meet someone."

"What do you mean?" Lupe asked.

"Someone like you have, like Javier."

"He's just a friend. Nothing else. I'd like him to be more, but I don't think he feels the same way about me as I do about him."

"You just have to keep at it. Show him a little of your charm. Or charms, I should say." Mercedes winked.

"He doesn't seem to respond to that or to anything else."

"You don't think he's...?" Mercedes said, pausing to let Lupe fill in the blank.

"Oh my God, no. Well, I don't have any proof. He kept his distance from everyone else in the desert. Never said much. But, no, I don't think that's his problem." The women walked a few steps further in silence. "Anyway, a boyfriend won't solve Ximena's problem," Lupe said, picking up the conversation after giving the topic more thought. "She's just having a hard time forgetting what happened."

"I still say, a boyfriend could fix everything."

"I don't think so."

"Even your father tried to tell her to settle—"

"My father? How do you know my father?" Lupe asked.

"He was here last week. I thought you knew."

"I had no idea. She told me she never wanted to see or speak to him again."

"Last week, when I came back from the mall, Mena was in the courtyard talking with a man I didn't know. They were arguing more than talking. I only caught the gist of what they were saying. Something about him mending his ways, finding God. When she saw me, she stopped talking and introduced me. But that was it because he left without another word."

"I can't believe it, Papa, here," Lupe said.

* * *

After services, instead of staying behind with Mercedes to chat with friends from the Latino community, Lupe rushed home. She took the stairs two by two and threw the door open.

"Mena?" she called. "Mena? Where are you?"

There was no answer. Lupe checked the bathroom and even Mercedes' room. Her sister was not in the apartment. Lupe stood beside Ximena's cot, her foot tapping the ground, her thoughts racing.

She took a deep breath and crossed the room to the small trunk Mena had bought for a chest of drawers. It was wrong to do what she was doing. She'd resent her sister doing the same, but she needed to find out what was wrong with Mena, what had changed her. Lupe lifted the lid. Inside were Mena's spare pair of sneakers and two stacks of neatly folded garments, her olive sweater, and a few sweatshirts in one pile and several tee-shirts on top of a couple of pairs of jeans in the other.

Beneath the jeans, an edge of black fabric caught Lupe's eye. She pushed aside the jeans and removed the black item she'd never seen Mena wear. The piece of fabric had an odd shape, a tube. Lupe ran her arm through it, slipped it off, then pulled the tube over her head. The knit fabric settled around her neck in folds. It appeared to be some sort of scarf. Using the mirror in the bathroom, Lupe looked at her reflection. She turned sideways and then back to the center. She reached behind her head and pulled the back edge of the scarf up and over her ponytail. The scarf fit snug around her head, allowing nothing but the oval of her face to show. Lupe took one glance at her reflection and tore the headscarf from her head.

She sat on her cot, faced the door, and waited for her sister to return.

38. CYRIL

At work, Cy had set two alarms for six o'clock, one on his phone and the other on his PC. He couldn't miss both of them, he thought. And, if he stopped at six, he'd have time to wrap up and still beat Yasmeen to the apartment.

Today, for once, his plan worked. He was home by seven. As soon as he heard keys jingle in the hallway, he ran to the door.

"Well, this is a surprise," Yasmeen said.

Cy pulled Yasmeen to him, gave her a hug, then kissed her on the lips. "I wanted to prove to you I do try to be here when I can," he said, holding the embrace.

"You don't have to prove anything to me."

"I know, but theoretically I'm the one with the nine-to-five desk job. Right?"

"Right. So, can I come in or are we going to stand here in the hall all night?"

"Sorry. Come on in. I missed you."

"And I missed you."

"Had dinner?"

"Nope. You?"

"Nope. I was waiting for you. Thought you might want baba ghanouj and taboule."

Yasmeen looked at Cy sideways. "That's a joke, right? You hate Mediterranean."

"Mediterranean food, maybe, but not everything Mediterranean," Cy said and winked.

Yasmeen had told Cy a few details of her past and how she'd come to the FBI. He'd learned the Fakhoury's had sent their daughter to London at an early age to live with an aunt, ostensibly for her education. Later, long after her parents' deaths, victims of the Israeli bombing of Lebanon during the July War in 2006, she realized the move had been for her safety as well. She didn't blame the Israelis or the Lebanese, or later the Iraqis, or Iranians, or Syrians, none of them and all of them. But she was determined to do something meaningful with her life, something to help stop the fighting and senseless killing. She graduated at the top of her class from a London university with a degree in political science and fluency in four languages and several Arabic dialects. Figuring she could do more good at the United Nations than with any of the other job offers she received, she moved to New York. Two weeks later, the FBI had made overtures.

"Okay, how about Chinese?" Yasmeen asked.

"Chinese it is."

"It's a safe ethnic," Yasmeen said. "Everyone loves Chinese food, no?"

Cy didn't, but if Yasmeen wanted Chinese, that was fine with him; at least he was spared a Mediterranean dinner.

Later, as Cy poured the last dregs from a pot of tea into Yasmeen's cup he said, "I worry about you."

"You do not," she said, nudging his arm playfully.

"I do," he said.

"You get so lost in your work, I bet you don't even eat when I'm gone, much less think of me," she said.

"I did miss a few dinners this week, but I made up for it tonight. And I never stop thinking about you. You're the one out there in the field. I'm just surrounded by big black boxes with yellow and green lights. The only danger I'm in is if one of them topples over on me."

"It's all training, Cy. If you've trained well and you know your role, it's nothing. Or, if not nothing, at least I'm comfortable with what I'm doing. And I believe in it and I believe it's providing a level of intelligence we wouldn't have otherwise. Here's what I can tell you. What would you guess is the fastest growing segment of the population adopting Islam?"

"Hispanics. Hispanic women to be exact," Cy said.

"What? Tell me that was more than a lucky guess."

"Actually, it's a small part of the work I'm doing. I'm tracking the assimilation patterns of legal and illegal immigrants."

"I guess we have more in common at work than I thought."

"Yeah, I guess so. Still, I don't get the attraction for Hispanic women, even if I see the statistics. It seems such an improbable choice."

"I haven't studied the numbers, but I've seen the faces," Yasmeen said. "And I've listened to the stories of the lives they're fleeing. I can absolutely understand the attraction, on the surface. There was a woman a while ago, devout, wearing a cross. She'd been abused. And she found herself far from home with no one to turn to, no one to understand how she feels. She's been visiting the mosque for weeks now. It's so predictable. We, that is, they offer such a sympathetic and respectful line, playing to just the right feelings. Sometimes I want to tell her 'run for your life,' or 'go home.' But of course I can't."

"And just how assimilated do they become?" Cy asked.

"What do you mean?"

"I mean," Cy said, "are the religious leaders content with having people convert, expanding their congregation, so to speak, or do they go further? Do they ever try to radicalize them?"

"Well, I'd say the overwhelming majority are happy to have people join the faith. I hope so, anyway. But some like Masjid Al-Raman want more. That's why I'm there."

The waitress brought the receipt and obligatory fortune cookies. Yasmeen cracked hers open. "The one you love is closer than you think," she read aloud.

"Let's go home," Cy said.

"What? So early on a Friday?" Yasmeen asked, smiling. "What's on your mind?"

"You'll have to wait and see," Cy said. As they rose to leave, he tossed his crumpled fortune to the table. It read, "You are on the right track."

39. JAVIER

"THREE BEEF TACOS," JAVIER SAID, PLACING HIS ORDER WITH THE Hispanic clerk, cook, janitor, and as far as he knew the owner of the taco stand near his house. When the order was ready, he grabbed the paper sack and left to find a sunny spot sheltered from the wind. Besides, he'd eaten before at one of the indoor tables and found them sticky with residue from untold numbers of meals. He was surprised he'd not become ill, but the stand was the nearest thing available and the food was cheap. Javier had eaten worse.

He squatted on an abandoned folding chair propped against the side of the building. After downing the three greasy tacos, he tilted his head back and closed his eyes.

"Hello?" It was a woman's voice. "Disculpe." Excuse me.

Javier bolted upright, nearly toppling his chair. In front of him stood Ximena, an inquisitive expression on her face. Her hand was still on his shoulder. Javier guessed he'd fallen asleep and that she'd jostled him to wake him. He cocked his head to one side and glanced toward the corner of the building, expecting Lupe to appear any minute.

"Lupe's not here," Ximena said, "if that's who you're looking for. It's just me."

Javier rose from his chair and offered it to Ximena.

"Thank you," she said, "but could we go sit there?" She pointed to a bench on the sidewalk in front of the restaurant.

Javier hesitated, still uncomfortable speaking with, much less being seen alone with, a woman. The bench was however more spacious and more public than the folding chairs stacked beside the taco stand. Javier followed Ximena to the bench and took a seat as close to the opposite end as he could. He kept his eyes straight ahead on the street.

Ximena sat in silence for so long Javier wondered if she would ever speak. He shot a glance in her direction. Her eyes were downcast, her hands in her lap. He noticed her thick dark hair, radiant like Lupe's, even when tied behind her head was barely visible under a cap. He saw, too, her arms were covered.

"I wanted to...to thank you. And to apologize," she said.

"You—"

"No, let me say this, please." Ximena looked up and then down again. "I spoke ill of you to Lupe. Warned her against you." Ximena took a deep breath. "Even after what you did for me."

"The man was a defiler."

"But, if you had not stopped him, he would have continued. He might have hurt Lupe and someone else, too. And for that I thank you."

Javier said nothing. He didn't need or want Ximena's thanks. He had done what he had done, killed Octavio because he had defiled a woman. Besides, Octavio would have killed Javier if Javier had not acted swiftly. Anyone would have done the same.

"And I have more reasons to thank you."

Javier eyed Ximena again. This time she looked back for a long moment before dropping her eyes to her lap.

"For taking me to the...the mosque and for introducing me to Yasmeen and the others. They are all very kind and understanding. I thought it would be only foreigners, but there were other women, Latinas like me. They told me their stories of their old lives and their new way of thinking and living. It's a way my church could never have shown them or me." Ximena paused. "Octavio." She spat the name. "My church sheltered Octavio and did nothing to help me live with what he did. My church allowed my father to worship one day and betray my mother the next." After another period of silence, she said, "I met a man, too. An imam."

"Ata Nahidian?"

"No. I met him, too, but this one never told me his name. He was kind and understanding, and more. I can't put it into words, it's just the way he is. His voice is odd, sometimes rough but then suddenly soft like his manner. When he speaks, he speaks to me as if I were the only person in the world, the only person that matters. He asked me to come back, and I did. Several times. I no longer go to my old church. And I have taken up the hijab."

Startled, Javier whipped his head toward Ximena. Her hair tucked under the cap, though it wasn't a hijab, leant her an air of modesty. The cap and the long sleeves made sense now.

"Not everywhere," Ximena continued. "Not yet. Yasmeen gave me one. I wear it when I go to the mosque, but not at work or at home, not yet. Not where everyone would see and ask questions."

"Lupe?" Javier asked.

"She knows. She found my scarf. She screamed and cried and asked me many questions. I tried to explain to her, but I couldn't make her understand. I tried to get her to come with me to the mosque and to meet the imam. Even once. But she refused. She says bad people go there and everything they have told me is a lie. Please understand, she says this only because of what others say." Ximena drew in a long breath before continuing. "Knowing how fond she is of you, I told her it was you who introduced me."

Javier sucked in air.

"I thought it would help her understand," Ximena continued. "But I don't know if it will or not. Anyway, that's what I came to say."

Without another word, Ximena rose and left Javier alone on the bench with his fears. Ximena had told Lupe about him. Next, Lupe would tell Mercedes, if she didn't know already. And then, who would Mercedes tell? He wondered how long it would be before word would reach Qasim and if Qasim, disappointed in Javier, would abandon him, and even if there were a man named Qasim.

40. JAVIER

FOR THE NEXT SEVERAL DAYS, JAVIER STAYED HOME, SPENDING THE hours inside in an endless cycle of prayer, exercise, meditation, and sleep. In the minutes before each of the five prescribed times for performing salaat, his daily prayers, Javier sat with his eyes closed, imagining he was at home and could hear the imam's voice broadcast over the village, calling him to prayer. At the designated time, he recited his prayers aloud but in a hushed voice, a mix of reverence and caution.

When he had to leave the house, he avoided any of the places he might see Lupe. He laundered his clothes in a different laundry, bought food and supplies from a different grocery store, ate meals at a different sandwich shop. He avoided both the Islamic Center and the mosque, figuring Ata Nahidian would call soon, anyway.

The one exception he made was to visit the mall, adhering to Ata's instructions. But he went during the day when Lupe and the others would be at work.

By now, he could follow the route from his house to the mall even if he were blind. He knew the exact number of minutes needed to go from his house to the south exit of Riverside Centre by bus or on foot. He could stand at the entrance and visualize each of the stores on his left and the food stands on his right, the carousel on the far side against the wall of floor-to-ceiling windows.

Whatever he did, his cell phone was with him. He kept the phone charged to one hundred percent and checked and re-checked to see it was not set to silence. Every so often, he pushed the "talk" button to ensure there was a connection, sighing in relief each time he heard a tone.

Soon, though, Javier's patience wore thin and his doubts grew. Several scenarios played in his head. Qasim had abandoned the plan, whatever the plan was, and Ata had neglected to tell Javier. Qasim had lost his trust in Javier and Ata had found someone to take his place. Even that Qasim or Ata had met with harm.

Doubt gave way to frustration and frustration to anger. On one particularly black day, Javier, his eyes aching from staring at the silent and motionless cell phone, flung the phone at the wall. It was a bad shot, and the phone fell short, landing on the carpet and coming to a rest in the corner. Javier left the phone where it fell.

In disgust, he set out for the mall, but not to his mark, the one labeled with a red triangle on Ata Nahidian's map. Today he would go to the other man's mark, the one labeled with a green triangle.

The north exit sat between the east and central sections of the mall, a hundred yards to the east of the south exit, and ringed with restaurants. Like the south exit, the north was a major ingress and egress point. It, too, faced one of the main thoroughfares from which cars entered and exited the property.

He spent two hours at the north exit, gazing at the merchandise in store windows, walking back and forth, and making a circuit of the cluster of restaurants. At one restaurant, he pretended to read the menu posted at the entrance, though he didn't understand many of the words or care what they meant. But the din of conversation, laughter, and the clatter of plates inside the restaurant made it impossible for him to concentrate.

He started to walk away, when a voice behind him asked, "May I help you?"

Javier turned to the voice. A young man about Javier's age, with hair the color of sand faced him. In the crook of his arm, he held a leather folder. The young man's eyes took in everything about Javier in one long look from head to toe, his rumpled sweatshirt, stained jeans, and worn sandals. The man's eyes said Javier was not welcome.

Javier pivoted and walked away. As he did, the door behind the young man swung open, flooding the area with the sound of laughter and music and the aroma of braised beef, garlic, and pepper. He glanced back over his shoulder. The waiter smiled and nodded as he greeted a group of well-dressed women toting shopping bags.

If this were a side street or alley and the waiter had given Javier the same glance he had earlier, Javier would have slit the man's throat and tossed him to the ground. Javier seethed and his anger clouded his head. He'd nearly forgotten why he'd come to the mall when he spotted his target. It was almost too easy, Javier thought, if you knew what to look for, the profile, the mannerisms, the pattern of behavior. The man Javier spotted was a young man of indefinite origin. He was well dressed, by Javier's standards, pressed pants and a shirt of western design, cuffs and a collar, buttons up the front. On the floor beside the bench where he sat was a tall white shopping bag.

Javier strode past the man and stopped at a directory with an illuminated map of the mall. He feigned interest in the map as if he were looking for a particular store. His eyes searched the long list of stores and every so often flicked back to the man on the bench.

Javier left the map and started a slow circuit of the nearby restaurants and stores while keeping the man in his sight. In front of a shoe store, Javier paused before the display of gleaming, finely-tooled, leather shoes and delicate slippers. He passed a jewelry store, the windows filled with suede-covered stands on which rings, bracelets, necklaces, and watches sparkled. Javier had never dreamed of being so close to such riches. He leaned forward to get a better look and the tip of his nose bumped the glass. Startled, he reeled back, looked left and right, and then, with the edge of his sleeve, he wiped the smudge from the glass.

When Javier checked again, the bench was empty. His heart skipped a beat. He crossed to the directory and pretended to search for something while he waited. In a few minutes, the man returned. This time he wore a hat and jacket and carried a black and gold shopping bag. He chose a different bench, one opposite from where he had been earlier.

Javier took a seat beside the man, but at a comfortable distance. The man glanced up and then away.

"Peace be with you," Javier said, in English.

The young man spun toward Javier, his eyes wide, his mouth parted as if he were about to speak but did not know what to say. He inhaled sharply then spoke in Arabic saying, "It is forbidden to meet." He reached for the black and gold shopping bag, fumbling with the loop with a claw-like hand, a hand with two fingers missing. He bolted out the exit, never looking back, never breaking his stride.

41. JAVIER

SEVERAL BLOCKS FROM RIVERSIDE, JAVIER WAS STILL REELING from the encounter with the man with the shopping bag. He was not looking where he was going and his head was spinning. What had he accomplished by finding his counterpart, he asked himself. If anything, he'd caused himself more trouble. Ata Nahidian would be furious.

As Javier stepped from the curb to cross the street, a horn blared and continued sounding long after it had passed. He shook his head and retook the curb. His heart was pounding. Javier steadied himself as he waited for the light, resting one hand on the pedestrian crosswalk marker. With the other hand, he wiped his forehead.

"Javier," the sound of his name found its way to him. It came from his left. He turned. It was Lupe.

"Oh my God, Javier," she said. "You were almost killed."

Javier had called enough attention to himself. And now, here Lupe was with her raised girlish voice and sensuous figure. A handful of pedestrians turned to stare, though she seemed not to notice.

"I yelled your name just as you stepped into the street. That car was inches from hitting you." Lupe leaned forward and put her arms around him. He stiffened. "For a moment, I was so scared," she said, continuing, oblivious to his discomfort.

Javier removed Lupe's arms from around his shoulder and

stepped back. "I'm fine. I have to go." When the light turned, he crossed the street and walked away as quickly as he could. He did not look back and prayed she had not followed. But from behind him, he heard her ask, "Where are you going?" She sprinted forward and tried to catch up to him.

"I have to go," he said over his shoulder.

"Where? To your mosque?" she asked.

Javier stopped and spun around, nearly colliding with Lupe. His gaff at the north entrance to Riverside had clouded his thinking. He'd forgotten Ximena had told Lupe of his mosque and of him being a Muslim.

"Yes, I know you're not Hispanic. We suspected that all along. The first day we met, Ximena and I knew you were different."

Javier looked over Lupe's shoulder. The other pedestrians had gone ahead. There was no one to overhear them. "It doesn't matter who I am or what I am."

"Why are you here? Why did you pretend to be Latino? Why did you come here with us from Mexico?"

"I'm here like you, to find a new life," he said.

"What kind of life? And what have you done to Ximena?"

"I don't know what you're talking about."

"She's changed. She's abandoned our church, our God, everything. All she talks about are her brothers and sisters. I tell her I am her sister. Me. Lupe. Her only sister. But she won't listen. And she talks about a man she calls 'imam.' It's as if she's fallen under a spell. Or a curse."

"Is she afraid?" Javier asked.

"Afraid? No. She says she's at peace."

"Then she's found what she was looking for. Praise be to God. Perhaps you should—"

"Oh no. I don't want anything to do with your religion. I've heard what your church does."

"You know nothing about us," Javier said. He looked skyward and shook his head. "I don't know why I'm even standing here talking to you. I have to go."

"Go then. Go to wherever you think you'll find your new life. But leave my sister alone. Leave me alone."

Javier walked away. Behind him, Lupe sobbed, whether for her sister, herself, or for him, he didn't know. He'd made a mess of things, a mess of everything. He'd called attention to himself. He'd allowed Lupe and Ximena and probably by now others to know he was not who he said he was. And he'd doubted those responsible for him. The doubt had caused him to take matters into his own hands, disobeying Ata Nahidian's orders to stay home and wait to be called. Worst of all, he'd made contact and jeopardized another brother.

Javier needed to see Ata Nahidian and tell him what had happened before someone else did.

* * *

This time, when Javier arrived at Masjid Al-Rahman he didn't knock. He tried the door handle. It gave, and he entered, startling four women in traditional black dress. Javier averted his eyes. He sat and removed his sandals.

"Brother Javier," a woman whispered. His head jerked up and around. "It is you, my brother." A woman approached, her hijab hiding all but the edge of the birthmark on her forehead.

"Ximena?" Javier asked.

She smiled. "Yes. It's me, Ximena. But not for long. I've asked Sister Yasmeen, here...," she paused, reached behind her, and pulled another woman forward. "I've asked her to help me choose a new name. Sister Yasmeen, this is the one I spoke to you about. This is—" She halted in mid-sentence, perhaps realizing for the first time "Javier" was not his real name.

This is the one I spoke to you about. Ximena's words echoed in Javier's head. His heart pounded. As he suspected, Ximena had not stopped spreading information about him.

Sister Yasmeen stood beside Ximena, her eyes lowered.

"Peace be with you," he said, swallowing hard.

"And unto you," Yasmeen said, raising her eyes. "My new sister is grateful for what you've done for her, both here and before."

Javier looked the woman full in the face. She did not look away and instead studied his face as if she were memorizing each feature's detail.

The door opened behind him and a handful of worshippers entered and, after stowing their shoes, passed into the prayer room. The sound of men greeting each other, pats on the backs, muffled greetings, and quiet conversations drifted to where he stood in the alcove.

"I must go," Javier said.

During the prayers, Javier's thoughts tormented him. He fought back, concentrating on each word of the Quran, enunciating each syllable, and glaring at the back of the person kneeling in front of him. Javier squeezed his eyes shut, but to no avail; he couldn't ignore the faces parading across the backs of his eyelids: Ximena, Lupe, Mercedes, his counterpart with the shopping bag.

Javier's eyes opened as if on a spring. He brought his hands to his head, palms turned skyward and, defying protocol, he turned his head to scan the rows of supplicants. He squinted at profiles and the backs of heads, hands, and feet, but did not find the man from the north exit among them. But as he leaned forward, ready to press his forehead to the floor, he found someone else. A man at the end of the first row cleared his throat.

Qasim Bousaid.

Javier listened intently, isolating the man's voice as they recited the next verse. Though Javier had only heard Qasim speak a few words, and those had been over a cell phone, he recognized the tone of voice. As the prayer continued, he detected the effort it took the man to speak. His words sounded as if they'd been forced around a stone in his throat. It was Qasim. It had to be him.

Just before Javier pressed his forehead to the floor the final time, though he doubted anyone else noticed, Qasim had angled his head a hair to the left toward where Javier knelt. He felt Qasim's wrath, his shoulders and back stinging as if he had been lashed. Javier kept his eyes on the spot where his forehead had touched the floor until the Maghrib prayer ended.

But he didn't flee the mosque with the group of men who left. Javier stayed behind, desperate to meet the man who had brought him to America, to explain his transgressions, and to plead his case.

Qasim had withdrawn to the back of the room where a handful of people waited in line to speak with him. One by one, they approached him, spoke for a few minutes, shook his hand and embraced him, touching shoulders. A woman was next in line. Javier listened as the man offered advice to her and to the child at her side, instructing the child how to tie her headscarf so it would not come undone. The supplicants nodded at his advice and smiled as they turned to leave. They called him "brother" but never used his name.

Qasim spoke to the last man in line and when they finished, Qasim stepped back and the man raised his hands to his shoulders, one hand a claw, missing two fingers. It was the man from the mall, the man whose mark was the green triangle, Javier's counterpart. He exited without a glance at Javier.

Everyone had gone. Javier rose and stepped forward, his hands raised, palms to the ceiling. "Brother Qasim, I ask your forgiveness. I am ready to do as you bid," Javier said.

"You have disobeyed your orders, Mohsan's orders, Ata Nahidian's orders, and my orders. Not once. Not twice. Your request is most welcome. But how do I know you can be trusted?"

"Because I swear it to you. On my life, Brother Qasim." Javier added, "By Allah." The sacred words would damn him were his promise to be a lie.

42. ALICIA

"Sure," he said as he wheeled his desk chair back and spun the seat towards her. Alicia pulled a vacant chair close and took a seat. She dropped a folder onto Carlo's desk, the word "Javier" scrawled across the cover.

"What's this?"

"My guy, the one I told you—"

"Oh no, not again. Alicia, I've told you—"

"If I remember correctly, you said, 'on my own time.'"

"I did. And," Carlo looked at the clock on the far wall, "we're still on my time, Ingram's time."

"All right. What if I come back at six?"

"Well, since you've already interrupted, go ahead, but this better be worth my while."

"Five minutes. I'll be quick." She removed a stack of photos from the folder and arranged them in a line in front of Carlo. The photos were printouts from the security cameras with the date and time stamp in the upper right hand corner. "Look at these. Can you see?"

"See what?" Carlo asked.

"He's the guy who was with our witness to the incident last month. He disappeared before we could question him, but I found the woman who he was with and her twin. The one who helped Polly. I talked to both of them."

"Did they identify him as the 'perp'?"

"Well, no."

"That's what I thought."

"They said he's not the one. And based on Polly's description, he's definitely not."

"Exactly."

"But I thought there was something more going on, so I hung around a while, and I finally met him face to face. He was wearing the jacket. The one with the stripes on the sleeve. Said he found it in the parking lot."

"And I suppose he won't talk either."

"No. He wouldn't say any more."

Carlo rocked back and forth in his chair, the springs groaning. "That's it?" he asked, the chair silent as he came forward and to a stop.

Alicia knew it would take more to impress Carlo, so she had shared only part of what she'd found. She had kept her best ammunition in reserve. "No, look at the time stamps. He comes here a lot."

"Yeah. So the guy likes to shop."

"That's just it. He doesn't shop. See? No packages. He comes in around five thirty, occasionally later, always through the south entrance. He takes a seat or stares at the directory or makes a circuit of the food court."

"Look, Alicia, I don't want to stir the pot again. We were lucky the local ambulance chasers didn't get hold of Polly's story. They'd like nothing better than to show Riverside with its 'won't happen here' attitude is not so special after all."

"I wasn't going to, I heard you, but, here's where it gets even more interesting. Something about him bothered me."

"Don't tell me."

"Wait a minute. His name is Javier, according to the woman. She says he's not Latino. But he's posing as one. And he didn't impress me as being too fond of talking to me."

"Surprise, surprise," Carlo said. "For all he knows, you're a cop, Alicia. And a dollar to a dime, he's illegal. What do you expect? You think he's going to ask you out to a movie?"

Alicia kept talking, ignoring Carlo's sarcasm and the chair's squeak, which had started up again at a more furious pace. "And then when I found him on the cameras so many times, lurking around the same place, I thought he might be stalking someone or something."

"Are you suggesting he's our parking lot guy or not?"

"No, we ruled that out. But take a look at these." Alicia picked up the folder and withdrew more photos. She lined them up below the others. "Last week, our man Javier shows up at the north exit."

"So, your man Javier grew tired of the shops on the south side."

"He hangs around and approaches a guy. Middle Eastern looking to me, though the camera's a bit fuzzy."

"And now, I suppose you're an expert in ethnic identities?"

Alicia ignored Carlo and continued, "Then, see here, the second guy gets up and leaves. Thirty seconds later."

"Looks like a better class of guy from the way he's dressed. Maybe he didn't want to sit next to a guy in jeans and a hoodie."

"Maybe, but guess what?"

"I have the distinct impression you're about to tell me anyway, so go ahead."

"I checked. The new guy has been hanging around, too. He's

been frequenting the north exit for a week, at least that's as far back as I've gone on the cameras. For now."

"So, you want me to call in the cops and say we have visitors to the mall who like to sit and enjoy their afternoon or evening in our atrium. What? And we don't like the way they look or dress or comb their hair?"

Alicia sighed. On more than one occasion, Carlo had let her know what he thought of feminine intuition. "That and a dollar won't get you half a cup of one of your coffees, much less solve a crime," he'd said.

She hadn't convinced him this time either. She'd have to wait until she had more to show or else find a way around her boss. Carlo ended the conversation by saying if she wanted to spend her evenings looking at security cameras instead of going home to her son that was her business, but her duty time was Ingram's. Still, Alicia thought, this was more than feminine intuition, this was just plain odd. And "odd" was one of the key behaviors she'd been advised to notice in working security, even mall security.

Seth had discussed odd behaviors in his line of duty. She remembered a conversation they'd had before he'd left on his second deployment. He'd lost friends, brothers really, people he looked out for and people who looked out for him. Seth said more than one of his friends' deaths could have been avoided had they not made stupid mistakes, overlooked something.

"And how can you be sure it won't be you this time?" she'd asked. Alicia's stomach knotted at the recollection.

"Because I'm careful," he'd said.

"Careful is not enough. You always said Don was careful; 'meticulous' was the word you used if I'm not mistaken." Don had been Seth's best friend, enlisting at the same time, going through basic training with Seth, and later deploying to the Middle East with him.

"He was, but he was also trusting. And he lacked situational awareness."

"And you don't?" Alicia had asked.

"I don't. My antennae are up twenty-four seven. I notice when a branch cracks, a stone rolls, or a note rings one decibel higher or lower than the background. When a light flashes. Or there's a whiff of perfume where there should be nothing—"

"I get it," she'd said.

"—A head turns, or a hand waves. Anomalies. Odd behaviors."

"I get it."

"Yours are up, too. Even if you don't know it."

"What do you mean?"

"Like when you watch over Kyle. You're always worrying when he's a degree warmer or colder than he should be. Or when he sleeps when he should be awake or he's awake when he should be asleep. Situational awareness. Odd behaviors."

"My instincts aren't a matter of life and death, though."

"Oh, but they are."

43. ALICIA

ALICIA GRABBED THE THREE RING BINDER HOLDING INGRAM SECU-rity employee policies and tore the cover off, replacing it with one she had created. On the new cover the words "Investigation Unit" sat in a prominent position, middle of the page, eighteen-point, Times Roman in bold letters under the Ingram Security logo.

Inside the binder, the logo and the words "Investigation Unit" appeared again and below them Case Number 4.62.9 and yesterday's date. She hoped no one would ask what Ingram's case numbering logic was or what the decimals signified, but she liked the air of precision they implied. The rest of the binder contained sets of photos encased in plastic covers, time stamped, three-hole-punched and organized by date, earliest to latest, followed by a synopsis of her observations.

The binder lay beside Alicia's briefcase on the front seat of her car as she entered the government building complex. She wanted to come across as a professional who'd done her homework. The last thing she wanted the FBI to think was Alicia Blake was a two-bit, mall cop out to prove she was every bit as good as a full-fledged member of law enforcement.

She'd told Carlo she had to take the morning off for a meeting and let him fill in the blank. He'd presume she was meeting with Kyle's teacher. She could not have told him her actual destination. He would never have condoned her jumping over several rungs of authority and taking her suspicions and feminine intuition straight to the FBI. He might have even fired her on the spot.

The complex was not at all what she had imagined. Each of the half-dozen red brick buildings looked like all the others. She had expected a more imposing building, marble maybe, stone at least. She was thankful she'd called ahead and asked for specific directions, as she might have missed the building altogether. There wasn't a sign on the map at the entrance to the complex, on the street, or on the building. You had to know where the FBI's offices were, or you had to ask. Alicia cringed at the thought of asking directions to the FBI, imagining the look in someone's eyes. They'd wonder which side of the law she was on, and that might have deterred her.

She entered the visitor's parking lot, which for security reasons was a good distance from the Bureau's Atlanta Field Office. And, though no armed guard with a bomb sniffing canine had checked her Chevrolet's chassis for explosives, once she entered the building, she faced several security check points.

The first was a gate similar to those she'd seen at airports. Alicia followed the familiar routine, handing her briefcase and binder to a guard who dropped both on the conveyer belt before ushering her through. Next, a receptionist checked Alicia's driver's license photo and name against the day's list of expected visitors. Thankfully, Alicia had made an appointment for ten o'clock with one of the agents, an agent named Cyril Westfall.

After having her photograph taken, her palm scanned, and being issued a temporary badge and the instructions to "wear this at all times," Alicia entered the elevator bank. It was five minutes to the top of the hour. On the fourth floor, the receptionist who fumbled with an intercom system on her desk said, "Mr. Westfall, there's a Mrs. Blake here to see you."

In a minute, a man who looked to be ten years her junior sauntered into the waiting room. He had a slight cowlick at his forehead, one that reminded Alicia of Kyle.

"Ms. Blake? Would you follow me?"

Mr. Westfall's assistant, Alicia thought. Halfway down the hall, he turned at an open door and stood aside for Alicia to enter. "Please have a seat," he said without specifying which of the dozen standard-issue, mesh chairs she should take. She lowered herself into one near the head of the table. "Oh, and here, let me give you my card." An FBI insignia in the top right corner and the name Cyril Westfall and a phone number centered on the front were the only two pieces of information on the card.

Alicia glanced at the card and back at the young man, his clean-shaven face, too clean, as if he might not need to shave. "You're Mr. Westfall?"

"I am," he said with his left eyebrow raised.

"Thank you for seeing me," she said, recovering quickly and hoping he hadn't realized her surprise.

"Not at all. Now, first, refresh my memory. Ingram Security sent you here for..." he said, leaving the end of the sentence open.

Alicia spoke for fifteen minutes without pausing except to direct Cy's attention to a few of the photographs in the binder. She covered every point of the outline she'd memorized and practiced twice last night after Kyle had gone to bed and again this morning after breakfast. On finishing, she sat back in her chair and congratulated herself for not cracking a smile. Midway through her remarks, she remembered Kyle with eyes half open coming into her bedroom last night, scanning the room for the person his mother had been lecturing. She'd laughed, mumbled a few words about practicing a speech, and put him back to bed.

Mr. Westfall was attentive, keeping eye contact except for the few times he jotted notes on a pad. It was an encouraging sign, Alicia thought, despite his not interrupting to ask a single question and his leg bouncing up and down the entire time. Whether excitement or boredom had brought on the tic, she didn't know. When she finished, Cyril Westfall leaned forward and flipped through the binder from front to back. Still, he gave no outward sign of interest or disinterest, no indication of whether, like Carlo, he thought she ought to focus her efforts on shoplifters and lost children.

"The one clue to the suspect's identity is a first name, Javier. Is that right?" he asked as he closed the binder.

"Yes, though, as I said, I suspect his first name isn't actually Javier. If you think it's worth pursuing, I could dig a little deeper."

"No. At this juncture, I'd suggest not putting any more of a spotlight on him," Cy said. "You could continue to have him observed, but beyond that, I'd ask you to sit tight and let me look into this. I'll get back to you as soon as I can."

Continue to have him observed. Alicia wanted to laugh. As if she had a staff to do observation. "Well, Mr. Westfall—"

"Cy. Please you can call me Cy."

"Cy. Thank you for your time."

"No, thank you."

Alicia bent to retrieve the folder. She was convinced Cy was polite enough to indulge her for a half-hour appointment, but was unlikely to spend time on her petty observations with what she imagined he had already on his plate. Cy reached for the binder. "Please. If you don't mind, or, rather if Ingram Security won't mind, could you let me borrow this? I may want to have another look."

44. CYRIL

AFTER ESCORTING THE INGRAM SECURITY REPRESENTATIVE BACK
to the reception area, Cy returned to his cubicle to check his
calendar. The rest of his day was booked. He had a weekly team
meeting at eleven and at one o'clock a mandatory Human Resources meeting on diversity training. Thankfully, that meeting
would last no longer than required for the Field Office's manager
to check a box on a compliance form. Still, it was another distraction from what he considered "real" work, a thought Cy kept to
himself. He was learning.

To get any work at all done it would have to be after hours, as
usual. The only time he could work on Cycle was lunch, meaning
he'd be eating junk food at his desk, again. There'd be no time to
think of looking at the Ingram woman's binder. The best he could
do, he thought, was take it home with him.

Yasmeen was in the shower when Cy arrived home. He had
half an inclination to jump in the shower with her. Instead, he
started a pot of coffee and collapsed on the sofa, propping his feet
on the cart he'd salvaged from a junk dealer, the cart doing double
duty as ottoman and coffee table. From the kitchen, white noise,
a hiss and then the gurgle of water dripping into the carafe. Cy
fell asleep.

When he opened his eyes, it was dark. He jolted upright,
blinked a few times, and shook his head. He never napped, hat-

ing the hangover a nap left him with, the slight disorientation and dizziness when he stood, and the taste of interrupted sleep in his mouth.

"Sleeping beauty awakes," Yasmeen said, handing him a cup of steaming coffee.

"What time is it?"

"Seven-thirty. Hungry?"

Cy sipped his coffee, the warm liquid soothing the momentary imbalance, the caffeine flooding his system. "I think so. Want to go out?"

"No. I made a salad. There's not much else here."

"Sorry. My plan was to stop on the way home, but..."

"I know. You got sidetracked. Busy day?"

"Boring day. Meeting after meeting. The usual. No time to get to anything I needed to do."

"I'm distracting you. If I weren't here, you'd have stayed late. Right?"

"Forget it. You're the best distraction there is." Cy set his cup on the cart and pulled Yasmeen to the sofa next to him. She placed her arms around his neck, crossed her legs over his and rested her head on his shoulder. He took a deep breath, drawing in the hibiscus and coconut scent in her hair. "You smell wonderful," he said as he pushed her back onto the sofa and kissed her.

"And you smell like a musty old office."

"I can shower."

"No, don't go anywhere," she said as she unbuttoned his shirt.

Cy pulled his arms from his sleeves and flung the shirt aside. The shirt landed on the arm of the chair beside the sofa and slid to the floor where it mounded over his briefcase and the work he had brought home. Later, he thought.

But after they had made love and taken a quick shower, this time together, there was a glass of wine, and dinner, and idle conversation while Cy watched Yasmeen pack. She had to go to D.C. in the morning for a staff meeting.

"What do you tell your Muslim friends?" Cy asked.

Yasmeen glanced up at Cy then back at her roll-aboard suitcase, open on the bed where he lounged with his second or third glass of wine.

"They're not my friends," she said as she tucked a garment inside the bag.

"I know. I know. I just wondered how you explain your absences to them."

"I tell them I'm kept prisoner by a very nosy boyfriend who lets me out once a week."

"Seriously," Cy said.

"Seriously. I say I married an infidel who would kill me if he found out I had never abandoned my religion. That I practice in private. That I come to the mosque only when he is out of town."

"And they buy your story?"

"Of course," she paused. "Really, Cy, I don't discuss it. The less said the better."

Yasmeen finished packing and set her suitcase beside the door. She'd be leaving early to make her flight.

Cy woke and glanced at the red numerals his projection clock displayed on the ceiling. It was two in the morning. He liked to know what time it was when he woke in the middle of the night and hated fumbling for the clock. It was much easier to peel open one eye, glance at the ceiling then go back to sleep. Or, lie there awake, as he did now.

Was it the third glass of wine? Or the thought he'd not set the alarm for Yasmeen, though he'd made a double and triple check, as usual. Was it Cycle and the variables he had wrestled with at work? Or the recordings he'd failed to complete?

Cy turned over in bed and tried once more to sleep. In minutes, his eyes went to the ceiling, checking the time again. It was no use. He eased himself from bed and padded barefoot to the living room. There, he turned on the light over the breakfast counter and perched on one of the bar stools. He rubbed his head back and forth a few times, wanting a cup of coffee but not badly enough to create a racket and wake Yasmeen. He'd try to work without one.

An idea had crept into his head while he slept. Strangely, those ideas had a habit of being some of his best work. He'd wondered if by adding a proximity parameter to Cycle whether he might see a closer correlation between the inputs and outputs. He needed to jot down the idea before it vanished. It took Cy a moment to locate his briefcase, hidden beneath his wrinkled dress shirt. He groaned, the shirt would need a good pressing before he could wear it again.

Cy reached inside his briefcase, but instead of his laptop, his fingers found the notebook he'd borrowed from the Ingram Security investigator. He sighed. He'd let one more thing interrupt his work on Cycle. He should have referred Alicia Blake to the local police and let them decide whether the circumstances merited bringing in the FBI. But the woman's passion and sincerity and the thoroughness with which she'd compiled her information had piqued his interest. There was a close enough parallel to what he was doing and enough data in her report to try running it through Cycle.

"What's that?" Yasmeen asked.

Cy jumped, startled by Yasmeen. "Good God. I thought you were asleep." Cy glanced at the clock on the stove.

"Well, it's time to get up, anyway."

"At four in the morning?"

"So, what have you been working on all night?" Yasmeen asked, ignoring Cy's comment.

"Oh. This? It's information a local security firm investigator came in with yesterday. She thought there was something odd going on here and I told her I'd take a look."

Yasmeen stepped behind Cy and looked over his shoulder as he thumbed through the pages. Strands of her dark hair fell across his arm. She brushed them out of the way, combing through her hair with her open fingers. "May I?"

"Sure."

Yasmeen flipped back one page. "Wow."

"What?"

"I can't believe it." She slid the notebook to the side and took a seat on the empty stool.

"What?"

"Wait a minute. Let me be sure." Yasmeen thumbed through a few more pages. She stopped on a full page photo and stabbed it with her forefinger. "It's him. Or, well, it might be him."

"Him who?"

"The guy who came to the mosque the other day. The Hispanic guy. Remember, the one I was telling you about?"

"No way."

"Way."

"Are you sure?"

"Well, my new best friend, the Hispanic woman. Remember?" Yasmeen had crooked the first two fingers of both hands in the air, signaling quote marks for the phrase, best friend. "She and I were discussing how happy she was and how she might help her sister. Anyway, we're deep in conversation when in walks this guy. This guy." Yasmeen tapped the photo. "She recognizes him and drags me over to introduce me. I'd swear it's the same person. Supposedly Hispanic, but I doubt it."

"Did she say who he was or anything about him?"

"His name. Let me see...Jose, Juan...no, Javier. That was it, Javier."

"And the guy in this other picture?" Cy asked, flipping back to the shot of the two men sitting on a bench at the mall.

"This one's the guy who claims to be Javier. And this one, I can't see him clearly enough, just enough to tell he's Middle Eastern."

"How can you tell?"

Yasmeen looked at Cy. "Really?"

45. JAVIER

QASIM BOUSAID HAD INSTRUCTED JAVIER TO WAIT AT HOME. HE'D told him twice not to go anywhere. He hadn't needed to though. Since meeting him face to face and receiving his reassurances, Javier had put his worries aside. He bought several days worth of food and went home to wait.

He gave thanks to Allah and fasted from sunrise to sundown as if it were Ramadan. After Isha'a, the last prayer of the day, he ate a few dates and settled in for the night, comforted by the knowledge his moment was approaching, the moment when he would realize his destiny and fulfill his promise to join his brother Nadheer in martyrdom. He'd told no one, not Selam, not his mother, and not his father. He hadn't wanted to put them through the anguish again. One day he had just not returned home. Still he hoped, perhaps through Qasim, news of his actions would reach his family and bring joy to them and honor to their name.

When Javier's knees grew sore from kneeling on the thin carpet, he sat, leaning his back against the wall.

Since he'd arrived in the United States, he'd made do without furniture, using the floor to pray or sleep and the wall to sit and think. He'd acquired nothing more than an extra jacket and pair of jeans, a bowl, a fork, a knife, a spoon, and a pot to cook, or rather warm his takeout meals. He'd bought the clothes for a dollar each at the Goodwill store and he'd stolen the few utensils he owned from the food court or saved them from his meals at the taquerias. Others simply tossed them in the trash with the rest of the packaging.

Javier needed nothing more. He hadn't planned to live in the house on Grant for long.

Qasim had given him hope. He'd said the word "soon" and to have "patience" and to "stay at home." Javier had assured Qasim that he had prepared well, boasting that he could walk through the mall with his eyes closed, asking Qasim to test him. But Qasim had declined and repeated his instructions. Qasim had not mentioned Javier's mistake in drawing attention to himself or his attempt to contact others. And by his silence, Javier interpreted forgiveness.

Javier stretched his legs in front of him and rubbed his hands along his thighs. The jeans were threadbare. Qasim must have realized too many more visits by Javier to Riverside looking like he did could draw unwelcome attention. Why had Qasim not asked Javier to dress like the man in pressed wool slacks and white shirt? Surely, clothes like his would have been a better choice. But, Javier reasoned, he knew only his small role. Or, he thought he did. He suspected even Ata Nahidian was privy only to parts of the plan and that Qasim Bousaid alone understood the whole, each of the parts and the whole. It was not Javier's position to question Qasim's decisions.

Javier took a drink of water from the kitchen faucet. As he cupped his hand under the faucet, he could not help but marvel at how easy it was to have a drink when he wanted one or to bathe when he wanted. Some days, when he thought of home, he wished these simple pleasures for Selam, but on others he feared she would become like Lupe and her friends, collecting trinkets, amassing clothes and perfume and jewelry, possessions they did not need. The temptations here were indeed great.

Just as Javier turned to go to the living room, something outside the window caught his eye. He stepped to the side of the window and peered out over the small expanse of thin grass, meager blades of brown now. The plot stretched uninterrupted to a fence and a stand of trees. The fence marked the edge of his landlord's property and kept people from the railroad tracks a few yards further. With the faint light from a sliver of the moon, he could see all the way to the fence.

Javier stood motionless and waited. He held his breath. Nothing in his field of vision moved, but off to the right and close by, a twig cracked. He strained to hear more. He'd seen deer foraging in the wooded area on the other side of the tracks once, but they'd never come to the house.

Another crack sounded. It was a foot fall, a single step, a human step.

Javier crept from the kitchen to his front door, keeping his head low and pausing only long enough to slip his feet into his sandals. Without making a sound, he twisted the front door handle and squeezed through, his hand easing the door into its frame behind him. Javier circled to his left, pausing at the corner of the house to check the side before he proceeded. The way was clear.

At the rear corner, he paused again, letting his ears do the work for his eyes. Footsteps ahead crunched a scatter of dry leaves on the concrete patio. Javier stooped and plucked a jagged rock from the ground. In one motion, he rose, rounded the corner, and came behind the figure in black holding a knife in his hand, drawn, ready to wield.

Javier swung the rock at the figure's head. The hood of the

man's sweatshirt blunted the blow, but the figure crumpled to the ground. The knife clattered as it hit the concrete. Javier struck again with as much force as he could.

The body lay motionless. Javier glanced at the rock in his hand. He tossed it as far as he could, letting the rock tumble into the leaves along the tree line. With his foot, he pushed the body, rolling it onto its side. The skull was crushed and blood poured from the wound, soaking the hood of the sweatshirt and trickling into the crevices of the broken concrete patio. Javier pulled back the hood and looked at the man's face.

His heart slammed in his chest.

How could this be? He shoved the body again with his foot, back toward the house, freeing the hand trapped beneath the torso. The hand was missing two fingers.

Javier retched then vomited his meager dinner over the concrete patio, the remnants of his dinner mixing with the blood. He retched again and then dared a second glance at the face of the fallen man, his counterpart. There was only one explanation. Someone had sent the man to eliminate Javier. Qasim.

Javier wiped his mouth with his sleeve and crouched beside the body. He paused while he contemplated what to do next. First, he assured himself no one had heard or seen anything. There were no lights in the windows of the other houses on Grant. There were no sounds of doors opening or closing, cars coming or going, no conversations.

Knock.

Javier flinched at the sound and wondered if it had been his imagination. A second knock followed. It wasn't his imagination. Someone was at his front door. Only one person had ever come to Javier's door before, his landlord. And his visit had been during the day. He'd said he'd come to check the furnace. And though Javier had assured the man the furnace was fine, he'd insisted on entering the house and seeing for himself. An unpleasant man, he'd sniffed at Javier and the air inside the house, Javier guessed to make certain he had not been smoking. He eyed Javier's meager possessions, the backpack against the wall, the folded extra pair of jeans and a jacket.

A third knock sounded and then a woman's voice. "Javier."

Lupe? How could she have found him? The only explanation was she'd followed him home one day after they had met at the mall. Javier wanted to know how he could have missed her, but he had no time to speculate. She called his name again, louder. He needed her to be quiet.

Javier picked up the knife and entered through the back door. As he crossed the front room to the door, he wiped his hands of nearly dried blood on the back of his pants. He held the knife behind his back and opened the door.

46. LUPE

"I HOPE YOU'RE NOT GOING TO BE MAD," LUPE SAID, NOTICING JAVI-
er's thin brows bunched and sitting as low on the bridge of his
nose as possible.

"I'm not mad," Javier said. "Give me a minute."

When Javier disappeared down the hall, Lupe took advantage
of the moment to survey his home. The living room was bare
except for a stack of clothing and his tattered backpack, the same
one he'd carried across the desert. To her left was a kitchen, little
more than a closet, and to her right the hallway where he'd gone.
She couldn't help but contrast Javier's circumstances with her
own and Ximena's. They had made a comfortable, if not pleasant,
place of the apartment where they lived. Javier might as well still
be sleeping in the desert.

In the kitchen, Lupe fumbled for the light switch, but before
she could find it, Javier had reappeared and grabbed her hand.

"Leave it alone."

"Okay," she said as she pulled two paper plates from a bag and
set them on the counter. "We can eat in the dark. I brought dinner,
so I hope you haven't eaten." Lupe avoided looking him in the face
and continued talking as if they were old friends. If she stopped,
she feared she'd lose her courage or worse, he'd ask her to leave. She
opened a drawer for cutlery. It was empty, as was a second drawer
she tried. "Just what I thought. No dishes. Men! You're all alike."

Javier said nothing, and with only a faint light coming from the window, Lupe had difficulty reading his face.

She continued, "That's okay. I brought knives and forks from the burrito place. Will you have dinner with me?"

"I'm not hungry. I ate." Javier looked behind him toward the short hallway.

Lupe gasped. "Oh, no." Her hand went to her mouth. "You have company." Heat rushed across her skin. She regretted not asking for permission before she'd barged uninvited inside the house. She turned and stared at the plates on the counter.

"No. I'm alone."

"Oh, my. Thank God. Maybe just a drink then." Lupe pulled a half empty bottle of clear liquid from the bag and held it aloft. The white letters M-O-N-T-E-Z-U-M-A on the label were legible even in the dark.

He shook his head.

Tears welled in her eyes. Mercedes had said to bring food. He was supposed to be glad to have dinner. "All men like to eat," Mercedes had said. "That was the secret to winning them over."

Still, despite Lupe's attempts to attract him with food and drink, Javier wasn't interested. Nothing was going as she had planned. Lupe figured she had one last chance before he asked her to go. She sniffled and slid the paper plates back inside the bag. She kept her face averted so he could not see her tears, or that she had no tears to show.

"Stop crying. I've eaten. But you can eat here. I'll sit with you."

"You mean that?" she asked.

"Yes."

His voice was not enthusiastic, but his face was no longer bunched, his brows no longer tense.

"You'll have to sit on the floor," he said, motioning to the carpet in the living room.

"That's okay." Lupe grabbed the paper sack and the bottle, two plastic cups inverted over its top. She squatted where Javier had pointed and sat, resting her back against the wall. He sat cross-legged across from her and watched as she ate.

"Tequila?"

Javier shook his head.

Lupe unscrewed the cap of the bottle and poured a couple of fingers into one of the cups. She drank between bites and the one sided conversation she maintained. Lupe talked of her work, the tedium, the inability to save money for the family she'd left behind in Saltillo. She talked of her father who had abandoned them, throwing Ximena and her out of the house where he lived with a woman. "I think she's American," Lupe said. "Ximena says he is going to marry her and become a United States citizen. Is that possible? He has a wife. But who will know? Who will tell?"

Javier shrugged.

"Are you sure you won't have a drink? Just a sip maybe?"

Again, Javier shook his head.

"Well, I can't let it go to waste." Lupe smiled and poured another drink. She continued her earlier conversation as if she had never stopped. At first nerves had prompted the tumble of words, but now the alcohol took charge. Lupe patted the floor next to her. "Come, sit beside me. It's more comfortable here against the wall."

Javier shifted position on the carpet and sat beside her.

"Better, no?" she asked.

"Yes."

Lupe set the cup on the floor and rested her hand on Javier's. He did not pull away. She sat without saying another word, her nerves robbing her of any thoughts of language. Lupe rose onto her knees and pivoted to face Javier. Keeping her eyes locked on his and hoping he would not move or rebuff her as he had before, she leaned closer and kissed him on the lips. He winced and touched the side of his mouth with the scar.

Lupe sat back on her heels. She kissed him again, trying to avoid the scar. Then, she placed her hands on his shoulders. Javier shifted. With one hand, he found the small of her back and drew her to him.

"Ja—"

The rest of his name, the words she wanted to say, the questions she wanted to ask, were smothered by his lips, pressing on hers, not flinching this time.

When he released her, Lupe pulled at her shirt and jacket, lifting them as one over her shoulders. She flung them to the ground then reached behind to unfasten the clasp of her brassiere, letting her breasts spill free. She put one knee across Javier and straddled his legs. As she kissed him again, her breasts rubbed against his shirt. Still with her lips on his, Lupe reached for the hem of his shirt, tugging it upwards.

Javier pushed her away and onto her back. He unzipped her pants and pulled them off, tossing them to the side. Then, he stood and removed his own jeans, never taking his eyes off her.

Later, Lupe lay with her back to Javier. Though she was breathing hard, his breaths came slow and even. She pressed her fingers against her lips and throat. Both were bruised and tender. The rest of her, her breasts, hips, thighs, and parts newly discovered and wakened, were numb.

She propped herself up on one elbow and groped in the shadows for her brassiere and her shirt and jacket.

"Don't go," Javier said.

"I'm not going. Just dressing. It's cold in here."

Javier moved behind her. He wrapped his arms around her, warming her. "Better?"

"Yes."

Lupe's thoughts circled in her head, unable to find a way forward. One minute, Javier had acted as if he wanted her to leave. The next he seemed not to care whether she stayed or went. Then, he allowed her what he had first refused. He'd kissed her hard, rubbing the stubble of his beard against her cheeks and her neck, scraping them as if he were scouring clothes against a rock in the river. And finally, he had pushed her to the carpet and entered her, jabbing, shoving, pushing, nothing she would describe as "making love." Those were the words Mercedes had used. But what Lupe had experienced was very different, not at all what she had imagined or how Mercedes said it would be. Still, what did either of them know about making love?

Javier's hands traveled up and down her arms. She was warm and cold at the same time, exhausted and stunned. She was certain she should run, but terrified to move.

"I should go," Lupe said. She dressed hurriedly, gathered the plates and utensils from the floor, and headed to the kitchen looking for a trashcan. Not finding one inside, she reached for the back door.

"No. Stop!" Javier said.

"I was just going to throw these away."

"Stop."

"What's wrong with you?" she asked, stepping onto the back patio. Clumsy with the alcohol coursing through her veins, she tripped and fell across a large object on the ground. Lupe looked to see what had caused her to fall, pushing against the object as she struggled to her feet. It was a body. As she opened her mouth to scream, Javier clamped his hand across her mouth.

"Quiet," he said. "Be very quiet," he held his free hand aloft, the index finger at his lips. "Okay?"

Lupe nodded.

"Can you help me? I need to move him to the woods over there," he said, pointing to a dark stand of trees a good distance from where they stood. "Can you take the feet?"

Lupe looked again at the form on the ground. She felt sick. Her heart was thundering.

"You must be quiet. Can you be quiet?" he asked.

Lupe nodded. She could keep from screaming, but she was powerless to silence her heart.

"Take a deep breath," Javier said.

Lupe did as he asked. She took two or three even breaths and kept her eyes averted from the body on the ground. "Who is it?" Lupe asked, her voice barely audible.

"No one."

"What happened to him?"

"He is dead."

"You—"

"Quiet."

Javier had killed again. Lupe did not know who or why or how. And now, he wanted her to help him hide the body. He needed her. She stooped and picked up the man's heels. Lupe would help Javier. She would do whatever he wanted.

47. LUPE

LUPE HAD MADE THE TRIP TO JAVIER'S HOME WITH A LIGHT STEP
and heart, singing to herself and occasionally aloud to allay her
fears and doubts. The return trip was filled with those same emo-
tions, layered with confusion. But Lupe didn't sing on the trip
home, on the contrary, she remained silent and watchful.

At the sound of an approaching vehicle or voices nearby, she
flattened herself against a storefront, or bank, or church, or whatever building gave her cover. She pressed her body against the
coarse brick or rested a hand on the ledge of a windowsill for
support until the sounds faded. Satisfied no one was pursuing
her, she continued. The fog of alcohol diminished with every step.
She was relieved, but dreaded the clarity to follow.

Lupe forced her thoughts to what lay ahead, to what she
would tell Ximena and Mercedes. She prayed one of them would
know what to do.

When she reached the foot of the stairs, Lupe drew a deep
breath before climbing to her apartment. She fumbled in her
jeans for her keys and then struggled for a minute to find the
keyhole in the dark. She took one more deep breath before opening the door and letting a shaft of dim light slice across the room
and the two beds. Ximena lay in hers, the far one, with her back
to the door. She did not move.

Lupe closed the door quietly. "Mena," she whispered. "Ximena." Lupe sat on the edge of her sister's bed and waited a moment. When Ximena did not respond, Lupe jiggled her sister's thigh.

"Go to sleep," Ximena said.

"Mena."

"Go to sleep."

Lupe moved to her own bed where she lay down fully clothed and stared at the ceiling or at a spot where the ceiling should be. She could see no further than a couple of feet into the dark. Sleep was impossible, she thought. But just before sunrise, she drifted into a half-sleep state. She was aware she was in her bed in the apartment yet the weight of the heels of the body she'd carried was palpable in her palms. In her nostrils the stench of decomposing vegetation lingered. In her mind, a series of muffled thumps echoed as she and Javier rolled the corpse to its resting spot near the railroad tracks.

When the corpse had settled into a swale, Javier had scattered debris over the area with his foot. She had left Javier there and fled, going across the yard and past the ramshackle gray house without looking back.

* * *

"Dios mío." Oh my God. "Lupe, what happened to you?"

Lupe raised herself to a sitting position and rubbed her eyes. Ximena stood over her bed, her mouth open. Lupe followed Ximena's gaze to the foot of the bed where clumps of dried mud lay in the shape of the cleats from Lupe's sneakers, to her jeans sullied with dirt, to the stain of unknown origin across her pink shirt.

Lupe half remembered stepping into a slippery patch on the patio behind Javier's house and later tripping over the railroad tracks. She half remembered a frenzied run home and falling into her bed.

"If you plan on working today, you better get up and shower. Unless you've found another way to make money."

Lupe ran her fingers through her tangled and loose hair. The pink band that held it behind her head was nowhere in sight. She rushed to the bathroom, passing Mercedes on her way to the kitchen.

"What happened to you?" Mercedes asked.

For the fifteen-minute walk to work, Lupe said nothing and kept her eyes on her feet. She was convinced if she spoke even one word, Ximena and Mercedes would know everything. But the two ignored Lupe. Their conversation wafted above her head. They spoke of everyday things, the long day ahead, the temperature, whether it would rain, and Mercedes's latest infatuation with Ricardo. She'd accepted and even encouraged the foreman's groping and gone out with him several times. But any time Mercedes was out of sight, Ricardo shifted his attention to one of the other females, whoever sat closest. Last week it had been a new girl. A girl on whose shoulder he rested his hand and into whose ear he whispered. Ricardo pinched the girl's cheek before moving down the row of workers at the table, his hand resting a moment too long on another girl's shoulder, or knee, or lap. Mercedes, Lupe realized, understood little about love.

The tedious repetition of potting occupied Lupe's hands but left her thoughts to wander. They roamed like a cloud of black birds swarming across the sky one moment and dropping as one to a rooftop in the next. Lupe's thoughts did not settle on a rooftop but on a woman on the floor of a dark room and on a man in a dank swale near a set of railroad tracks.

She thought of going to the police. If she went today after work, it might not be too late. She could tell them. She'd say Javier had killed a man. That Javier had hidden a body in the woods. And that she, Lupe, had been forced to help Javier conceal the body. She wondered what the police would ask her in return. Why she had helped? Could she show them where the body was? Where did he live? Where did she live? Where were her papers?

Lupe could not conceive a scenario ending in anything but disaster. She decided to wait until the break when she could take Ximena aside and tell her what had happened. She'd tell her about the body. Ximena would know what to do—not for the dead man—but for Lupe's part in covering up the crime. Lupe would not tell Ximena about the other thing. It was lost forever.

When she finished her account of the night before, or at least parts of the night, Lupe sat back and waited to hear Ximena's reaction.

"This can't be...," Ximena said, pausing, unable to finish her thought.

"It is. It's true. Every word," Lupe said, anticipating her sister's thought. "I don't know what to do."

"Why on earth—"

"Because...because of what he did for us. For you."

"That's not a good enough reason."

"I didn't see Javier kill the man. The body was just there on the ground. Maybe someone else killed him."

Ximena's eyes narrowed and bored into her twin's. Ximena could see into Lupe's heart, and into her soul. She had to know there was more Lupe was not saying.

"You'll have to live with his. You can't do anything about it now. You can't bring this into our lives," Ximena said.

"But I have to do something. The police are bound to find out. There'll be more questions."

"I don't want any more trouble. You can't tell anyone. Not even Mercedes. And you cannot see him again. Ever."

Lupe hung her head.

"Do you hear me?" Ximena asked, grabbing Lupe by the arm and shaking her.

"Yes."

"Swear it to me."

"I swear."

The women returned to work, Lupe taking a seat as far from Ximena and Mercedes as she could. As she worked, she prayed. She said the rosary as she grabbed pots and filled them with soil. She repeated the words as she tamped a plug into the earth and covered its roots as Javier had covered the body. Once, she looked up and found Ximena staring at her as if she were checking her thoughts. Lupe recited the rosary again, faster, louder, screaming the words in her head, drowning out every other thought.

After work, as they made their way home, Lupe spotted Javier ahead. He must have followed them to work that morning and waited all day for them.

"Lupe," Ximena said, the one word enough to remind Lupe of Ximena's earlier admonition. And of Lupe's promise.

Javier stepped forward as they approached, but Ximena clasped her hand around Lupe's arm and pulled her along. Lupe kept to her sister's side and did not look back.

"What was that about?" Mercedes asked as they entered the apartment.

"Nothing," Ximena said. "Lupe is finished with him."

48. ALICIA

CARLO PICKED UP THE PHONE. "INGRAM SECURITY," HE SAID, THEN paused. "Yes. Yes, just a minute." He swiveled in his chair and said, "It's for you."

Alicia blinked. No one ever called her at work. Her thoughts went to Kyle. But the school used her cell phone, not her work number. "For me?" she asked. Carlo extended the phone in her direction. "Hello?"

"Alicia? It's Cy Westfall from the FBI. We met the other day?"

"Oh, yes. Ah..."

"I'm sorry. Did I catch you at a bad time?"

"Ah..." Though Carlo had turned back to his PC, his hands sat poised over his keyboard, motionless. "Ah, yes. Can I call you in a bit?"

"Sure. Do you have the number?"

"Yes. Thank you." After a quick glance at the phone's display, Alicia passed the phone back to Carlo. The display had shown just the ten-digit number, nothing else to indicate the call had come from the FBI.

"A problem?"

"No, just the school reminding me of a meeting tonight," Alicia said, gambling Cy had not said more than his name, if that, to Carlo. The last thing she needed now was for Carlo to find out she'd gone to the FBI with her "feminine intuition."

Out of the corner of her eye, Carlo sat rocking back and forth in his chair. Alicia unlocked her computer screen, found where she'd left off earlier, and typed furiously for several minutes. When she reached a stopping point, she sent her report to the printer, retrieved it and tossed it on her desk, announcing for Carlo's benefit that she was heading to the restroom in the corridor.

With her cell phone and Cy's business card in hand, Alicia exited the office and assessed her options. The hallway on the second floor of the mall was designed for shoppers, not for private phone calls. Alicia settled for a spot in front of an empty storefront, one whose windows were covered in paper. Most shoppers stayed on the opposite side where the stores were open for business. The empty storefront was as private a place as there was. She keyed Cy's number from his card.

Cy answered and cut to the chase. "Have you seen the young man Javier today?"

"No. Not for a couple of days as a matter of fact. But he usually shows on Saturdays," Alicia said. "So maybe he'll show today."

"And the other one. The clean cut one."

"No sign of him either. Was the information I gave you helpful?"

"Perhaps. I'm still looking it over."

"Oh," Alicia said, her momentary excitement dashed.

"But I'd like to ask you to do something for me, if I may?"

"Of course," Alicia said.

"Could you let me know if either of them shows? I might be able to come by and take a look. Let me give you my cell phone. Call me there as soon as you spot them."

She'd been right. She knew it. After they'd hung up, Alicia wanted to shout for joy but satisfied herself with a "Yes!" and one short pump of her fist.

With the shadow of a smile on her face, Alicia slid back into her desk chair and tried to ignore the quizzical look Carlo shot her way. At six, he rose to go, stuffing his arms into his plain-clothes raincoat. Carlo didn't like leaving the office in uniform—it attracted people and he'd said it took him twice as long to get to his car if he did. "Thought you had a meeting," he said.

"Meeting?" Alicia couldn't remember having a meeting or even mentioning one. "Oh, yes. School." She remembered just as Carlo's eyebrows were about to reach the ceiling. "I took care of it over the phone. So, no worries, I can close out tonight."

When the door closed behind him, Alicia exhaled, a long slow breath. She wanted a coffee, but before going for one, she flipped to the cameras, focusing on two of the dozen she could command from her desk. In one, she had a view of the north exit and in the other the south exit and the food court.

The usual scenes played out, people entered and exited, empty handed coming in, armfuls of packages going out, unsupervised children ran through the aisles fighting with each other, their parents God only knows where. In the food court, people lined up for fast food and balanced trays as they looked for a table. A minute later, heads in the food court swiveled to the far side of the room. Something had drawn their attention. Alicia switched to a different camera. A woman had spilled what looked like a full tray of food to the floor. The empty tray, cocked at a precipitous angle was in one of her hands, a child in the other. A second child stamped his feet and wailed, the monitor silent but capturing the wide oval of his open mouth.

She returned to the earlier view. A family of five lingered at a table near La Parilla where Alicia had found the Mexican twins on multiple Saturday nights. The wife pushed her chair back and headed toward the ice cream stand, one of her children in tow. The husband stayed with the other children. Two women took a seat at the table next to his. One woman resembled Mercedes with her plump waistline and tight clothing. But Alicia didn't recognize the other. The second woman wore a patterned scarf with bold colors rendered in high-contrast black and white on the screen. A few seconds later, the woman in the scarf turned her head to speak to her companion. The camera caught a glimpse of her face, part of the birthmark visible at the edge of the scarf.

Alicia eyed her cell phone. She had put Cy's number into her contact list and on speed dial. It was all she could do to avoid calling him. But what did she have to say at this point other than two young women were enjoying their dinner on a Saturday night?

She needed Javier to show. Alicia waited, fidgeting and fighting to stay calm. She paced back and forth across the tiny office, checking the camera each time she passed. Nothing changed. Alicia poured a coffee from the office coffee pot and then slumped in her chair to wait.

Not five minutes later, the now familiar figure in a hoodie entered the mall. "Bingo," Alicia said aloud, though she was alone in the office. On the camera, Javier headed toward the two women, stopping every so often to look around.

"Cy?" Alicia asked when he picked up the phone, even though she knew who it was. "It's Alicia Blake," she said, confirming what she realized he already knew. She winced.

"Yes?" he asked.

"He's here. Javier."

"Okay." There was a considerable pause. Alicia imagined Cy sitting at his desk with his leg beating time to music only he could hear. "Unfortunately," he said, "I don't think I can make it to the mall right now. See if you can find a reason to engage him and get him to reveal anything more specific about his background. That could be very helpful."

Cy didn't have to ask twice.

49. ALICIA

ALICIA'S INTUITION AND SITUATIONAL AWARENESS HAD PANNED out, or she thought it had, and apparently so did Cy. She'd found something and it was enough to pique the FBI's interest. Maybe it wouldn't turn out to be anything big. On the one hand she hoped it wasn't, but on the other, well...

Her thoughts spun through her head as she walked toward the atrium, a walk that seemed to take much longer than usual. She pushed the button for the elevator, but nothing happened. Alicia peered over the rail and saw a line of shoppers, several with baby carriages, jostling to board the elevator on the first floor landing below. As she contemplated taking the escalator at the far side of the food court, Alicia heard a slow grinding of gears. The elevator was rising.

When the elevator car opened, though she wanted to flash her badge and ask for preference in boarding, Alicia waited her turn, her fingers tapping a fast beat against the side of her radio. She kept her place by the doors and once they reached the first floor, Alicia exited before anyone else. Without so much as a quick glance toward the food court, she headed to Starbucks, sighing with relief on seeing only one person in line.

"Hi Alicia," the barista said, "double with—"

"No, just a small regular coffee, black."

"Whoa, that's a new one."

Alicia bit her tongue. Just pour the coffee, she thought, and skip the cream, the caramel, the sprinkles, and the chatter.

With her coffee in hand, Alicia walked to the far side of the food court, away from her target. She stopped and spoke to a familiar face before circling back.

"Good evening, ladies." The two women looked up and smiled. Javier was standing with his back to her. He turned his head, his eyes flicking to her badge and back to her face. "And gentleman. Good to see you again. It's a great night out, no?"

The women nodded. Alicia took a sip of her coffee. She hovered beside the table and took a second sip.

"Would you like to join us?" Ximena asked.

"Oh thank you. I've been on my feet since this morning. Just thought I'd take a break."

Javier looked over his shoulder. He turned.

"Oh, don't go on account of me. I won't be here but a sec." Another sip, avoiding his face. "In fact, I'm sorry, did I take your seat?" Alicia asked, arranging her most innocent smile on her face.

"No. Not at all," Ximena said, answering for Javier who said nothing and glanced over his shoulder again.

Alicia swiveled to face Ximena and Mercedes as if she were uninterested in Javier. Thankfully, the women chatted without prompting. In one break in the conversation, Alicia ventured a question, "So, are you all from Saltillo or did you meet here?"

"We're both from Saltillo," Mercedes said, "Lupe, too, of course. But we didn't meet each other until we came here to Atlanta."

Mercedes and Alicia turned to Javier.

"No," Javier said.

"Look, there's Lupe," Mercedes said, raising an arm over her head and signaling their whereabouts to Lupe. Lupe smiled and approached the table, but when she came within a few feet of the group, her demeanor changed. Her smile vanished. She pulled a chair to the opposite side of the table, the side away from Javier.

Alicia did her best to balance her dual roles, friendly guard just taking a break to talk with customers versus law enforcement official. And so, though she was pushing the bounds of polite chatter, she made one more attempt to gather information. Alicia picked up the thread of their earlier conversation, asking, "Do you live in the same place, too?"

"We live pretty close," Mercedes said. "Just across Chatta-hoochee."

"Oh, really? At Ashland?" Alicia said, mentioning the nearby apartment complex popular with first and second generation immigrants.

"Yes," Ximena said. "You know it?"

"I do," Alicia said. She turned to Javier and arched her brows.

Javier said nothing and kept his attention focused elsewhere, as if the question had not been asked of him. But Alicia did not move or flinch. After a long interlude, Javier turned, glared at her and said, "Where do you live?"

Alicia shivered but held his gaze for as long as she could, Then, she looked away and laughed as if he'd made a joke.

Alicia raised her cup of coffee to her lips. With the lid still on, only she was aware the cup had been empty for the last five minutes. "Well. I suppose my break is over," she said, rising from the table. "Thanks for letting me join you."

As she ambled away, Alicia paused to greet customers at a few other tables, as if it were her routine. But she kept an ear tuned to the group behind her, straining to hear any snippets of their conversation. From what she could tell, though, the silence continued.

Just outside Security, Alicia's cell phone rang. The screen read, C. Westfall. "Cy," she said, "are you here?"

"Sorry, no. Did you have any luck?"

"He's here but I'm afraid I couldn't get any information out of him. I didn't want to seem too interested. I guess I don't have much experience in interrogating suspects."

"That's okay. I'm sure you did fine," he said, his tone flat. "We'll try again next time."

"I don't know. Maybe," Alicia said, dejected and reflecting the tone of disappointment she heard in Cy's voice.

Javier's stare stayed with Alicia. At her desk, she sat motionless, her eyes closed and her fingertips pressed to her eyelids. It took her several minutes to shake off the uneasy feeling Javier had read her mind and was even now in the room. If that weren't troublesome enough, she'd also given him a reason to be interested in where she lived. With Kyle.

"You okay?" one of the night shift guards asked. He was making his way to his station, a large soda in his hand.

"What?"

"You look a little pale. Are you sick?" he asked.

"No. I'm fine." Alicia wriggled her shoulders as if to work out a kink. She clenched and unclenched her hands while the desktop woke from its sleep setting. On the cameras, Alicia found the women as they were leaving, Mercedes and Ximena leading the way, Lupe following with Javier.

Alicia shut off her computer and gathered her coat and keys. "Can you guys close out?" she asked. Both guards in the room nodded and gave her a wave.

Rather than pass through the atrium again, Alicia took a shorter route and exited the mall through Macy's. She circled back to the south entrance and crossed the parking lot headed for Chattahoochee River Avenue where she guessed the women were headed. She did her best to avoid being seen, keeping to the edge of the circles from the overhead spotlights. By the time she reached Chattahoochee, it had begun to mist. She ducked under a bus stop shelter, more to avoid being seen than to escape the weather. Closing time was minutes away and already people streamed through the exits, most headed to their cars, while others made their way to the neighborhoods around Riverside on foot.

Alicia fixed "yellow" in her mind, the color of the parka Lupe had had with her earlier. Though she was looking for a young man in a dark hooded sweatshirt, she'd have a better chance of success if she concentrated on finding someone dressed in yellow. Alicia realized Javier might not still be with Lupe but she'd have to take that chance. Seconds later, she saw a flash of yellow. It was Lupe. She was half-walking half-running toward Chattahoochee. Ahead of her were Mercedes and Ximena and a few steps behind was Javier. Lupe spun on her heels as if reacting to something Javier had said. The two stopped and chatted. Lupe gestured wildly in the air. Javier caught her arm and pulled it to her side then put his arm around her. Lupe pushed away, turned, and sprinted off to join her sister. When the three women reached and passed the bus stop where she sheltered, Alicia turned her back to them but kept her eye on Javier.

Javier did not pursue Lupe. He waited in the light rain for a moment. When Lupe disappeared from sight, he turned and walked the other way on Chattahoochee. Alicia went after him, thankful for the darkness and the coat she'd put over her uniform with its metallic badges, straps, and buckles, all reflective surfaces. She thought of Carlo and realized he might well have taught her a valuable lesson.

50. JAVIER

A FEW MINUTES AFTER THE SECURITY GUARD WITH HER ANNOYING questions went back to work, Mercedes and Ximena rose to leave. Javier reached for Lupe's hand, hoping she'd stay behind, but she pulled away and rose to follow the others. Javier pretended not to notice. He kept in step with her through the exit and across the parking lot, trying to engage her in conversation.

"Lupe. The other night..." he said, letting his words drift away, unsure of what to say.

"I don't want to talk about the other night," she answered. "At least not part of it."

Javier wondered which part he was supposed to avoid. "I want to see you again," he ventured.

"You're seeing me now."

"You know what I mean."

"What are you going to do?" she asked.

"About?"

"About the...the person."

"It's done. There's nothing more to do," Javier said.

"You can't just turn your back and hope this will go away. Someone will find him. You should go to the police."

Javier scanned the area in the parking lot where they stood, ensuring no one was near enough to overhear their conversation. "Was that what tonight was about? Were you going to tell the cop?"

"She's not a cop."

"Close enough. You want to be deported?"

"No. Of course not. It's just that Ximena—"

"Ximena? Did you tell her? Did you tell your sister?"

"No. I just asked her what she would do if she found something. Or if something terrible had happened, like if someone was badly hurt."

"And? What did she say?" Javier asked.

"She said I should look the other way and not get involved."

"But you know better? You think you should go to the cops?"

"No. Well. I don't know."

Lupe's response left Javier perplexed. She would not listen to any more of his arguments and would not agree to come home with him. Still, he wasn't sure what he would have done if she had. Would he have sex with her again, or what?

When he hesitated, Lupe flung her arms in the air, turned, and ran to catch up to Ximena and Mercedes who were by this time well down the sidewalk. She was going home, he thought. And, if nothing else, there her sister and friend would keep her from doing something stupid, like saying something to the wrong people. If she didn't understand it now, maybe they could convince her of how naive she was to even think of going to the police.

The mist changed to a light rain. Javier snagged the rim of his hood and pulled it over his head, still watching Lupe until her yellow jacket disappeared. Allah was most provident, he thought. Javier had arrived at the mall tonight in time to ward off any discussion Lupe or the others might have had with the cop or the guard or whatever she was.

He stomped off toward home.

By the time Javier turned onto Grant, the rain had stopped. Ahead, lights shone from the front window of his landlord's house. Those further down the block, including his, were dark. Behind him a drawn out swish from tires along the damp pavement and then quiet. In the brief silence before a second car passed behind him, he heard a sound and had the uneasy feeling he was being followed. Without breaking his stride, he continued but with his head cocked slightly to the right.

There it was again—the patter of footsteps on the sidewalk, unhurried, matching his pace. He slowed. The footsteps slowed. With his house just a few more yards ahead, he kept going.

As he inserted his key in the door, Javier caught a reflection in the half-moon of glass set in the top of the door. There was someone behind him on the far side of the street, a sliver of the person reflected in each of the three panes. Without turning around or looking back, he entered and went through the house and out the back door. He circled to his left and crept along the side of the house, treading across the damp vegetation to absorb the sound of his footsteps. Using the corner of the house as cover, Javier peered across the street. He half expected to see Lupe, but it wasn't her.

Opposite him, at the edge of the road and partially obscured by the overhang of tree branches, a woman in a long raincoat stood holding something in front of her, chest high. He squinted. As best he could tell, she was writing on a pad of paper. She opened the top of her coat to put the pad away and Javier caught a glint of light on her badge. It was the guard.

She turned and walked away, heading back on Grant to Beechwood.

Javier fingered the hilt of the knife he'd grabbed as he'd passed through the house. He came out of his hiding place and headed after the woman, closing the distance between them, no longer caring if she heard him approach. In fact, he intended for her to hear him.

The sound of voices broke the silence as the door to 1005 opened. Two women stepped onto the porch. One tossed a bottle into the yard and the other came after it, raucous laughter ensuing from both. The one in the yard spied Javier. She laughed again.

Ahead, the guard turned the corner at Beechwood and then hurried away along the busy thoroughfare. Javier sprinted after her. When he caught up to her, he grabbed her shoulder and spun her around to face him.

"Ah!"

"What are you doing here?" he asked.

She opened her mouth. For a moment, he thought she might scream, but she regained her composure. "Oh my goodness. You scared me," she said, trying to smile. She raised a hand to her chest and placed it against her heart.

"Why are you following me? What do you want?"

She hesitated and watched as a car approached and then passed. Javier didn't turn but he could hear the swish of another approaching.

"What do you want?" he repeated.

"I'm sorry. I...I thought this might be yours," she said, pulling her hand from her pocket. She held a single key on a plain key ring in her palm.

Javier glanced at the key and back at her face. A muscle on the right side of her temple pulsed. Her breaths were even but short. He waited. He wanted to see what she would say next.

"I thought I saw you drop the key in the parking lot in the mall. I...I tried to catch up to you but—"

"Thank you. It is mine." He grabbed the key ring and stuffed it in his pocket.

Javier could tell he'd startled her. He wondered whose key he now possessed.

"Good," she said. "Well, Good night."

She turned and hurried away without looking back.

Javier stayed where he was, staring after her long after she'd disappeared. He returned home, passing the two women from 1005 who were arguing now in their front yard. Without turning on a light, Javier loaded his backpack with his clothes and his prayer rug. When he reached for his phone, the screen was lit and held a two-word text message.

"Fajr. Come."

The message did not show the sender's identity, but Javier knew it was Qasim inviting him to the mosque for the prayers at dawn.

Javier slipped out the front door and into the night.

51. CYRIL

CY WAS HOME WHEN HIS PHONE RANG. HE DIDN'T RECOGNIZE THE number, but answered. Wind noise pummeled through the speaker together with the sound of someone breathing hard, trying to catch a breath.

"Cy? Cy?"

"Alicia?"

"Yes. I have an address for you. Oh my God. Wait a minute." A horn blared in the background, then footsteps and more heavy breathing.

"Alicia! Are you all right?"

"Yes. I think so."

"What do you mean, you think so? Has something happened?"

"I followed Javier from the mall."

"You did what?"

"I followed him. And I have his address."

"Yes. But what were you doing following him?"

"There's something strange going on here. I'm certain of it. And we just didn't have enough to go on, so I thought I'd try to find out where he lived."

"Well, I am sure an address will help. Go ahead, give it to me." Cy took down the address on Grant Street and tore the page from his notepad. Alicia was silent, but Cy could hear her rapid breaths through the phone. "Was there something else?" he asked as he folded the note.

"It's only, he, well, he caught me. I didn't think he'd seen me. I was just leaving when he came up behind me. I had to improvise." She paused, took another breath, and continued. "It wasn't my best effort. And I'm afraid I may have tipped him off. I don't know."

Cy cursed to himself, realizing for a moment how much her efforts were like his and Greg's during the botched sting and remembering the tongue-lashing afterward. He'd try to be a bit more understanding. "That's okay," he said. "Are you all right?"

"Yes. I'm back on the main drag. I can catch a bus home from just up the street." Her breathing calmed.

"Do you want me to come pick you up?"

"No. There are plenty of people here. I'll be fine."

"You shouldn't have put yourself in jeopardy. But the address will help, I'll definitely check into it. Thank you again." Cy hung up the phone and slipped the folded piece of notepad paper into his briefcase.

"What was that about?" Yasmeen asked.

To Cy's delight, she'd arrived back in town with a one-month extension of her assignment. He liked having someone around, or rather having Yasmeen around. Also, he was reaching the point where he wanted to approach his boss about Cycle. Yasmeen had a good sense of how to deal with people and could advise him on how to handle Druitt. If he didn't broach the subject the right way, Druitt might refuse to discuss any topic but Cy's performance and, worse, he might pull the plug on Cy's extracurricular work. Cy had to assure Druitt he was not wasting time chasing unfounded suppositions and tinkering with programs outside the boundaries of his job.

"The woman who brought me the photos. The security guard I told you about." After their earlier meeting, Cy had done a background check on Alicia Blake. He'd discovered she was a security guard and not the inspector she'd tried to make him believe she was.

"So what's your protégé doing now? Don't tell me she's been arrested for stalking her man?"

"Not quite, but she might have come close. Still, you have to admit, she did some good work pulling the pieces together. And now, she managed to get an address." Cy avoided mentioning Alicia's close call, as he'd encouraged her to go after more information. He'd been lucky she hadn't been arrested, harmed, or worse.

"Amazing. So now what?"

"I was thinking I might run the address in with my test tomorrow. It's not likely to come to anything, but it can't hurt."

"Tomorrow's Sunday."

"Yeah, I know. I'm sorry, but I'm running short of time and I'm at a crucial point."

"Don't apologize. I don't suppose it's work you can do here?" Yasmeen asked with a hopeful tone in her voice.

"No. I wish it were, but I need to access the mainframe. I made a lot of changes this week and I'm hoping this next run will stand up to expert scrutiny."

* * *

It was three-fifteen and Cy was wide awake, staring at the ceiling. His mind would not rest. The timing couldn't be better, he thought, considering the rumors circulating in the office in the last week—rumors of a potential terrorist attack. For now, all the FBI had to go on was increased over-the-air chatter, but as a precautionary action, the Bureau was stepping up surveillance activities across the board.

Three forty-five. Yasmeen stirred but didn't wake. He'd promised to take her out to dinner on Sunday, and maybe he still could. He counted on his fingers, an hour to the office, one or two hours to run and test the program, another to pull a report together. He could be back by mid-afternoon.

Four o'clock. It was no use trying to sleep.

"Yasmeen."

"Yes?"

"I'm getting up."

"What time is it?"

"Early. But I can't sleep. I might as well go to the office now. I'll try to be back around noon."

Yasmeen raised her head from her pillow and gave him a sideways look as he rolled out of bed. Then, she let her head fall back to the pillow. "Go," she said.

OCTOBER 30

52. CYRIL

FOUR OR FIVE PEOPLE WERE IN THE OFFICE WHEN CY ARRIVED A little after five in the morning on Sunday. He nodded at Thad Norvell, an Assistant Special Agent to the Field Office's most senior executive, Ken Bordogna. Cy was not surprised to see Thad at his desk. The guy always beat Cy to the office during the week; was there when Cy went home, and, so Cy heard, Thad worked most weekends.

Thad nodded back, adjusted his headset, and returned to his PC. Thad spoke just about every language in the book, at least every language Cy had ever asked him about. His language skills made him indispensable in the Atlanta Field Office. With Thad, they could translate most of what they needed on the spot, avoiding having to transmit files to D.C. or one of the other labs and waiting, sometimes days, for a response.

Cy took his seat in his cubicle and rocked back and forth while he stared at the FBI logo tracking across his computer screen like a Pac Man figure. For as technically sophisticated as the department was, Cy mused, it took an extraordinarily long time for his computer to boot. Then again, layers and layers of security software had to be navigated for everything from submitting his expenses to crawling through terabytes of sensitive data.

The login screen popped up and Cy signed in just as Special Agent-in-Charge Ken Bordogna passed through the aisle beside

Cy's cubicle. The SAC? On a Sunday? Cy sat up straight in his chair and craned his neck to see over the tops of the cubicles. The lights in Druitt's office, one of the corner offices, were lit. Druitt and Bordogna never came in on the weekend unless something was up and now both were here. Bordogna entered Druitt's office and closed the door behind him.

With the pretext of needing an infusion of caffeine, Cy headed for the break room on the far side of the third floor. On the return trip, he stopped at Thad's cubicle. If anyone had a clue what was going on, Thad would.

Thad looked up, tapped a few keys, and pulled his headset off one ear. "What's up?" he asked.

"I was about to ask you the same thing," Cy said. "What's your boss doing here on a Sunday?"

"Same as yours. Chatter. Washington did a data dump yesterday, lots and lots of gigs, and we were summoned to help sort through the info. Some of us have been here since yesterday."

"Well, I came in to get some other work done, but if I can lend a hand..."

"Hey, we need everyone we can get. Check with Moira, she's organizing the whole thing for Bordogna."

Cy signaled "thumbs up" and sped off to Moira Hadorn's cubicle. He left his full can of Monster Energy Drink on Thad's desk and the note with the address on Grant Street, the reason he'd come to the office to begin with, in his briefcase. He hadn't made a conscious decision to ignore it, but data from Washington took precedence over someone's hunch and his own tinkering.

"Soft targets," Moira said. As the SAC's assistant, she had a work area twice the size of Cy's, forcing her to rise from her seat and cross to an upright file. She unlocked the cabinet and pulled out a stack of manila folders, picked through them, and then handed several to Cy.

"Go through these as soon as you can. We'll meet with Ken in the executive conference room at ten o'clock. He wants to know everything we have. As always."

"As always," Cy repeated.

"There's a briefing online to get you up to speed. The login details are in the top folder. If you need anything else, just let me know."

By nine-thirty, Cy had gone through Moira's files. He'd found a few items of interest, made a few notes, and set them aside for the meeting. Once the team had finished a preliminary scan of everything they had, they'd talk through their findings, identify the most promising pieces of information, then divvy the work up for a second, more detailed, pass.

At the sound of his cell phone vibrating, Cy reached in his briefcase and found both the phone and the folded note with the Grant Street address.

It was Yasmeen. "How's it going?" she asked.

"Oh fine. You up?" Absentmindedly, as he chatted Cy fingered the note, folding it over again to form a triangle.

"I just wanted you to know, I have to go in, too. I received a call just a minute ago and have to go. So, it might be me who's late," she said.

"What's going on?" Cy asked as he tapered the sides of the note and then sailed the now aerodynamic piece of paper across his desk.

"I don't know exactly, but I need to show my face. Whatever. Do what I do."

"Same here," Cy said, not wanting to say more on the phone.

"Be careful."

"You, too," Cy said. He hung up the phone and drummed his fingers on his desk when he spied the miniature paper plane lodged nose-first into his keyboard.

He sat up abruptly, nearly knocking the remnants of a day-old, soda can off the desk. It was nine-thirty, leaving him little time to do more than enter the address and run a search. Cy closed out the files on his computer and switched to his authorized sector of the server, scrolling through the online folders until he reached the one labeled, Cycle.

Although Cy could have loaded data from any metropolitan area or even the entire United States into Cycle, to keep it responsive he'd restricted the test data to a single county, Fulton County. Fulton was one of the nineteen in the Atlanta metropolitan area and the one in which he lived. He'd thought having knowledge of the names of streets and landmarks would streamline his efforts. As it so happened, Grant Street ran through Fulton. Had it not been for his fortunate choice, he'd have had to load new data and that would have taken well more than the half hour he had left before Bordogna's meeting.

You are on the right track. The fortune cookie's words popped into his head. Maybe there was something to them after all, Cy thought.

* * *

The progress bar at the bottom of the screen registered twenty percent complete. Cy needed to leave for the SAC's meeting in fifteen minutes. He tapped his fingers on the desk and glared at the progress bar at the bottom of his screen. Twenty-five percent. Beneath the desk, his leg vibrated in double time.

The progress bar froze. The program aborted and a dialog box popped up with the words: Error. No Address Match.

Cy slammed his fist on the table. What? He looked at the handwritten address on the note pad, 905 Grant Street. He toggled back through several screens to the input box to check what he'd typed, 905 Grand Street. Cy cursed under his breath. He corrected the misspelling, hit enter, and watched the progress bar restart. For his next iteration, he'd add a few logic checks for typos and unknown addresses before having Cycle initiate the search process. While he waited, he jotted a reminder to himself.

Twelve minutes. Cy did not take his eyes off the progress bar, holding his breath as it hit twenty percent, twenty-five percent, and then kept going, crawling pixel by pixel to the right. Cycle was running through a huge amount of data, by design. The program, even this simulation, had to approximate the real world experience with millions of pieces of data, even many millions. Only a robust test could get him the green light he needed.

Five minutes. This time, Cycle completed the run and filled three screens with results. Cy was out of time. He sent the report to print, gathered his files for the meeting, and left, passing the printer on his way to the elevators.

53. CYRIL

CY SKIRTED THE CONFERENCE TABLE AND PICKED AN EMPTY CHAIR
at the back of the room. As an extra pair of hands on this assignment, he thought it best to let Bordogna's team members have
the seats at the table. Plus, sitting at the back and out of the direct
line of sight from the head of the room offered another advantage. If anyone droned on too long or went off topic, he'd have a
chance to sneak a peek at Cycle's results.

Bordogna began the meeting saying, "Ladies and gentlemen,
as you know, we've been working closely with my counterpart
Special Agent-in-Charge Blatchly out of New York since the attacks in Mumbai and Nairobi, and more recently Paris and Germany. Those incidents involved a variety of soft targets, a mall, a
hotel, a concert hall, a nightclub. We've assumed all along the
attacks were mere exercises in preparation for something on a
larger scale, an attack closer to home—soft targets here in the
United States.

"And of course, we're swimming in data. Our own and, since
Germany, the information our partners abroad have made available. Last week Blatchly's team identified increased and wide-
spread chatter, making the job that much more difficult. The
Bureau began parsing the data to certain field offices yesterday—
offices they believe are connected to this threat.

"Last night, our office's Counter-Terrorism Group, my group,

243

started combing through the data we received, which includes the last three months of intercepts. The rest of you who are here have graciously volunteered to lend your time. And I thank you. If anyone needs me to clear your assistance up the line, let me know.

"Now, there's a handout going around. You'll have access to it in the project file by the time you get back to your desks." A shuffle of papers ensued as each person peeled a copy from the stack circulating through the room. Cy slid his copy underneath the Cycle printouts. If all they were going to do was discuss what was legible from the handout and soon to be on their computers, he had a minute to sneak a look at the results. Besides, Cy was familiar with the information Blatchly's team used. They worked with data captured from phones and email, and social media sites, including internet chats, gaming sites, and the supposedly self-destructing message sites. They also mined activity on the Bureau's own "honey pots," sites the FBI operated to entice radicals and potential terrorists. They would have looked for connections between the individuals using the sites, even very loose connections. And they'd have sorted through airline, hotel, and car rental records, credit card and online payment records, driver's licenses, rental agreements, job applications, and background checks. For the most part, they used the same data Cy had loaded into Cycle's database.

"To the normal due diligence," Bordogna continued, "we're asking you to consider the major venues with upcoming events, including stadiums, concert halls, theaters, shopping malls, conference facilities, hotels."

Cy looked up, thinking he'd heard something, but Bordogna had continued, and moved on to his signature lecture on imagination.

"We don't want to stop with just the usual suspects. Look at both the usual and the unusual. Look at every piece of data twice, then look at it again from a different angle, and a third or fourth. Straight up analysis won't get the job done. You'll have to use your imagination. Finally, though we'll go over this at noon, we have reason to believe one of our most wanted terrorists is involved. Qasim Bousaid. If he is, we need to locate him. We can't let him slip back underground again."

The lecture was one Cy had heard several times and could practically recite the key lines. He sighed. By volunteering his help, he'd have to delay sifting through Cycle's results. He'd—

"Westfall?"

Hearing his name, Cy jerked. All eyes in the room were on him.

"Sorry, sir. I think my imagination was taking hold."

Bordogna said nothing and though Cy had not meant to be flippant, he realized too late his words had come across that way.

Bordogna frowned but continued, "I was asking if you have time for this? Or do I need to clear it with ASAC Druitt?"

"No. I'm fine. I'm on board."

"Good. Thanks."

"Niehoff?"

"Good here, sir," Chris Niehoff said. Chris was, like Cy, in Druitt's chain of command.

"Okay. Back at noon with your lists. Let's go."

Cy wasn't sure which lists Bordogna was referring to, but Thad Norvell would know. As everyone rose and headed to the elevators, Cy held back, trying to remember what had caught his attention earlier. Was it a word or two someone had said before Bordogna had called on him or was it something on the report?

He wanted to find it again before he became absorbed in Bordogna's assignment. Cy ran his finger along the rows of information on the first page of Cycle's reports. He couldn't see what he was looking for; perhaps he'd been mistaken.

"So, you ready to meet?" It was Thad Norvell, hovering over him.

"Ah, can you give me ten?" Cy asked.

"You got it. I'll meet you downstairs."

Cy needed far more than ten minutes, but with Bordogna's deadline looming, ten was all he would have for now. Thad Norvell was not about to give Cy more. Thad was obsessed and considered it a matter of pride to be the one to find more relevant information than anyone else and to find it long before they did. And, with the nagging black mark on Cy's performance record hanging over his head, Cy wanted to be on Norvell's team, a winning team.

But, he thought, maybe Cycle would be a winner, too.

Back at his cubicle, Cy spread Cycle's findings across his desk. Cycle had flagged three high priority possibilities. The first name he'd expected, it was based on a known case of terrorism Cy had loaded on purpose. It was a two year old case, ending in the arrest, capture, and conviction of the perpetrators, two students who'd become pawns of a foreign terrorist cell planning to bomb Philips Arena in downtown Atlanta.

Cy moved on to the second possibility. When Cy read Rasil Khan's name there, his eyebrows shot up on his forehead: Rasil Khan, the contact Cy and Greg had pursued for Peter Olson in the botched sting. Unfortunately, there was no new information on Khan, at least nothing new Cy could see without digging deeper.

On reading the name listed on the third entry, Cy dropped to his chair. He stared in disbelief. Qasim Bousaid. And beside the name, the priority Cycle had assigned, "High."

The report listed several variables supporting the flagging of Qasim Bousaid. At the top of the list was Changes in Communications. Among other variables, Cy had directed Cycle to look for sparing use of land or wireless telephones, short, cryptic messages, and communications between identified parties occurring over a brief period and ending abruptly. Change was key.

A second variable was Ordinary Activities. Here, Cycle looked for activities that appeared to be legitimate, ordinary everyday activities, similar to what the FBI and other intelligence agencies did. After all, Cycle had to be consistent with the FBI's standard approach. But what Cycle did differently was to look for a set of multiple normal activities from the specific activities Cy had flagged. Property rental was one of those.

Cycle had identified Qasim Bousaid, but it also connected Bousaid to the Grant Street address he had entered, 905 Grant Street as well as two others on Grant, 1105 and 805. One of the Bureau's most wanted terrorists had acquired each of these properties and a dozen more around the Atlanta area in the last year. The fifteen properties had been vacant for a lengthy period, but 1105 and 905 leased in the last three months.

Alicia Blake's man was living in one of Bousaid's properties.

Cy congratulated himself on one other aspect. The test had produced three entries, not dozens or tens of dozens, some valid some invalid, like many of the Bureau's analysis reports, or for that matter any computer search. As there was no way to know which were right and which were wrong, Agents spent hours following each lead, hours of wasted effort that could be avoided with fewer "false positives," in computer lingo.

"Ready?" Thad asked, he'd returned with a stack of folders in his hand and his PC and an expression that said he wasn't waiting a minute more.

"Oh. Sure. Sorry," Cy said. Validating whether he had made a breakthrough would have to wait. He gathered the papers strewn across his desk and stuffed them in the drawer. The results were promising, he was ecstatic, but it was not enough to go to Druitt or even Bordogna with yet. Still, as Cy walked away with Thad, he recalled his father's comments on looking for a needle in a haystack. Cycle had cut the haystack down to size.

54. ALICIA

"KYLE?" ALICIA CALLED FROM THE BATHROOM. SHE TOOK ONE MORE
look in the mirror, leaned closer and groaned, not liking what
she saw. When, she wondered, had the tiny lines appeared at the
outer edges of her eyes? And the gray hairs strewn among the
auburn beside her right temple? Alicia pulled tweezers from the
drawer and plucked a hair. It was gray, undeniably, depressingly
gray. She dropped the strand and watched the hair float into the
waste bin. "Kyle?" She plucked the other four matching hairs, but
had no time to look for more. And if she found them, what would
she do, she asked herself, pluck them until she had no hair left?

Alicia pursed her lips, still not satisfied. Color. She needed
color. Alicia fumbled through a drawer for a tube of lipstick. She
was spending too much time indoors, which accounted for the
pallor, but the lines and the gray were signs of stress, as was the
pit at the bottom of her stomach.

For an hour here and there since last night, she'd managed to
block the memory of her encounter with Javier. But it returned,
his eyes full of hate and anger and more. His stare said he saw
through her pretense and knew what she was doing. Another thought haunted her, too. Javier had her key to the Security
Office—even if he didn't know what door the key opened. On
Monday, she'd be taking a lot of grief from Carlo for losing the
office key. Losing, was the word she'd chosen to use. Last night,

when facing Javier on Beechwood, she'd groped inside her pocket and her fingers had first landed on the key ring with her car and apartment keys. She would never have handed those over, no matter what, so she had dug deeper and found the office key on its own key ring.

"Mom?"

Alicia jumped, her hand going to her chest. "Kyle! You scared me. Don't go sneaking up on people like that."

"I wasn't sneaking up on you. I've been standing here for an hour."

"You have not."

"Well maybe not an hour, but forever. So, what do you think?" Kyle asked, turning around to give Alicia a full view of his Halloween costume.

Tears welled in Alicia's eyes. Kyle had raided the closet in her bedroom to create his costume. He wore the shirt to his father's uniform, sleeves rolled up and Seth's belt cinched tight around his waist. Seth's cap was in his hand. The uniform had not been out of the closet for years. In the first few months after Seth's death, she'd take the uniform out and lay it on Seth's side of the bed at night. She'd bury her face in the coarse fabric and inhale the fading scent of him. She hadn't wanted to share it with anyone, not even Kyle. Yet, from the way he wore the shirt, standing with his shoulders back and as tall as his four feet six inches allowed, she could imagine no better person to wear it now.

"You look great," Alicia said, "but what happened to Spiderman and Fifty Cents and the other costumes you were trying out."

Kyle rolled his eyes. "Colin is going as Fifty Cent, so I had to find a different costume."

"I think you found a much better one. Your daddy would be proud. It's missing something though."

"What?"

"Hmm, let me see." Alicia made a circle in the air with her index finger. "Turn around."

"What?"

"Come with me," Alicia said, leading the way to her bedroom. She pulled open the top drawer of her bureau and felt for the clam-shell box. She plucked the medal from the box and pinned it to Kyle's chest.

"Wow," Kyle said, his chin to his chest, his fingertips running over the medal.

"Just for tonight, though. Now, we had better get going or we'll be late."

"Colin said he'd be there at five."

"No. I spoke to his mom earlier. Nancy and Colin are meeting us at six. We'll make it in plenty of time." From commuting to and from the mall for years, Alicia had the time it took to go from her home to Riverside down to the minute.

Nancy was the one who had suggested taking the boys to the mall for the Halloween party. Alicia had hesitated at first. She wanted to keep trick or treating low key, escorting Kyle to a few of the neighbors, but once the boys heard about the mall's party, Alicia knew she'd lost.

Riverside Centre management had plastered every billboard for miles around with notices. They'd strung huge holiday banners at each entrance and flags bearing images of skeletons on the lampposts in the Blue lot, pumpkins in the Orange lot. Newspaper and radio ads had added to the marketing blitz, making the event impossible to miss.

Worn down by the media and Kyle's constant pleading, Alicia surrendered.

* * *

Alicia and Kyle arrived at the mall and stood under the clock in the center of the atrium. She spotted Nancy with her son Colin on the far side of the food court and waved a hand high over her head.

The ladies greeted each other, touching cheeks, while the boys ogled each other's costumes. Colin and Kyle started toward the entertainment booths set up along the perimeter of the food court.

"Whoa there," Nancy said, catching the boys before they'd taken more than a few steps. "Rules. No running. No leaving this area. See that pillar over there?" Nancy said. She pointed a finger toward a white column beside the escalator. "And the other one over there?" Colin nodded. "Okay, that's the boundary. Here." Nancy handed each of the boys a few dollars. "Now, go have fun." She turned to Alicia, "How about a cup of coffee?"

"I thought you'd never ask."

"What's with the police?" Nancy asked as they waited for the barista to finish their coffee orders, two double caramel macchiatos. Sprinkles on both.

Alicia glanced in the direction Nancy had cocked her head. One city policeman stood along the wall near the restrooms, a second near the escalators, and a third at the south entrance door.

"I'm not sure. We asked anyone without kids to work tonight, but I didn't know Carlo was asking for city law enforcement, too.

He never mentioned needing extra security. But Halloween, you know. And tricks."

As they took their seats at one of the remaining vacant tables in the food court, Alicia's phone buzzed in her pocket. The words "C. Westfall" were backlit on the display.

"Excuse me," Alicia said to Nancy. "I have to take this."

"I thought this was your day off?"

Alicia grimaced. "Me, too," she said before pressing the "accept" key.

"Alicia, thanks for taking my call. I tried to reach you earlier but had to run to a meeting. Your address. We ran it through with other information and it appears you might have been on to something."

"What do you mean?"

"Well, I'm not at liberty to say much. But I wanted you to know we're raising the threat level in the city from Elevated to Imminent. We've just made the mayor and heads of the police department and other security partners aware."

"And imminent means?"

"It means we have more than just general information about a threat. It means we have credible and specific information and that an attack might occur soon. We're beefing up security at key locations, soft target locations... you know, theaters, stadiums, malls—"

"Malls? So, you think—"

"No reason to rush to conclusions. It's still very preliminary, but any of the sites with scheduled public events over the next few days will have an increased police presence. Riverside Centre included."

"I noticed. I'm here for the Halloween party and saw quite a few people in uniform."

"Ah, sorry I've got to go. I just wanted to thank you and to say how helpful you've been. We'll take it from here."

Alicia retook her seat next to Nancy. "Do you see the boys?" She craned her neck, looking left and right.

"They were over there a minute ago," Nancy said, flicking her hand toward an inflatable amusement funhouse, the entrance, a wide-open shark's jaw. "I guess they went on in. Everything all right?"

"Huh? Oh. Oh yeah. Fine."

55. LUPE

"XIMENA, YOU HAVE TO GET UP NOW OR WE'LL BE LATE," LUPE SAID.

Lupe ran to the shower and then dressed. When she returned to her room, her sister had not moved. She lay as Lupe had left her, facing the wall. Lupe called her sister's name and waited for a response. Ximena did not answer or move. Lupe bent over and nudged her sister's shoulder. "Mena, are you all right?"

"You go without me."

"What? Are you sick?" Lupe perched on the edge of the bed and placed her palm against her sister's forehead, testing for signs of a fever.

"I'm not sick."

"Then you must come to church with us."

"I can't."

"That's nonsense. You haven't been in weeks. You're not still thinking about those...others, Javier's people?" Lupe asked. She couldn't bring herself to say the word "Muslims."

Mercedes came in the room. "What's going on?"

"Nothing. Mena says she's not going. Again."

Ximena rose and Lupe breathed a sigh of relief. Her sister had been quiet and withdrawn of late, even missing work and risking being let go. Two days ago, Ximena had sat stoically as Ricardo passed their table, ran his hands along her shoulder, and put his lips an inch from her ear. Ximena had not reacted other than to pause in her work, a small maroon-splashed yellow pansy in one hand, a clump of dirt in the other. Lupe had come to her defense, telling the nursery foreman to leave her sister alone. Ricardo had left Ximena alone, but switched his focus to Lupe who ignored his taunts, brushing them away as she would a scatter of loose fertilizer granules.

But Lupe's relief was short-lived. Though she'd climbed out of bed, Ximena did not gather her toiletries and head to the bathroom. Instead, she stooped and pulled a small box from beneath her cot. It was a plastic box from the greenhouse that once held labels for pansies and snapdragons. With the box in her hand, Ximena came and sat beside Lupe.

She opened the lid and withdrew her rosary. "Take this," she said as she handed the rosary to Lupe.

"What would I want with your rosary? I have my own."

"It was mother's rosary."

"I know whose it was. But I have one. This is yours. She gave it to you."

Ximena did not reply but looked at her sister straight on, no smile, no frown. She bent over the box again and picked through the assortment of treasures. From the bottom, she removed a prayer card.

"Mercedes, I want you to have this."

Mercedes accepted the card from Ximena's outstretched hand. She held the card with the image of Saint Theresa surrounded by a bouquet of roses to her heart, then slid the card into her purse. Ximena glanced from Mercedes to Lupe and back again. "Go now. Go or you'll be late."

At the corner, Lupe grabbed Mercedes' arm. "Go ahead without me. I don't know what's bothering Ximena, but she's worse than ever. I'm going back."

Mercedes gave Lupe a look. "You can't do anything. She has to work this out on her own."

"Just go. It's okay. You're not responsible," Lupe said.

Lupe waited until Mercedes rounded the corner before turning back. Then, instead of climbing the stairs to her apartment, she waited beneath the stairs on a small landing. If she were right, Ximena would leave soon, thinking Lupe and Mercedes had gone.

Thirty minutes passed. Lupe was on the verge of admitting she was wrong, torn between running to catch the end of the church service and going upstairs to talk sense into her sister, when the door above opened. Hidden from Ximena's view, Lupe watched her sister come down the iron rail stairs, dressed in black, the hem of her abaya, a full-length robe, trailing behind her on the stairs. Lupe bit the back of her hand to stifle a cry of disbelief.

Once Ximena reached the corner, Lupe emerged from her hiding place and followed. For several blocks, she stayed well back. She had no fear of losing sight of Ximena, not in the hijab and abaya. But Ximena must have felt Lupe's presence because, without warning, she turned around and waited for Lupe to approach. "Lupe. Why are you following me?"

"Why are you dressed like that?" Lupe asked. "Where are you going?"

"You wouldn't understand. I've found a place where I belong and where I feel safe. If you want, you could come with me."

"Look at you," Lupe said, still shocked at the sight of her sister and ignoring Ximena's comments. The light that once flickered in Ximena's eyes had gone. The oval visible beneath the hijab was blank. "Why are you hiding yourself under those clothes?"

"I'm not hiding. I'm being what I want to be, respectful and modest."

"Are you afraid someone might see how beautiful you are?"

"I am not afraid. Not anymore. I don't care if people see me as beautiful or not. I want them to see me for what's in my heart."

"Mena, what happened in the desert was terrible. But—"

"The desert is in the past. I'm only thinking of the future now, as my friends have taught me. I'm looking ahead, not back. Come with me, just once. You can see for yourself."

"No. Those people are not your friends. I know who they are and what they do. I want no part of them or their church."

"I'll pray for you," Ximena said.

With those words, Ximena, or what Lupe could see of her sister, shut the door to the world. Lupe stepped forward, put her arms around her sister and kissed her on the cheek. Ximena did not acknowledge or respond to Lupe's touch, her shoulders and arms remained as lifeless as a rag doll. When Lupe withdrew her arms, Ximena walked away.

Lupe let her sister go half a block, then followed behind. She was not ready to surrender Ximena. Fifteen minutes later, Lupe watched Ximena cross the street to the mosque, the same one Ximena had shown Lupe weeks ago when Lupe had challenged her to show proof of Javier's identity. Lupe found an alcove at the front of a store a few doors away. There, partially hidden from view, she squatted on the cold cement floor to wait.

Shortly, three women exited the mosque. It was Ximena, flanked by two others. For the first time in her life, Lupe was glad her sister had a distinguishing feature. Were it not for the birthmark, she would not have been able to tell one from the other of the women. Ximena was right. She would not be seen again as beautiful or even remarkable. She was safe from the prying eyes of strangers. No one would give her a second glance.

The shrouded women moved as one. They went four blocks, never pausing, never looking right or left or back. They entered a small storefront, this one without a sign, blinds drawn over the windows.

Noon. Lupe had missed breakfast and now would forego lunch as well. Were it not for her new watch telling her it was time to eat, the thought of food would not have crossed her mind. Two o'clock came and went. Then four o'clock. Absentmindedly, Lupe reached in her pocket, finding Ximena's rosary. She prayed, eyes open, fingers working the beads. She prayed again. At five, two women left the building. Too tall. Minutes later, a man and a woman emerged and approached a parked vehicle. The man held the door for the woman and as she bent to enter, Lupe caught sight of Ximena's face with its mark. When she was seated, the man placed a tall white shopping bag in the back seat. On the side of the bag in gold were the capital letters N-O-R-D-S-T-R-O-M.

56. JAVIER

JAVIER WAS OUTSIDE THE MASJID AL-RAHMAN WHERE HE'D BEEN most of the night. He stood with his back against the wall on the lee side, shifting from one foot to the other, then pacing up and down the block to ward off the late October chill. He retreated at the sight of anyone who gave him a second glance and kept an eye out for city cops patrolling the area and sweeping it of vagrants and would-be criminals. The last thing he needed was to have Ata or Qasim show up while one of the city's deputies was questioning him.

A white Toyota turned up the drive. Javier turned and hunched his shoulders. As the car passed he caught sight of Ata Nahidian at the wheel. The car came to a stop at the back of the building, its tires catching and tossing a few of the loose pebbles across the pavement. Javier followed and stood nearby as two men exited, Ata Nahidian from the driver's side, Qasim Bousaid opposite.

"Brother Ata," Javier said.

Ata Nahidian turned toward the sound of Javier's voice. "Who's there?"

"My brothers, it's me. Shafra."

Ata and Qasim looked at each other and then at Javier. Ata smiled. "Brother Shafra, you are early. Come. We must prepare for the Fajr."

Javier followed the two inside where they removed their shoes and set them beside the door. "Wait here," Ata said. "Your brothers will be here soon. Today, we worship together, as one, Inshallah."

Javier took a seat on the bench, his socked feet relishing the warmth of the wool rug. From where he was, he had a glimpse into the prayer room and watched as Ata spread a few prayer rugs. It was nearly time for the Fajr prayer. Qasim, though, had disappeared.

Soon, he said to himself. Soon, I'll meet the others and do what I came to do. Allah, give me strength to see my duty through. Javier closed his eyes. He rested his head against the wall and fell asleep.

Voices from outside woke Javier. He blinked and shook his head and watched as a handful of people entered. One of them was an old man who leaned on another for support. Both had to sit to remove their shoes. A woman with two children stood behind them. They removed their shoes and passed to the right of the screen partitioning the room. These could not be his cohorts.

Fajr, he remembered. The text had said Fajr. Of course, any number of people would have come for prayers at this hour. Javier set his worries aside and followed the old men into the prayer room.

As he stepped into place in a row the men had started, the door behind him opened again. Four young men entered the mosque and took their places at the back in a row of their own. Ata reappeared and beckoned Javier, motioning for him to join the four young men in the last row.

When the Fajr prayer was over, the mosque cleared, leaving Ata, the four young men, and Javier.

Ata locked the front door, then in a voice soft as a prayer, he asked the five men to kneel in a semicircle at one side of the room. When they were assembled, a door at the back of the room opened. Qasim emerged and knelt facing the five men. Ata excused himself and took up a position near the entrance to the mosque.

"Brothers," Qasim began, then stopped and cleared his throat. "Today is the day we have been looking forward to. The day you achieve your greatest desire. Today we will be together. We will fast together, meditate together, and pray together."

Javier's heart filled with joy. At last, he thought. Praise be to Allah.

Qasim coughed again but continued speaking to the five men with intermittent interruptions to clear his throat. "We have prepared well, but we are being watched. When you leave today, you must be especially vigilant. The infidels have information about our objective. How they found this information, we do not know. That is for another day and for other people. Your duty is all you need to remember and to savor.

"Now, I beg each of you to purify yourself. You will find a basin there," Qasim pointed to the back of the mosque, "and new clothes for each of you. Go. In silence. When you are ready, come back and we will pray together."

Javier followed the others into a room, empty, except for folding tables set against three walls. On the tables, someone had placed stacks of clothes, clean, pressed, and neatly folded. A piece of paper with a name lay on top the clothes. Javier stood in front of the stack with his name, Shafra.

One by one, the five took their clothes to the bathroom, washed, shaved, and dressed. When they emerged, except for the different colors of their sweaters and pants they could have been twins, one to another. Their heads and cheeks were shaved clean, and below their clothes their chests, arms and legs, and pubic area as bare as the day they entered this life. Each bore the same expression, one of calm and reverence, eyes looking ahead but seeing nothing.

They returned to the prayer room where Qasim waited. Ata had joined him, and both sat with their hands uplifted in prayer. As he knelt again in his place, Javier ran his hand along the crease of his new trousers, the wool smooth and soft to his touch. From his shirt, an unfamiliar scent, a crisp smell, not from having been laundered and ironed, but, he guessed, from being recently purchased and never worn by anyone but him. He let his fingertips linger on the cuff.

On the floor in front of each of the men were more clothes, outerwear. None of them men acknowledged or made a move to touch the piles of sweaters and jackets.

Ata rose and handed each a pen and a slip of paper. "You may leave a note for your families." He stepped aside but watched expectantly as each of the young men bent over to write, each one except Javier. He held the pen poised in the air thinking to whom he could write and what he could say to his father, his mother, or Selam. What was the point, he asked himself, he doubted the letters would find their way across an ocean and a continent. Nevertheless, he scrawled a word and then for some minutes moved the pen over the paper, mimicking the others. Ata passed down the line and collected the papers, including Javier's folded in half and containing a single word, "Nadheer."

Qasim rose and walked to the first young man, the one farthest from Javier. The others turned their heads to watch. Qasim called the young man's name, Behrooz, and held out his hand.

Behrooz rose. Qasim embraced him, then stooped and picked up the pile of clothes at Behrooz's feet. He separated the pieces of clothing, handing the topmost, a brown jacket, to Ata. Qasim held the other item in front of him at arm's length for all to see. It was a vest with duct tape holding wires and a string of gray cylinders to the front and back. As deftly as an experienced valet, Qasim placed the vest on Behrooz, circling him and patting the vest against the young man's torso.

Standing again face to face, Qasim lashed the end of a strand of wire to Behrooz's sleeve. Then Ata helped the first jihadist into his jacket. When the jacket was buttoned, it hid the vest. The only sign was a wire with a switch at its end protruding from the sleeve.

Qasim stepped back, placed his hands on Behrooz's shoulders. He paused for a moment and then clasped the young man, touching shoulders. Qasim moved to the next in line. When the first two men were dressed, and spoke each other's names, they embraced, clasping each other's shoulders as they had with Qasim. Ata led them to the door.

A second pair, dressed, greeted each other by name, and left.

Qasim stepped in front of Javier, the one man remaining. Javier's eyes darted around the room, wondering if another partner would materialize. He searched Qasim's face for the answer. Qasim said nothing but gazed at Javier as if he were the only person in the world that mattered. He dressed Javier as he had the others. The ritual the same, except for the step sideways Javier took when he felt the full weight of the vest on his shoulders. Qasim steadied him.

"Am I to go alone?" Javier asked, daring to speak before Qasim did.

"No, Brother Shafra. Your partner will be here in a moment."

"But—" Javier stopped. He knew his partner was not going to show. He was lying face down in the brush in a swale by the railroad tracks. Javier studied Qasim's face to see if Qasim knew, knew the man was not coming, knew where Javier's partner was, and knew who had put him there.

Qasim held Javier's gaze but said nothing more.

"I am ready to do my duty, Brother Qasim, God willing."

"You have had doubts, Brother Shafra. I know. Fear takes hold of some of our brothers at the hour of their duty. They are the weak ones. We know them and take them aside." Qasim raised his head, the light from a ceiling panel fell across his spectacles, concealing his eyes.

Javier feared Qasim might have a different plan for him than one of glory. He feared Qasim might ask him to martyr himself on the spot and prevent him from fulfilling his role.

"I have no doubts. I —" Javier stopped in mid-sentence. He could not lie at a moment like this. "I had doubts, but I have none now."

"It is understandable. There is no need to be ashamed."

"I have asked Allah for forgiveness. I am ready. By Allah, I am ready. I want to liberate my people. I want to fulfill my sacred oath. I want to be a source of pride to you, Brother Qasim, and to Brother Ata, to my father, my mother, my sister, and to my brother Nadheer."

"May Allah protect you. Clear your head of everything. Think about your oath. Think of paradise. Think of your reward waiting for you there."

"And the honor I will bring to my family."

"And the honor you will bring, yes. Think of your life here on earth as nothing more than a journey to your next life. The next life is the true life. The life for those who are worthy. As worthy as you are now, Brother Shafra."

Javier's eyes watered, his heart swelled. "Praise be to Allah."

"I believe you are ready," Qasim said. "And we are most fortunate Allah has given us brave and faithful brothers and sisters." A hint of a smile crossed Qasim's face. He cleared his throat and said, "Come, you will not be alone. We have someone to go with you. Come meet your companion in glory."

Qasim took Javier's hand. Together they walked toward the door.

"Who? Who do you want me to meet?"

"Sister Nafis," Qasim called, his voice soft, the rasp gone.

A dark figure emerged from behind the screen. A woman in a hijab and abaya. Everything was covered but the oval of her face with the birthmark on her forehead.

57. CYRIL

THEY'D MET AT NOON FOR LUNCH AND TO ASSESS WHERE THE team's work should focus for the rest of the afternoon. Completely unproductive, Cy thought, his leg twitching in high gear. As it turned out, there were no changes to the work assigned to Cy and Thad. The interruption had wasted precious time. Dinner with Yasmeen, even Yasmeen herself, and Cycle had slipped from Cy's thoughts. Then, at five, Bordogna summoned everyone back to the conference room.

Bordogna passed a sheet of paper to each of the agents on the ad hoc team.

"Sorry to interrupt what you were doing, but we have an update everyone needs to hear. Moira?"

"Thank you, Ken," Moira said. "The call came in a few minutes ago. No name of course. We have audio loaded for you in the group project folder. Female, broken English, presumed Hispanic, but she was speaking softly and holding something over the phone so the recording is not clear. This is the best we could do for now."

Moira played the audio of the captured call.

"Location?" Chris Niehoff asked.

"Pay phone at a gas station on the corner of Peachtree Parkway and Ashland Road," Moira said. "We have someone on it now, checking the station's cameras and any other video in the area. There's a bank across the street. It's possible the ATM camera has a shot. A team is on the way to question the station attendant, but I doubt they'll have seen much, if anything.

"As you heard," she continued, "the caller mentioned a mosque, but didn't say which one or give us an address. There are two within a five mile radius of the gas station."

A map of the city was tacked to the wall and a dozen red circles drawn around the city's major public gathering sites. The largest circle encompassed downtown Atlanta's key sites—Centennial Olympic Park, the Falcon's football stadium, Philips Arena, and Underground. Smaller circles were scattered across the map into the surrounding communities.

"The gas station is here," Moira said, stabbing her forefinger at a point north and east of downtown. She held her finger in place and with her thumb tapped on a point nearby. "The Islamic Center is here. And Masjid Al-Rahman over here."

"Riverside Centre," Mike Lott said, identifying the nearest red-circled venue.

Shopping mall. The words that had been sitting at the back of Cy's head since the morning meeting, jangled into his consciousness.

Bordogna nodded at Mike, an agent on his team. "Exactly," the SAC said. "We're sending three teams out, everyone we can spare, one to each of the two Islamic sites and their imams' houses, and the third to Riverside, the nearest mall. We'll keep a skeleton crew here for now, but everyone else needs to get moving. We don't know if our big fish Qasim Bousaid will be at one or the other site. But even if he's not there, you can be sure one of his lieutenants is, acting in his place. They'll be likely to link back to him at some point. So, we'll be monitoring communications.

"Lott, you have the Islamic Center. Slater, you have Al-Rahman. And Norvell, Riverside. Take what support you need."

Cy knew his skills were best used sifting through the data to help locate Qasim Bousaid if he were not apprehended at one of the mosques. But he also thought having eyes on the venues, his own eyes, might yield even more. And he was convinced Riverside was the target and that one of those involved, Alicia's man, might still be at the Grant address. If Cy could reach the man before he did something drastic, Javier might lead them to Qasim. Cy shuffled the papers in his lap and rose to follow George Slater, the third of Bordogna's lieutenants, back to their offices.

"Chris, Cy?" Thad Norvell said, "meet me downstairs in five."

"You don't think I'd be better off helping Slater?" Cy asked Thad, though his inquiry was half-hearted.

"Probably, but I think Slater has it covered. We need everyone we can out in the field."

* * *

They left the parking lot in one of the department's nondescript Sport Utility Vehicles. Cy, the odd man on the team, rode in back. Thad Norvell and Chris Niehoff rode upfront, with Chris in the driver's seat.

"Humor me, Norvell," Cy said.

"What do you mean?"

"I have an address we should check."

"An address? Would you care to be more specific?"

"Nine-oh-five Grant Street."

"I mean, as in why we should take a detour. We're expected on the site, pronto. Did you see the look on Bordogna's face? I've never seen him this wound up. He's laser focused on this. It's the most credible threat and possible link to Bousaid we've ever handled."

"I know, but there's something we should check out."

"Yeah, but..." Norvell said.

Hesitation in his voice was evident. Cy wondered if he was considering Cy's tenuous position. He was sure Norvell was aware of Cy's performance issues. He had to put more of his cards on the table, even at the risk of exposing the hunches he'd been pursuing and his tinkering. "I know who called this in."

Both heads in the front seat turned.

Cy leaned as far forward as the seat belt allowed. "One of Qasim's guys lives there. If we can get to him before he goes to the mall, we might get lucky. He could lead us to Qasim."

"Grant?" Thad tapped the address into the GPS system. "What was the number again?"

"Nine, zero, five. And it's on the way to Riverside," Cy said.

"How'd you get this?" Chris asked.

"Long story. But from multiple sources. And I checked it against a program I designed."

"Off the grid?"

"Off the grid," Cy said. "I've been working on it, testing it, and perfecting it in my spare time."

"You're not wasting our time on a wild goose chase, are you? There'll be hell to pay if you are."

Cy swallowed hard. "No," he said with as much conviction as he could muster. "This is solid."

"Man, you know if you are wrong, you'll take us down with you."

There it was, Cy thought. Thad knew. "I'm not wrong," Cy said. The botched sting was a black mark Cy could only shake with one big eraser. He was gambling everything on this.

Chris pulled the SUV into the dirt and gravel driveway of 905 Grant Street. "Doesn't look like anyone's home," he said.

"Five minutes," Thad said. "That's all the time I'm giving you. Five. Not six. Not seven. Five. Let's go."

The three stepped from the SUV and approached the house.

"I'll take the back," Cy said and broke away to his right. He tuned out the crunch of his footsteps on the gravel drive and listened for other footfalls, someone opening or closing a door or window, hitting the ground and making for the cover of the woods behind the house. There was only silence. The back of the house had the same look of abandonment as the front. The blinds were drawn. A plastic Adirondack-style chair, lay on its side, one leg snapped. Leaves lay strewn across the intermittent strands of grass in the back yard.

"Empty," Chris said as he emerged from the back door. "If your guy was here, he's gone now. The front door's wide open and there's nothing in any of the rooms."

"Damn," Cy said, glancing around, looking one more time at the house and at the area behind the house. Nothing but a small slope leading to the woods and a set of railroad tracks.

"Let's go," Thad called as he joined Chris and Cy on the concrete pad.

"All right," Cy said, but he let his feet go toward the tracks, making a sweep left to right across the perimeter of the yard. He slapped his leg and turned to catch up with his team when his eye caught a glimpse of color, nothing more than an anomaly, but anomalies were what he was trained to spot.

Cy took a few steps closer to the tracks and then stooped to examine the piece of pink fabric that had caught his eye. With a stick, he tugged at the pink ribbon, drawing it out of the brush. As he rose again, he spotted the shoe a few yards away.

"Over here," he yelled and knelt to look closer. He heard Chris and Thad come at a run.

"That's disgusting. Is it him?" Thad asked. "Can you tell?"

Cy stared at the head of the corpse lying on its side. Blood and dirt caked the side of the skull where it had been crushed and damp leaves adhered to the cheeks and forehead. Cy used the stick to pick a clump of loose leaves from the face.

"Shine a light over here," he said.

Thad held his light over the head and panned it back and forth while Cy did his best to make out the face. "Is it your guy?" Thad asked again.

Cy edged lower, examining the mouth and jaw. He could find no evidence of the scar in Alicia's photos. "I can't be sure, but I don't think so." He glanced at the body and back at the house.

"How long would you guess?" Chris asked.

"A few days to a week, give or take would be my guess," Thad said.

"It's not our guy, which is not necessarily good news," Cy said. "He's still out there."

"Let's call it in and go," Thad said. He glanced at his watch. They'd stayed well past the five minutes allotted for Cy's excursion.

58. SHAFRA

BECAUSE OF THE HALLOWEEN PARTY, ETOWAH RIVER DRIVE WAS closed to vehicular traffic for the evening. Ata Nahidian was forced to make a last minute change to the plan. He pulled the Toyota to a stop on Chattahoochee on the south side of Riverside Centre. Shafra exited the vehicle and checked his watch.

Ata said, "Remember. You are to go to the north side. Ali will be here in a few minutes with Sister Nafis. She'll take your place at the south entrance. Go now. You have plenty of time to circle the mall and enter on the north side." Then, he nodded and said, "May the peace and mercy of Allah be with you." It was the simple, everyday greeting and was said as if he would be back to pick Shafra up later.

Shafra replied, "Wa 'Alaykum Asalaam," and took a last look at the imam as he drove off and was swallowed by the traffic.

It took Shafra a moment to fight the urge to go directly to the south entrance as he had practiced so many times, but his duty now, Qasim had said, was to take Jamil's place at the north entrance.

As Shafra headed across the parking lot toward the mall, he recited a verse from the Quran,

and we have put a barrier before them and a barrier behind them and we have covered them up so that they cannot see.

He said the verse over and over, reinforcing Qasim's message—he and his brothers would be invisible and even if found, they would be protected from attempts to deter them from their duty.

Shafra stopped halfway across the parking lot. He set the heavy shopping bag on the pavement and folded back his sleeve to check the time again. He had a half an hour to reach his mark. As he rolled his sleeve back in place, the tips of his fingers passed over the clean-shaven skin of his forearm. It would be better to go through the mall, he thought. He'd save time. Shafra picked up the bag and headed for the Macy's entrance.

Ahead of him, a man approached, dressed in an identical sweater and trousers, carrying an identical package. Shafra raised his free hand to his forehead. The figure did the same. He squeezed his eyes shut, then blinked several times. It was his reflection in the glass. On any other day at any other hour, he might have found the illusion and his surprise humorous, but not on this day, not at this hour.

The glass door swung outward, toward Shafra, but stopped with a bang.

A woman's voice. "I'm so sorry." She stood inside, half-hidden from Shafra by the glare of the overhead lights bouncing off the glass. Her eyes went to the front wheel of a tandem stroller carrying two young children, two boys dressed in matching blue shirts. The younger looked startled and ready to cry from the jolt of the stroller against the door. Shafra stepped back and held the door for the woman while she freed the stroller. "Thanks. I'm sorry, I'm not very good at this yet," she said as she passed. Shafra watched the woman and the two boys until she stepped behind a van in the parking lot.

"Come on. You'll be out there all night if you don't come on in." Another woman's voice broke Shafra's trance. He swiveled to see a heavy-set woman holding the door for him. "Come on. I have the door."

Shafra slid past the woman and into the mall without looking back.

"You're welcome," she said, her cynicism lost on him.

59. ALICIA

ALICIA DOWNED THE LAST OF HER COFFEE. "CAN YOU WATCH OUT for them for a minute?" she asked.

"Sure, going for a refill already?" Nancy asked, knowing Alicia's penchant for caffeine.

"Ah, no. I just want to call in and see what's up with the police."

Once away from the din of the food court, Alicia dialed Carlo from her cell phone. There was no answer. Across the atrium, everything seemed normal, that is, normal for a children's party on Halloween. If she hurried, she thought, really hurried, she could make it to Security and back in ten minutes or less. Alicia hit redial. Again, no one answered. She scrolled through her address book, while dodging the oncoming tide of shoppers and party goers, skeletons, ghosts, cowboys, ninja turtles, and princesses. Somewhere deep inside her head, the idea of the costumes being a perfect foil for a terrorist crossed her mind.

She found Wade's number and dialed him. He answered on the first ring. "Thank God. I was beginning to wonder if anyone was here," she said.

"Alicia?"

"Yes."

"I thought this was your day off."

Alicia sighed for the tenth time this evening. "It is. But you won't believe it; I'm here with Kyle for the Halloween thing. Where's Carlo?"

"He should be in Central, but maybe he's patrolling. You need me to reach him?"

"No. I just tried. He's not there. No one's answering. So, tell me, what's up with the extra security?"

"We got a call this afternoon. City's raised the threat level. Twice."

"I heard that," Alicia said.

"Carlo brought in the local police. Well, actually, I doubt he was given a choice. They started showing up around three."

"Can you—" Alicia halted in mid-sentence. A face in the oncoming throng caught her eye. He had changed. His head was shaved and he wore a clean white shirt and a neatly pressed pair of slacks, but Alicia recognized the scar on his cheek. It was Javier.

"Alicia?" It was Wade.

She put a hand to her forehead, concealing her face as Javier passed. She reversed course and took off, following him, keeping him in sight. He was heading for the atrium. Between the intervening arms and legs and torsos of the crowd, Alicia spied something in his hand. She cocked her head one way and then the other, until, through a small gap, she caught a glimpse of a white shopping bag with the Nordstrom logo in gold capital letters on its side.

"Alicia?"

"Sorry. I'll call you back," Alicia said to Wade. She shoved the phone into her pants pocket and took the nearest service hallway. She could make better time through there, exit through the fire doors, and come back in through the south entrance.

60. LUPE

LUPE COULD NOT TELL IF XIMENA HAD HEARD HER SO SHE CALLED out again, "Ximena!" this time louder. Lupe caught up with Ximena halfway across the Riverside Centre parking lot. After watching the car in which Ximena sat leave the mosque and head in the direction of the mall, Lupe emerged from her hiding spot and ran to Riverside as fast as she could.

She'd been lucky. With a few of the roads closed around the mall, traffic was at a standstill. Lupe spotted Ximena as she was crossing the parking lot. Lupe sprinted and caught up to Ximena near the south entrance. When she placed her hand on her sister's shoulder, rather than jumping as Lupe thought she might, Ximena pivoted in place.

"What are you doing?" Lupe asked. Ximena had a quizzical expression on her face. It was as if she did not recognize Lupe. "Mena. It's me. Lupe," she said, jostling Ximena's shoulder. Ximena smiled as if she were staring at a far away object, a kite, a rainbow, or the moon, but otherwise her expression did not change. "Mena. I know what you are doing." Lupe could not resist a quick glance at the white shopping bag in Ximena's right hand. A piece of fabric was stuffed into the top of the package, preventing Lupe from seeing the contents.

Ximena turned and started toward the mall again.

At the same time, a woman came toward them from across the parking lot. Her hand was raised in front of her as if she were directing traffic. She had an air of familiarity with her auburn hair and thin frame. It took Lupe another second to realize the woman was Alicia Blake. Lupe had never seen her out of uniform.

"Guadalupe. Ximena," Alicia said, calling to the sisters. She stopped beside them and put her hand to her heart. She'd been hurrying across the lot, her hair was blown back from her face and her face was flushed. When she caught her breath, she said, "Don't go. Let me talk to you a minute." Her glance at the Nordstrom's shopping bag was quick and, after that one glance, she kept her eyes averted from the bag.

Ximena made a move to leave, but Lupe grabbed her arm and held her back.

"Ximena, it's me, Alicia Blake." The guard had stepped to the right to block Ximena's way. "Do you remember me? We met a few weeks ago." Alicia kept up a slow one-sided conversation, short sentences in a deliberate, non-threatening voice. "We had coffee in the mall a few weeks ago. Do you remember?"

Again, Ximena tried to pull away. She looked at Lupe's hand on her arm and at the shopping bag. Lupe's eyes widened in panic.

Alicia turned to Lupe. "It's all right. Everything is going to be all right. Isn't it Ximena?"

A million thoughts swirled in Lupe's head, but not one of them were that everything was going to be all right.

"Ximena, why don't you give the shopping bag to Lupe?" Alicia asked.

Lupe shook her head violently from side to side to warn Alicia the bag held something dangerous

"It's okay. I know." Alicia Blake smiled then pivoted back to Ximena. "Do you remember the first time we met? Weeks ago now. You helped a woman here one night," Alicia said. "You kept her safe. Right here in this parking lot. Remember?"

Nothing was happening. Ximena continued to look from one of them to the other with a blank expression, almost as if she'd been drugged. Where were the police, Lupe wondered. She'd called them hours ago and tried to tell them something bad was about to happen, though she hadn't known it would be at the mall.

"I knew something was wrong," Lupe said, half whispering her confession to Alicia. "I knew something terrible was going to happen. I called the..." Lupe stopped. She was afraid to say the word "police" in front of Ximena.

"That was good," Alicia said in a reassuring tone. Then Alicia resumed her conversation with Ximena. "I know you don't want to hurt anyone. You want to keep them safe like you kept Polly safe. You don't want to hurt anyone, not the mothers and children inside the mall, not your sister."

At the word "sister," Ximena looked at Lupe. With Ximena momentarily distracted, Alicia seized the opportunity and placed her hand over Ximena's, folding her fingers over Ximena's fingers and under the handle of the bag. Ximena turned her gaze back to Alicia.

"You can give me the package. It's okay."

Ximena did not move or relax her grasp.

"Here," Lupe said. She dangled a rosary in front of Ximena and swung it back and forth to catch Ximena's eye. "Give the lady the package and you can have this back."

Alicia tugged at the handle of the shopping bag and took it from Ximena. Alicia moved away, awkwardly, not at a run but at a quick pace, the bag at arm's length, her eyes fixed on the bag.

Lupe placed the rosary in Ximena's empty hand and bent

close, stretching her arms around Ximena's shoulder. Only then did Lupe feel the hard shell beneath Ximena's abaya.

"Don't!" It was Alicia. She had come back but without the bag.

At the hint of alarm in Alicia's voice, Lupe dropped her arms and stepped back. Now that she knew something was there, Lupe wondered how she had missed it earlier. The outline of the suicide vest rippled across Ximena's midriff.

"Lupe, can you help your sister sit on the ground?" Alicia asked.

Lupe nodded. She put her hand under Ximena's elbow and helped her to the pavement, then squatted beside her. When Ximena slumped against the side of a car, her hand fell open, revealing a small black tube in her palm.

Sirens sounded at some distance. They were coming, Lupe thought, finally. She looked from the tube in Ximena's palm to Alicia.

"Lupe, I want you to go now. I want you to get up and walk away. I want you to go find help. Find the nearest person with a badge and bring them here."

Lupe shook her head. "I can't leave her."

"She'll be okay. I'll keep her safe, I promise. But I need your help, too."

Lupe rose from where she had squatted beside Ximena and backed away. Flashes of blue and white light split the night sky over the tops of the cars in the parking lot. Lupe took one more glance at her sister propped against the car and the security guard crouched a few feet away, her lips moving slowly, her voice calm. Then Lupe sprinted toward the lights.

61. SHAFRA

SHAFRA WANTED TO CHECK HIS WATCH AGAIN, BUT REFRAINED. BY entering the mall through Macy's, the west anchor, rather than circling around and entering through the north entrance, he had added at least fifteen minutes to his cushion. He had plenty of time, more than he had planned.

Shafra saw the open dome of the atrium ahead. He would have to pass through the atrium and down the next corridor to reach the north exit. But everything had changed and he lost his bearings. Every wall and storefront bore orange and black balloons, banners, and streamers. The colors swirled and clashed in front of his eyes. The only familiar sight was the carousel turning with every horse, carriage, and bench on its platform occupied. Shafra guessed the familiar music was playing but he could not hear it above the din of the crowd.

There were so many people filling the atrium, he saw none of them, only a mass of shapes of tall figures and small figures, shapes standing, or sitting, or eating, or running, and all of them talking at once.

Above his head, lights were strung through the glass dome's rafters. He stared at the lights, mesmerized by their twinkling against the dark sky beyond the dome. For an instant, he thought he spotted a familiar pattern, Taurus, maybe, though it was too high in the sky. He reached out for Selam to bring her close and to ask her to find Orion with his belt of stars. Orion was her favorite and the first he had shown her.

Shafra's fingers found cold metal, a handrail. He started and stared at his empty hand. Selam was not there. And above him, there was nothing to see but a string of lights.

A drop of sweat trickled down the back of his neck and melted into his cotton shirt, another dripped from his forehead into his eyes. Shafra wiped his forehead on the sleeve of the jacket. By the clock visible above the crowd, he would have to wait six more minutes. He stared at the second hand as it circled the dial. He had five more minutes.

He was unbearably hot and when he waded into the middle of the atrium, into the middle of the jumble of arms and legs, sweat poured from his forehead. The back of his neck was wet, the trail of one bead was now a sheet of moisture.

Shafra unzipped his jacket and felt a breath of cool air across his neck and chest.

A scream echoed through the corridor and was joined by another. The shapes backed away, turned and ran, fleeing up the stairs, along the corridors, or out the exit. All of them headed away from the man beside the pillar with the bomb attached to his chest and a large shopping bag in his hand.

62. ALICIA

ALICIA KEPT UP THE ONE-WAY CONVERSATION WITH XIMENA. SHE dared not move and cause the woman to panic, not yet; they were not out of danger. She had to keep herself in the moment, at least outwardly. Though every ounce of her being wanted to run toward the mall to stop Javier and to find Kyle, she could not. She prayed silently in snippets, saying "Please, God. Keep Kyle safe. Please, God," and interspersing her prayers between the words she said to Ximena.

Even were it not for the device, what Alicia supposed was a trigger lying in her open palm, Alicia could tell Ximena wore a suicide vest. The form of a half dozen cylinders stood out clearly under the abaya as it lay limp against Ximena's chest.

"You were very brave to do this, but you are even braver now. You saved many, many people from being hurt," Alicia said, praying and wondering where the police were. She couldn't risk taking a look around or rising to signal someone. She could only hope Lupe had not run away.

Then, in the distance, Alicia heard the distinctive blare of a fire truck rounding the corner and heading in her direction. Still, she thought, there should be more. There should be everything the city could throw at this place. It should be crawling with emergency vehicles. Except, it wasn't. Something was terribly wrong.

Then, across the parking lot came the sound of footsteps slapping on the pavement and the jingle of keys, buckles, radios, and holsters. They were coming at a run. The steps halted, then spread left and right. One figure stepped into Alicia's line of sight. Relief flooded her body. "We need some help here," she said.

"I can see that," the cop said.

"This is Ximena."

The cop knelt beside Alicia. "Hello, Ximena, I'm Officer Frank Twery," he said, his voice as calm as a priest's at mass on a Sunday morning. "But you can just call me Frank. Francisco. Okay?"

"Ma'am?" It took a second for Alicia to realize the officer was speaking to her. "Ma'am," he said again. "You can go now." When she hesitated, her eyes flicking back and forth from Ximena to Officer Twery, he said with a bit more emphasis, "I'd like you to go now. Just back away slowly."

Alicia retreated, threading her way between two rows of cars and to two policemen who stood with arms outstretched trying to cordon off the area. Beyond them were several police cars, blue and white lights flashing. They'd come, finally.

"I'm with Security," she said to one of the officers. "There's a shopping bag, over there, at the base of that light pole," Alicia said, pointing over the officer's shoulder. "It's a package the woman was carrying, and I think it's a bomb."

The cop called a few of his fellow officers together then motioned for Alicia to go to where their squad car sat. He opened his mouth as if to tell her to stay where they could question her later. Alicia gambled. She sprinted away.

As she neared the mall's entrance, the crowd grew thick with people fleeing the atrium. Only now, this close, could she hear the screams. People were running, shoving, pushing her to the side.

"It's a bomb. He's got a bomb."

Others joined in the screaming.

"Come this way," a man yelled.

"Get out, get out," a cry from someone else.

"Over here," Alicia yelled, pointing toward the exit. In their panic, the crowd could not distinguish a glass door from a glass wall or a way in from a way out.

Alicia craned her neck to see behind and between the people in the crowd. She scanned the faces for someone familiar and grabbed the arm of a woman who hesitated as she passed, "Have you seen a little boy? About this high." Alicia held her hand just above her waist. The woman, eyes wide, stared at Alicia unseeing. "My boy. A young boy. Have you seen him?" she asked the next person who passed by but did not stop to answer.

Alicia searched the faces for reassurance. Her eyes flicked from one to the next, one face drawn, its jaw slack, another bunched tight, brows furrowed, eyes darting left and right. But there were no cuts or bruises or other signs of injury.

As the crowd thinned, Alicia saw her chance and burst inside the mall. In front of her, the food court lay in shambles. Chairs and tables were scattered and overturned, black and orange streamers had been snapped from the walls, and a sea of spilled food, paper bags, and cups littered the marble floor.

"Praise be to Allah."

Alicia pivoted toward the sound of the man's voice and spied the lone figure in the middle of the atrium, his hands at his head, his face skyward. It was Javier. Behind him, on the carousel, rider-less horses rose and fell in silence.

Javier arched his head back and glanced upward at the ceiling, then at the small crowd behind him, trapped in the place they'd sheltered. The dozen or so people, mostly children, stood wide eyed at the scene unfolding in front of them, panic on their faces. Alicia could afford no more than one quick glance to spot a child alone among them, a child left behind, a child in army fatigues. Kyle was not there.

Please, God. Keep him safe. Please, God.

Javier showed no sign of recognition of where he was. He seemed oblivious to everything and everyone as if he were standing alone in a desert.

"Javier," Alicia said, trying to catch his attention. He turned and stared at her, or in her direction. Inside the open jacket, Alicia could see the tubes she guessed were filled with ball bearings or nails or other objects capable of becoming projectiles. "Wait. Please," Alicia said.

From the corner of her eye, Alicia saw three men in dark uniforms approach, weapons drawn but at their sides. She recognized one, the thin one with the stand up hair, Cy. Placing their feet carefully and soundlessly on the marble floor, they separated and formed a wide arc to her right.

"Javier," she said, her voice low without a trace of urgency. "Please. Think for a minute. You don't have to do this."

Javier did not move. He continued to stare at her.

A commotion erupted near the entrance, but this time Alicia could not turn to look. She feared Javier would follow her glance and see more FBI agents, police, or firemen, which could frighten him. She was still speaking to Javier when Cy broke from the arc and came to her side.

"Keep going," he whispered. "You're doing great."

"Javier, let the people behind you go. Okay? There's no need to harm them. They're just children. They haven't hurt anyone."

Two more figures joined the arc. Alicia could see they weren't cops. They were two women in traditional Muslim dress, black from head to toe. One stood tall, seeming sure of herself. She had her arm around the other who appeared hesitant, stumbling. The tall one steadied her.

Cy nodded to them and made a motion, signaling them to go forward.

"There's someone here to see you, Javier," Alicia said. She forced her lips into a smile and nodded at the women she assumed were friends or translators. Though she did not know how Javier would respond, she had to follow Cy's lead. As they stepped forward, Alicia caught a glimpse of the smaller woman's face. Alicia gasped audibly. It was Ximena. She had no idea how the FBI had removed the vest or how they had talked Ximena into cooperating.

"Shafra," Ximena said, softly.

On his face, Javier showed a flicker of recognition and surprise.

The taller woman spoke to Javier in Arabic, the words indecipherable to Alicia, but the tone similar to the one Alicia had used with Ximena earlier, unrushed, but firm.

The atrium had grown eerily quiet.

Cy tapped Alicia's arm. "Go slowly," he whispered, "very slowly now. Back away with me."

Alicia held her ground.

"We have this," he said.

"But the women. Those people."

"Trust me."

Alicia was not convinced.

"Look," Cy said.

Alicia followed his eyes. The man, woman, and the group of children who had been trapped behind filed out the exit with an FBI escort.

63. ALICIA

WHEN SHE REACHED THE EXIT, AN AGENT GRABBED ALICIA'S ARM and ushered her through a cordon of police and police vehicles surrounding the mall entrance. Where had they come from, she wondered. It was as if the city's entire police force had assembled outside the entrance.

"What are you going to do?" Alicia asked one of the men crouched on a knee behind a police car's open door. His gun was drawn and aimed at the entrance to the mall.

"Ma'am, you need to get back," he said.

"No—"

"It's all right," a second agent said. "She's with Cy." He turned to her and said, "Mrs. Blake, you can stay here as long as you stand behind me. But if I tell you to back away, you'll have to do that without hesitating."

The first agent eyed Alicia then resumed his position.

The doors opened, an agent in an FBI marked vest showed himself. A radio squawked, "We're clear."

"Okay," the agent beside Alicia said into his radio. "Mall is clear."

"Clear?" Alicia asked.

"No more civilians. Just us and the terrorist," the agent explained.

"And the two women."

"Yes. And the two women. One's ours. Agent Fakhoury."

Minutes passed with no apparent progress inside the mall. Alicia heard more vehicles arrive and come to a halt in the lot behind the others, but she could not tear her eyes from the glass doors.

After another period of silence, the radio squawked again. "Coming out." Two figures in black emerged.

Alicia exhaled just as an explosion from deep inside the mall reverberated into the air. For an instant, there was only the sound of the world coming apart, a roar that rumbled in Alicia's chest and echoed in her head. There was a moment of absolute silence after which smoke billowed from the top of the mall, above the atrium, or where the atrium once stood.

"Oh, my God, no," Alicia said. Instinctively, and before the agent could stop her, she ran toward the entrance where the two figures in black lay on the ground. When she reached them, one was kneeling above the other. The one on the ground, Ximena, was crying.

Ximena yanked at her hijab, sobbing as she did, flinging it to the ground. Her dark hair fell free. Her hands went to her head and to a forehead free of a birthmark.

"Oh, my God. Lupe! It's you," Alicia said, realizing in an instant that the FBI had brought Lupe dressed as Ximena to appeal to Javier and keep him from detonating the bomb.

Hands reached in from all directions, pulling the women to their feet, pulling Alicia away. Sirens wailed. Radios squawked. The cordon of police inched forward, ready to enter the mall as soon as someone gave the word.

"Ma'am. Ma'am," someone was calling to Alicia. "You have to come with us. You have to clear the area."

Alicia nodded and turned as if to go. Satisfied, the policeman loosened his grasp on her arm. A couple of medics pushed passed her and to the two women, Lupe and the woman who had spoken to Javier in Arabic. Both their heads were scarf-less, like witches who'd lost their hats. Two hatless and broom-less Halloween witches. Halloween. "Kyle!" Alicia screamed and headed for the atrium.

"You can't go in there," someone behind her yelled. "Stop! Stop her."

Alicia ignored the pleas and ran at top speed. As she approached the entrance, or what was left of the entrance, a figure emerged. It was Cy, covered in dust, coughing. Three other Agents, staggered out behind him.

"Kyle!" Alicia said, her hands clawing at Cy and the Agents.

"What?" Cy asked.

"My son. He's inside the mall."

"Your son?"

"Yes, I was here with him. I left him with..." Alicia paused, confused, trying to remember. "Oh my God, I don't know where he is. I have to find him."

"Wait a minute. He can't be in there. I'm sure he was evacuated with the others." Cy motioned to an agent with a phone to his ear. "Chris," he said, "where'd they take the civilians?"

Chris, still holding the phone, squinted. "What?" he asked.

"The children," Cy said. "Where are they?"

"Oh! Couldn't hear you. Most of them are over there, behind the barricades. We set up a spot for families." Chris turned and squinted again at his phone as if it were not working. "Just a sec, I'll show you," he said.

"It's okay, I'll take her," Cy said. He guided Alicia through the chaos of first responders and their emergency vehicles and through the rapidly clearing parking lot to the southwest side of the mall. They reached another cordoned off area, and stepped around a cop car to find an ambulance with its rear doors open and medics talking to several people.

"Kyle!" Alicia shouted. "Kyle!" It was useless. She dashed from one group of costumed children to another, looking for the right face. She spied an Ingram Security guard to one side of the group. His head was bent, looking at someone, and nodding. She pushed her way through. It was Wade talking to a diminutive figure in army fatigues with a medal pinned to his chest. "Kyle. Oh, thank you, God."

NOVEMBER

64. ALICIA

IN THE FRONT ROW OF THE AUDITORIUM, ALICIA AND KYLE SAT TO-
gether, surrounded by local dignitaries. Kyle wore a new suit and
fumbled with his young-boy's tie, his first. Alicia skimmed a
hand across the top of his head, slicking down his cowlick, but it
popped up again. She smiled.

Behind them, in the second row, Cy Westfall sat beside his
father, a bigwig with the FBI. Cy had made the introductions
moments ago.

Alicia had almost missed the start of the ceremonies as she
struggled to pick out an outfit for the occasion. Kyle had watched
and grown more frustrated with every change. "Mom. You looked
great in the first one," he said. And so, she'd returned to the con-
servative gray jacket and skirt now at the bottom of the pile on
her bed. After all, a cop should look serious, not sexy or frivolous.

A cop. She shook her head from side to side and returned
her attention to the man at the dais. Another of the Field Office
executives was speaking.

"The scope of the October 30 terrorist attacks, as you know,
was unprecedented. While we were fortunate to have had advance notice, enough to increase the threat level and bring more
law enforcement individuals to bear than we otherwise would
have, we could not prevent the attacks from occurring. They were
a staggering blow to homeland security.

"We suffered losses. And we will avenge them. The perpetrators will be brought to justice.

"We mourn for those who are no longer with us and pray for those left behind, hoping they will find comfort and peace in the days to come. And we thank God for those who were spared. But, for one brief hour today, we are setting our sorrows aside, because fate did smile on this fine city that day, too. Fate in the form of a few people from the community. People who saw something not quite right. People who looked twice. People who prevented the senseless killing of many, many more."

Alicia let her thoughts drift. Like everyone else, she'd missed the larger picture that day, never imagining multiple attacks. She'd focused on preventing the two people she suspected were going to detonate a bomb at Riverside. The first was Javier and the second a Middle Eastern terrorist whose identity she never learned, whose place apparently Ximena had taken. The city credited Alicia with stopping Ximena and delaying Javier long enough to allow evacuation of the atrium. Both actions prevented a catastrophic loss of life.

A few days after the event, she figured out why the first responders took so long to get to Riverside. Terrorists had detonated bombs at a first site at seven o'clock, drawing the city's resources to that location, only to have half of them called to a second site a half hour later. The resources were stretched thin and strewn across the city limits by eight, leaving few resources to respond to the third call for help at Riverside.

She'd tried to follow up with Lupe and Ximena, though she could not see either of them. Ximena had been arrested and was in police custody. Lupe too, though Cy told Alicia because Lupe had tried to stop her sister, the authorities would go light on her.

She'd be sent back to Mexico, but be given assistance and priority to apply for a visa to return through approved channels.

Cy told her, too, he'd be working in Washington for a couple of months. Besides the commendation he received for helping to delay the suicide bomber from detonating his device, the FBI had expressed interest in a computer program he'd developed, something he called Cycle. They thought the program had promise and might improve their ability to identify potential terrorists and perhaps even lead to the capture of the head of the cell.

They'd brought in two local imams for questioning and detained one, Ata Nahidian, who they identified through Riverside Centre security cameras as the man who dropped Javier off at the mall on Halloween, and Ali Ahmed, another of the Muslim conspirators who Ximena had helped identify and locate. But Qasim Bousaid had vanished, melting back into the wall of lies that protected him.

The mayor had called Alicia a hero and introduced her to everyone who was anyone in Atlanta's government and law enforcement. After that, she'd been polite but refused further public spectacles, allowing only one brief interview. It made the papers and the late night news on television. Alicia had let Kyle stay up to watch.

Alicia didn't want to be a called a hero. She'd done what she'd done because it was right and it was her job. She wanted life to get back to normal and return to Riverside as quickly as she could until Cy approached her. He'd waited until the immediate shock had worn off and until the city and country settled down to dealing with the political, economic, and military aftermath of the attacks.

They'd met for lunch, Cy bringing Atlanta's Chief of Police

with him. An odd guest, she'd thought at the time. The combination made sense only when Cy explained that his father AEAD Jerald Westfall had convinced the local police to extend an offer to Alicia to join the force.

When the surprise wore off, she dabbed her napkin at her eyes. She thanked both of them several times and started to say she couldn't accept the offer when Cy interrupted.

"Wait a minute, before you answer," he'd said. "The FBI is funding your training. And the City of Atlanta, by way of Chief Hendrickson here, is assuring you a position in law enforcement, pending successful completion of the training, of course. But neither he nor I have any doubts about that."

Somehow, Cy had known she couldn't afford the expense or the investment in time without a guarantee of a paying job on the other end.

Alicia had one more hurdle to overcome before deciding. She had to wrestle with the dangers of the job and the risks she'd be taking. In the end, she decided to give it a try for six months, if Kyle approved. When she told him about the opportunity, his face had lit up and Kyle left her with one word, "Cool."

Officer Blake. She'd said those words, aloud, a hundred times in front of the mirror and had liked the sound every single time. She'd join and start out like everyone else, at the bottom of the ladder. That was a given, but Alicia had started planning ahead.

As the speech came to a close, the spokesperson called for a moment of prayer for the fallen. Alicia took one of Kyle's hands in hers. She closed her eyes and bowed her head. Seth would be proud, very, very proud.

Notes & Acknowledgements

WRITING THE MARTYR'S BROTHER WAS LIKE EMBARKING ON A round-the-world journey without a map. With two novels of historical fiction to my credit, the easiest next step would have been to write another story set in the same between-the-wars era. And, though I will most likely return there one day, taking the detour to write a contemporary "thriller" was a chance to examine the world around me rather than one gone by, and to shape, but not lose, my writer's voice into the requirements of a new genre.

In telling this story, I have no doubt violated someone's "ten rules of thriller writing." I simply began with the images and headlines that keep me up at night, slathered on a layer of research, and molded four squares of clay into characters I fell in love with. "You can't do that," one critic said of my alternating points of view and word count devoted to villains and minor characters. "Why not?" I asked. "Whose story is this, anyway?" a reader asked. "Whichever character you'd like it to be," I said.

If I had a purpose in writing this particular story, I'd use Alicia Blake's words when she said, "people had forgotten there was a day in the not too distant past when they'd not seen or heard of bombings, and suicide vests, and snipers." I am fortunate to have lived in a time and place where terrorism didn't happen in our backyards. I hope people don't forget, and I pray that terrorism does not define our future.

* * *

For readers who finish the book and think it is unlikely that Middle Eastern terrorists, or for that matter, any terrorists, might enter the United States through our southern border—though the claims have been called into question—or for those who say I stretched their credulity by having a character in the book convert from Catholicism to Islam, I offer the following comments:

In the course of my research, I found credible news reports of potential terrorists entering the US from Mexico and, to a lesser degree, Canada. Several of these sources reported ranchers and US Border Patrol members finding Urdu dictionaries and Islamic prayer rugs abandoned in the desert along our southern border, though the claims have been called into question.

On the second point, Islamic councils in the US report there were 250,000 Latino Muslims living in the US in 2011, and about half of those are women. Islamic scholars claim Hispanics are the fastest growing segment of Islam, though of course the growth is from a small initial base. As a reason for the attraction, they cite the simplicity of Islam's theology, its structured belief system, and a cultural familiarity.

* * *

Thank you to the many people who made this book possible and better than it would have been, including: the North Atlanta Writers Critique Group, all those who read advance copies, who agreed to an interview, who wrote the numerous articles, books, and websites that provided the story's backbone, who offered opinions on titles and covers, and who en-dorsed the book, to the security guard at a local mall who I tailed for hours, and to the forty-three people who inspired or men-tored me during my thirty-plus year career in corporate America, (yes, that character is named for you).

And, as always, my deepest gratitude goes to my husband, to whom this book is dedicated, for all the things in life that matter, but also for listening as I read one of my many drafts aloud, yawning to indicate a slow spot, saying "uh-oh" on cue when danger loomed, and being there at the end.

If you enjoyed *The Martyr's Brother*, I encourage you to send me a comment or question, leave a review, and mark your calendars for the next book in the series featuring Alicia Blake, coming in 2017-2018.

About the Author

Rona Simmons is the author of *The Quiet Room* and *Postcards from Wonderland*. Both novels were set outside the south, yet she considers herself a southern writer. Both were historical fiction, yet she thinks of them as stories that just by happenstance took place in the past. For *The Martyr's Brother,* she ripped a topic from today's headlines and set it in present day Atlanta, Georgia, her adopted home in the South. When not planning to write, writing, or talking about writing, Rona "slow blogs" about women in the creative arts and her other passion — travel — as well as this and that on *The Huffington Post Blog.* Her short stories, articles, and interviews have been published in literary journals and online magazines, including *Deep South Magazine, Points North,* and *The Persimmon Tree.*

Read more about Rona Simmons at ronasimmons.com.